OWEN

Book One of The Tudor Trilogy

By

TONY RICHES

Published by
Preseli Press

Tony Riches asserts the moral right
to be identified as the author of this work.

ISBN-13: 978-1502901019
ISBN-10: 1502901013
BISAC: Fiction / Historical

Tony Riches is a full-time writer and lives with his wife in Pembrokeshire, West Wales UK. For more information about Tony's other published work please see:

www.tonyriches.co.uk

For my daughter
Caroline

The martlet device of Owen Tudor,
signifying a restless quest for
knowledge, learning and adventure.

Chapter One

Winter of 1422

I tense at the sound of approaching footsteps as I wait to meet my new mistress, the young widow of King Henry V, Queen Catherine of Valois. Colourful Flemish tapestries decorate the royal apartments of Windsor Castle, dazzling my senses and reminding me how life in the royal household presents new opportunities. My life will change forever, if she finds me acceptable, yet doubt nags at my mind.

The doors open and Queen Catherine's usher appears. I have been told to approach the queen and bow, but must not look directly at her or speak, other than to say my name, until spoken to. Taking a deep breath I enter the queen's private rooms where she sits surrounded by her sharp-eyed ladies-in-waiting. I have the briefest glimpse of azure silk, gold brocade, gleaming pearls and a breath of exotic perfume. I remove my hat and bow, my eyes cast down to her velvet-slippered feet.

'Owen Tudor, Your Highness, Keeper of your Wardrobe.' My voice echoes in the high-ceilinged room.

One of her ladies fails to suppress her giggle, a sweet enough sound, if you are not the reason for it. I forget my instruction and look up to see the queen regarding me with confident, ice-blue eyes.

'You are a Welshman?' Her words sound like an accusation.

'My full name is Owain ap Maredydd ap Tudur, although the English call me Owen Tudor. I come from a long line of Welsh noblemen, Your Highness.' I regret my boast as soon as I say the words.

'Owen Tudor...' This time her voice carries a hint of amusement.

I put on my hat and pull my shoulders back. She examines me, as one might study a horse before offering a price. After years of hard work I have secured a position worthy of my skills, yet it means nothing without the approval of the queen.

'You look more like a soldier than a servant?' The challenge in her words seems to tease me.

'I have served in the king's army as a soldier.' I feel all their eyes upon me.

'Yet... you have no sword?' She sounds curious.

'Welshmen are not permitted to carry a sword in England, Your Highness.' I am still bitter at this injustice.

I remember the last time I saw her, at the king's state funeral in Westminster. Her face veiled, she rode in a gilded carriage drawn by a team of black horses. I followed on foot as the funeral procession passed through sombre crowds, carrying the king's standard and wearing the red, blue and gold livery of the royal household.

'You fought in France?'

'With the king's bowmen, Your Highness, before I became a squire.'

The queen has none of the air of sadness I expected. Slim, almost too thin, her childlike wrists and delicate fingers are adorned with gold rings sparkling with diamonds and rubies. Her neck is long and slender, her skin pale with the whiteness of a woman who rarely sees the sun. Her golden-brown hair is gathered in tight plaits at the back of her head and her headdress fashionably emphasises her smooth, high forehead.

King Henry V chose as his bride the youngest daughter of the man they called the 'mad king', Charles VI. They said King Charles feared he was made of glass and would shatter if he didn't take care. Charles promised Henry he would inherit the throne and become the next King of France and there were rumours of a secret wedding dowry, a fortune in gold.

Barely a year into his marriage, the king left his new wife pregnant and alone in Windsor. He returned to fight his war in France, capturing the castle of Dreux before marching on the fortress at Meaux, defended by Jean de Gast, the Bastard of Vaurus, a cruel, brave captain. The king never saw his son and heir, his namesake.

The siege of Meaux was hard won and he suffered the bloody flux, the dreaded curse of the battlefield. Men had been known to recover, if they were strong and lucky. Many did not, despite the bloodletting and leeches. The flux is an inglorious way to die, poisoned by your own body, especially for a victorious warrior king who would never now be King of France.

The queen has an appraising look in her eyes. She has buried her hopes for the future along with her husband. I remember I am looking at the mother of the new king, once he comes of age. One thing is certain; she will not be left to raise the prince alone. Ambitious men are already vying for their share of power and influence.

At last she speaks. 'And now you are in my household?'

'My appointment to your service was made by Sir Walter Hungerford, Steward of the King's Household and constable here at Windsor.'

'Sir Walter was one of my husband's most trusted men—
the executor of the king's will.'

'I worked as squire to Sir Walter for many years, in
England and France.'

'You speak French?'

'A little, Your Highness.' I answer in French.

'Were you with King Henry at the siege of Rouen?' Now
she speaks in French.

'I was, Your Highness. I will never forget it.' I answer
again in French. I learned the language on the battlefield
and in the taverns of Paris and can swear as well as any
Frenchman.

'I heard the people of Rouen were starving... before they
surrendered.' Her voice is softer now and she speaks in
English.

I hesitate to admit she is right. The townspeople of the
great city of Rouen were eating cats and dogs at the end,
whatever they could find. Hundreds of good men and
women starved to death to give her husband his victory. I
drank foul ditch water to survive and the sights of the siege
of Rouen are forever engraved on my memory.

'War is cruel, yet now there is less appetite for it.'

'I pray to God that is true.' She glances back at her ladies,
who are watching and listening, as ladies-in-waiting do.
Queen Catherine regards me, giving nothing away. 'I
welcome you to our household, Master Tudor.'

'Thank you, Your Highness.'

Our first meeting is over. She is unlike any woman I have
known, fascinating, intriguing and beautiful. More than
that; there is something about her I find deeply attractive, a
dangerous thing to admit. Perhaps my fascination is with
the glimpse I'd seen of the real woman, the same age as
myself, behind the title of Dowager Queen of England.

'Aim high, boy,' my garrulous longbow tutor once
advised me, his voice gruff from too much shouting. 'It's

not the Welsh way to play safe and wait until you have a clear shot!' The man spits hard on the ground to add emphasis and stares knowingly into my eyes, standing so close I can almost feel the coarse grey stubble of his beard. 'When you aim high,' he points an imaginary bow up at the sky, 'your arrow will fly far into the enemy ranks and strike with the full vengeance of God.'

'Who, of course, is on our side.' A daring, foolhardy thing for a boy like me to say to a man who can punch me to the ground or worse.

For a moment I see the old man's mind working as he tries to decide if I am being disrespectful, sacrilegious or both. The moment passes. I notch a new arrow into the powerful yew longbow and fire it high into the sky, without a care for where it will fall.

I smile at the memory as I return down the long passage to the servants' hall. Life as a king's archer was hard, but I enjoyed the camaraderie of the other men and it taught me many things. As well as how to use a longbow, I learned to watch my back, when to speak up and when to remain silent. My tutor died in the thick mud of Normandy, yet his lesson serves me well. I know to aim high.

That night, wide awake in the darkness, I reflect on the unthinkable turn my life has taken. I always imagined I would become a merchant, setting up shop somewhere in the narrow, dirty streets of London, or perhaps an adventurer, sailing off to seek my fortune. I remain a servant, yet for the first time I have my own lodging room, however small and cramped.

My reward for long and loyal service as squire to Sir Walter has been this new appointment, a position of great responsibility. The queen's wardrobe is a treasure store of priceless gold and jewels, as well as all her expensive clothes and most valuable possessions. Such a senior post in the royal household pays more than I have earned in my life and carries influence, allowing me regular and privileged access to the queen.

I resolve to become indispensable to her. High and mighty lords and dukes will come and go, with their false concerns and self-serving advice, yet I will see her every day, tending to her needs. I recall how she referred to Sir Walter as one of the king's most trusted men. That is what I wish to become; Queen Catherine's most trusted man.

✷ ✷ ✷

Life begins to settle into a routine and I soon learn what the queen likes—and what she does not. I have never worked so hard and expand my role to all aspects of the royal household, dividing my time between the army of servants who wait on the queen and the many demands of keeping the palace of Windsor running smoothly. The castle employs so many staff and servants it is almost independent of the outside world. Every day I must make decisions and resolve disputes between them.

One of the most important of my daily duties is to visit the royal nursery and check all is well with the infant Prince Henry. Although he was crowned king in September, everyone in the household refers to him as 'the prince', as he is still not one year old. Each morning I make my way down the long corridors with ornate, tiled floors and high, leaded-glass windows, to the prince's apartments. The nursery occupies an entire wing of the castle, with its own guards and staff to care for the future king.

King Henry V permitted Queen Catherine two maids and three noble ladies to accompany her to England. Juliette, at sixteen the youngest of the queen's chosen maids, greets me. She dresses plainly and covers her hair with a white headscarf, her only jewellery a silver crucifix around her neck. She looks more like a nun than a maidservant, yet I understand why the queen trusts her with the care of the young prince. There is a spark of ambition in Juliette's hazel eyes and she is always the first to notice me when I visit.

Juliette smiles in welcome. 'Good morning, sir.'

I look forward to seeing her on my daily rounds. Although I am four years older than her, she gives the impression she thinks me young for such an important post. I wish to prove myself well-organised and skilled at getting the best from the servants. Sometimes I hear them saying the most inappropriate things behind my back, but Juliette is different and I admire her easy modesty.

Juliette sees me looking at the prince. 'He has slept well, sir,' she says. 'We all give thanks to God he has passed the worst of his teething. His little teeth were keeping him awake every night.'

I look across to where the prince sits with his nursemaid. She keeps his attention with a red ribbon attached to a silver bell, which tinkles musically as she shakes it. Harry is able to sit upright now and has a full head of blond hair. He shows little sign of the thin-faced Plantagenet features of his father, although I expect these will develop with time.

'Has the queen been to visit him today?'

Juliette shakes her head. 'Not yet, sir, although we are always ready for her.'

I am happy for an excuse to stay a little longer than usual in the nursery and take my chance to know Juliette a little better. I am careful to maintain my professional distance from the servants and miss the camaraderie I shared before I came to Windsor Castle.

'I wondered... if you would help me with the arrangements for Christmas and New Year?'

She looks surprised. 'I will be happy to, sir.'

'We need to meet, to discuss what needs to be done.' I know this will be seen by the other servants as a sign of favouritism. There will be gossiping in the corridors, but Christmas will mean many visitors coming and going, extra tradesmen to negotiate with and a thousand decisions to be made.

'I have some time tomorrow morning, if that will suit you, sir?'

'Thank you Juliette. I will see you tomorrow.'

I hum a tune as I head for the next stop on my tour of the castle, the Great Kitchen, with its high arched ceiling, steaming cauldrons and cooks shouting orders over the noise of clanging pots and pans. At first I found the scale of the kitchens overwhelming, particularly when there are banquets to be arranged. I soon learned to plan several months ahead and to take care about relying on the advice of Samuel Cleaver, the head cook, who runs the Great Kitchen.

Cleaver is a heavily built, ox of a man, with a shiny, shaven head, a thick neck and deep-set, questioning eyes. The head cook is obstructive and difficult, and regards the Great Kitchen as his personal empire. He rules over his army of minions with a harsh, bullying manner, bellowing orders to the cooks in his strong northern accent.

There are rumours he has amassed considerable wealth over his years at Windsor Castle. The vast quantities of food produced in the Great Kitchen mean there is plenty of scope for theft and I sense that Samuel Cleaver is a man with something to hide. I have no wish to make an enemy of him, yet am certain evidence of his crimes will eventually come to light.

Hearing a commotion of raised voices, I investigate and find a red-faced palace guard being rebuked by a suave nobleman in riding clothes. I recognise the visitor as Duke Humphrey of Gloucester, youngest brother of the late king, who has been appointed Lord Protector of the Realm and Regent of England.

'What seems to be the problem, my lord?'

The duke scowls. 'Who might you be?'

'I am the keeper of the queen's household, Owen Tudor, my lord.'

I feel the duke's sharp eyes judging me. 'I wish to see the queen.' He points an accusing finger at the guard. 'This man had the impertinence to challenge me.'

'My apologies, my lord. We have to be most careful.' It seems a reasonable mistake, as the duke arrived unannounced and looks dressed for hunting.

Duke Humphrey seems placated yet his tone is strident. 'From now on, I expect the palace household to know who I am, is that understood?'

'Yes, my lord. May I enquire if the queen will be expecting you to call today?'

The duke gives me a scathing look. 'I doubt it.'

I lead the duke down the corridor to the queen's apartments, wondering what she will say when she sees her visitor. It is another reminder of how little control she has over her life from now on. She is going to need to keep powerful and influential men like Duke Humphrey on her side, for they can send her to Leeds Castle in Kent and have the prince raised by nursemaids and tutors of their choosing.

The duke waits impatiently while I knock and enter the queen's private rooms, where she sits with her ladies-in-waiting. Queen Catherine looks up when she sees it is me.

'A visitor, Your Highness. Duke Humphrey of Gloucester.'

The queen seems unsurprised and dismisses her ladies. I show the duke in and wait outside in the hall, ready to escort him back after the meeting. The duke is talking in a raised voice and I struggle to make out his words through the closed doors, although his sentiment is clear. He is telling the queen how she must conduct herself.

When he finally emerges the duke orders me to take him somewhere we can talk privately. I lead him to one of the rooms set aside for visiting dignitaries. The air is musty and cold with the winter chill, as the room is unused and no fire has been lit in the hearth. The duke gestures for me to close the door and takes a seat, indicating that I do the same. I feel a sense of foreboding about what Duke Humphrey is about to say. As Protector of the Realm he has the right to appoint new staff and servants to the queen's household as he wishes or to dismiss them.

'Queen Catherine tells me she is pleased with the way you run her household.'

'Thank you, my lord.'

'You have done well here.' His tone is friendlier than before. 'Now... there is something I need you to do for me.'

'What is that, my lord?'

'I am responsible for safeguarding the young king. It will be a long time before he reaches his majority.' His tone becomes conspiratorial. 'And I have to spend most of my time in London. I need someone to act as my eyes and ears, here in Windsor and at the other royal residences, particularly when the queen is travelling. I need to be certain everything is as it should be—behind closed doors.'

I must think quickly, as to agree will put me in an impossible position. 'You are asking me... to spy on the queen, my lord?'

The duke's eyes narrow. 'You will simply tell me who visits her and when. There are... factions who will seek to influence the queen for their own ends. This matter must stay between us. You are to mention it to no one. Do you understand?'

'I do, my lord.'

Duke Humphrey looks pleased. 'I will send a man every two weeks to receive your reports. If there is a problem I expect you to send a message to me.'

I watch from the grand entrance of Windsor Castle as the duke rides away and make one of the hardest decisions since I arrived at Windsor. Returning to the queen's apartments, I ask to see her alone, on a confidential matter concerning the royal household. The queen looks at me in surprise and dismisses her ladies-in-waiting a second time. This is the first time I am alone with Queen Catherine since I arrived—and possibly the last.

The queen looks at me. 'What is this mysterious matter, Master Tudor, that is so confidential?'

'Your visitor, Duke Humphrey...' I must explain, if I am to stand any chance of winning the queen's trust and confidence. 'He asked me to keep him informed of everyone who visits you, my lady.'

'And what was your answer?' There is a sharp edge to her voice.

'If I refused he would have found someone else to do his work. At least now you are aware of this, you can decide what he is to be told.'

The queen looks deep in thought. 'You are right. It is better this way. I am sure the duke is only interested in protecting my son.'

'From what I know of him, Duke Humphrey takes his responsibilities very seriously.'

'The duke has overstepped his duty. My guardian is Henry Beaufort, Bishop of Winchester.'

'I understand...' I know the two men are fierce rivals and it seems Duke Humphrey has a talent for making enemies. As well as openly opposing the Bishop Beaufort, the most powerful man in the parliament and council, the duke is also engaged in a bitter dispute with his elder brother, John Duke of Bedford, now Regent of France.

The queen's diamond necklace sparkles as it catches the light. 'I am grateful you told me this. Did he offer you payment?'

'No, he did not, my lady.'

A flicker of concern crosses her face. 'You must take care, Master Tudor. The duke will make a dangerous enemy if you cross him.' Queen Catherine looks at me with wide blue eyes. 'Let us hope you never have to.'

Chapter Two

Christmas at Windsor Castle is a great disruption to my well-ordered routine. The queen's invited guests descend on the castle at short notice, expecting to be fed and found lodgings in keeping with their status. I note Duke Humphrey is not amongst them and has yet to send his man to question me about the queen's visitors.

After discussion with Queen Catherine, I engage a clerk, a monkish young man named Nathaniel Kemp, to record the details of everyone visiting for the Christmas and New Year celebrations. Nathaniel has been told to be discreet, although as far as he knows the records are only for housekeeping. There are now so many on his list it fills the sheet of yellow parchment, which will serve its purpose in showing Duke Humphrey he made the right choice of informer.

Although I am celebrating my first New Year's Eve at Windsor I decide not to join the servants' drinking party. It is important to maintain my reputation and I don't relish the prospect of dealing with drunken subordinates. As keeper of the household I still keep my distance from the servants and staff. This doesn't trouble me though, as I enjoy my role at Windsor and am glad to loosen my tunic and warm my feet by the fire.

I like having my own room, despite the low ceiling and sparse furniture. The bunk is comfortable, with thick woollen blankets to keep out the winter chill. The wash stand has a pewter bowl I looted from a deserted farmhouse in Normandy, as well as an earthenware jug of clean water, a luxury I will never take for granted. My sturdy oak table is functional enough and I have two old chairs of padded leather, one each side of the stone hearth. The room is my home now and reminds me of a captain's sea cabin, with its single oval window looking out over the green expanse of Windsor Park.

There is a tentative knock at my door as I settle in front of the fire and I groan as I prepare to deal with another minor emergency. Fastening my tunic I open the door to find Juliette carrying a folded white cloth.

'This is for you.' Juliette hesitates, then hands me the cloth. 'It's a New Year's gift,' she explains.

'Thank you.' I'd not thought of giving anyone a New Year's gift, even Juliette, who has become indispensable, as she always seems to know what the queen would wish. Over the past month there has been a subtle shift in our relationship, as she no longer calls me 'sir' although Juliette has yet to call me by my name.

'Are you going to ask me to come in?'

I hesitate to agree, as the household staff and servants already presume there is a deeper reason for my choice of the young French maid to act as my assistant. Tongues will wag if anyone sees her entering or leaving my room. At least this is one evening of the year when they have better things to do than note who visits me.

'It is New Year's Eve. Perhaps you'll join me in a goblet of mulled wine?'

Juliette enters, closing the door behind her. She sits in the chair on the opposite side of the fire to me and I am glad my room is tidy and my bed made. A substantial log crackles in the flames, providing plenty of heat on the cold winter night.

She pulls off her headscarf and shakes loose her dark auburn hair. It reaches to her shoulders, attractively framing her face. I am surprised at the transformation in her. Without her headscarf Juliette is more beautiful than I imagined and I feel an unexpected frisson of desire.

Pouring spiced wine into an earthenware bowl I place it in the hearth to warm, then return to the chair opposite her and unfold her gift. She has made me a linen handkerchief, embroidered with a red dragon.

'Thank you, Juliette.' I am touched by her gesture and lost for words, as I can't remember the last time anyone has taken so much trouble for me.

'It is only... a keepsake.' Juliette plays with a long strand of her hair.

I can tell she has put a great deal of thought into her gift. It must have been difficult to find a picture of the emblem of the Welsh, even in this castle with its library of magnificent illuminated books. The embroidery must have taken her many hours, working in poor candlelight.

I take the warmed bowl of mulled wine and fill two pewter goblets. The heady aroma of precious cloves and cinnamon drifts in the air like an exotic promise. Handing one to Juliette I realise it is over filled. It feels good to hear her laugh as I nearly spill wine on her dress and I am glad not to be spending New Year's Eve alone.

I raise my goblet. 'Here's to a successful New Year.' The wine is good and the spices give it an intoxicating flavour. I am enjoying her company and feel a tingle of anticipation as I wonder where it will lead. After all, she has chosen to come knocking on my door at this late hour and could have given me her gift on New Year's Day.

Juliette raises her goblet in the air. 'To 1423!' She takes a drink. 'This wine is strong... I can feel it going to my head. It reminds me of Christmas. When I was a girl we called it *vin chaud* and used the cheapest red wines, with lemons.'

'I'm not in the habit of drinking alone in my room. This wine is a gift from the queen.'

'Well, thank you for sharing it with me.' Juliette looks across at me with a mischievous twinkle in her eye. 'You know Queen Catherine thinks highly of you?'

'She hides her opinions well.'

Juliette takes another sip of her wine. 'I think... she hides her feelings about everything.' She leans forward conspiratorially. 'Can I tell you something?'

'Of course.'

'She wasn't like this before the death of the king. It is as if she has... shut out the world.'

I am intrigued, as the better I understand the queen the more I can be of use and earn her trust. 'I forget you have known the queen longer than most of us.' I take the iron poker and prod the log on the fire. It crackles and spits glowing sparks into the air. 'When did you first enter her service?'

Juliette looks into the flames. 'My parents were killed in the war. I was a girl when I first went to work for the royal family.'

'I'm sorry. My own father died when I was a boy.' I refill both goblets, not bothering to warm the mulled wine this time. 'He survived all the battles for Welsh freedom... only to be killed in a brawl in London.'

Juliette is silent for a moment. 'Do you have any other family?'

'My mother was the daughter of a lord and lived in Beaumaris, on the island of Ynys Môn on the north coast of Wales, which is where she met and married my father. He came from a nearby village and was descended from the princes of North Wales.' I smile as I remember my father. 'As a fourth son, he had to make his own way in the world.'

'What work did your father do?'

I hold up my goblet. 'He told me once he was a master brewer of the finest ales in Ynys Môn. Then he became squire to the Bishop of Bangor. That's what I could have been doing now, except somehow... he killed a man.'

'In a fight?'

'All I know is a man died. We had to run to the mountains of Snowdonia. My father lived as an outlaw there, fighting the English with his cousin, Owain Glyndŵr.'

'Is your mother still alive?'

'We were overrun by the English. My father and I had to flee for our lives—and leave my mother and family behind in Wales.'

'You were a child at the time though?'

'Yes. I went back there when I could... they were all gone.'

'Did anyone know where?'

I watch the dancing flames for a moment, remembering. 'Our house was burned to the ground by the English soldiers. I expect they took what they could first. Even the stones of the walls were robbed. I doubt if I will ever learn what became of my family.'

This is the first time I have spoken of my past to anyone and doing so brings bitter memories. 'Defeat by the English meant our lands were confiscated and my father died leaving me with little more than the clothes on my back. My first stroke of luck was when I found a place as a royal page. I was seven years old—but it was the making of me.'

'Well, I for one am glad you survived it all—and ended up in Windsor Castle, Owen Tudor.'

I smile at her compliment, the first time she has used my name. She has shown her hand first and is good company on a winter evening. Most importantly, Juliette is available. For a second I feel regret that Queen Catherine is so far out of reach, and then dismiss the ridiculous thought.

The bells in the castle chapel sound in the distance, interrupting my thoughts. They are marking the midnight hour, celebrating a special mass for the dawn of the New Year. I look across at Juliette. She reminds me now of a girl I knew in Normandy, the closest I have ever been to falling in love. I lost her to another through my indecision, only realising too late. I am not going to make that mistake again.

Juliette sets down her empty goblet on the flagstone of the hearth and crosses over to me, taking my hand and pulling me over to the bed. I obey as if entranced, as she embraces me, slowly undresses me, then kisses me. The first of many kisses that winter night.

✳ ✳ ✳

I wake alone, my mind a whirl of powerful, sensual images and serious consequences. I am sure it hasn't been a dream. The fire in the hearth has long since turned to a pile of grey ash, yet there on the flagstones stand two goblets. On the table is the folded square of white linen with its proud red dragon, so carefully sewn. I pick it up and take it to the window to study it in the bright winter dawn. The craftsmanship is impressive. Juliette used red silk, with stitches so neat they are hard to see.

I have to think about what I will say to Juliette when I see her next. I smile as I recall how I thought her so prim and proper, like a nun in the pristine white headscarf she wears in the nursery. I could not have been more wrong. Juliette planned the whole thing, knocking at my door at the perfect time. I have never been seduced before.

I dress in my riding clothes and walk to the stables. Although I don't own a horse, the late king's horses are kept here at Windsor. They are officially the property of the new King Henry, although at barely one year old he has little use for them. I ride them as often as I wish, as the horses need regular exercise. I choose my favourite, a fine black gelding, and fit it with a bridle and saddle.

The horse's powerful hooves crunch rhythmically on the frosty turf as I canter across the open pastures of Windsor Park. The brisk ride helps clear my head. There are important decisions to be made, choices which could change my life for better or worse. The most pressing of these is to come to terms with what happened the previous night.

There are no rules against relationships between household servants, as long as it does not compromise their work. That is the problem. As one of only two maids the queen chose to bring to England with her from France, some servants envy Juliette's status within the royal household. It would be easier if she were older and less attractive. People like to make mischief and will imply I have abused my position to take advantage of a vulnerable young maiden.

The other problem on my mind is the need to visit Duke Humphrey. I look up, trying to recall what snow clouds look like. The winter sky is clear and bright, a good omen, and I decide not to wait until he summons me. It has been some months since my last visit to London, twenty-five miles from Windsor. It is a cold ride in the middle of winter, yet it will show good faith.

My clerk, Nathaniel, has drawn up a comprehensive list of visitors, detailing when they arrived and how long they stayed. The clerk has made a good impression with his attention to detail and understated manner. I showed his list of visitors to the queen, who agreed it should satisfy the duke's curiosity.

I slow my pace and ride around the perimeter of the castle, noting things that need repairing or attending to. Even though this is my morning off, I have so little life outside the household I am always working or thinking about work. My attention is drawn to two men with a wagon at the rear entrance to the castle kitchens. I keep my distance and see they are busy loading something into the back of the wagon, rather than unloading supplies.

There is a furtive look about them which suggests they are up to no good. At last, it seems I could have the evidence to be rid of the bullying Samuel Cleaver. The trouble is it will be my word against that of the head cook, who would deny any involvement. Rather than let the men know I am on to them, I curse and ride away with yet another thing to think about.

Returning to the stables I hand my horse over to a stable lad who appears more than a little worse for wear. I have a fair idea Nathaniel will be already working, even on New Year's morning, and soon spot the thin figure of the clerk. He is stooped over his writing desk in the castle library, which also serves as a scriptorium where scribes copy important documents.

The servants have yet to light a fire in the grate and the library is chilly. I am warm from my ride but the young clerk is seemingly unconcerned at the coldness of the room.

'Happy New Year, Nathaniel!'

The clerk looks up from his work, apparently unsurprised to see me so early in the morning. 'And to you, sir.'

I try to make a judgement about how much to tell him. Nathaniel has dealt with the list of visitors with quiet efficiency, missing nothing, yet never raising questions by his actions. He is something of a loner, with a talent for blending into the background which is useful to me now.

'Did you join in with the festivities last night?'

'No, sir,' he grimaces at the thought. 'Those household celebrations are not to my taste. I prefer an early night.'

'Me too.' My answer is only half a lie. That had been my intention. 'I have another task for you, Nathaniel, one which requires your usual discretion.'

'I am happy to be of service, sir.'

'Good. This concerns a serious matter. I suspect there might be thieves within the household, stealing supplies from the kitchens.'

The clerk raises his eyebrows in surprise. 'How can I help?'

'I need proof, Nathaniel. It must be good enough to stand the test of a court, if necessary. I need you to look at the records of what should be in the stores—and what is actually there.'

'So we can see if there is anything that can't be accounted for?'

'That's right, and keep your wits about you, Nathaniel. The head cook has a reputation for dealing harshly with his staff. It would not be wise to anger him.'

Nathaniel nods. 'I understand. They must not suspect my real purpose. I will make a start today, sir.'

'Good—and remember to take care.' I recall the men with the wagon I saw earlier that morning. 'Let me know if you see or hear anything I need to be aware of. Is that understood?'

'Of course, sir.'

I leave in search of Juliette, satisfied at least one of my problems is on the way to being addressed. I worry about how Cleaver will react to Nathaniel's task, but the work is clerical and Nathaniel is, after all, a clerk. As I approach the nursery I realise I will be lucky to find Juliette there alone. The prince's nursemaid seems to live in the nursery and there are always other maids coming and going.

I am right, the nursery is as busy as ever, with the young prince surrounded by servants as they wash and dress him for the first day of the year. Juliette glances up as I enter and approaches, looking as correct as ever in her white headscarf. The only sign of what happened the previous night is the briefest twinkle in her eyes as she speaks.

'Good morning, sir—and a happy New Year to you.'

I raise a hand to show I am addressing the whole room. 'Happy New Year to you all.' The prince is now dressed and beaming up at me. 'And to you, my king.' There is a trace of irony in my tone, which amuses the nursemaids.

Juliette speaks for them. 'The queen has asked for him to be at her side for the New Year's feasting. It will be his first banquet.'

'We should discuss the arrangements, if you have the time?' I try to sound casual, although I am holding my breath as I wait for her answer.

'Of course, sir. I will walk with you.'

We walk side by side down the corridor in silence, through shafts of winter sunlight from high leaded-glass windows which make bright patterns of light and shadow on the tiled floor. One of the strange qualities of the corridors at Windsor Castle is the way even whispered voices carry great distances. Good for men guarding the doors but not for people with secrets to discuss.

I am pleased Juliette has agreed to see me now, rather than make me wait before we can discuss what happened. It would have distracted me for the rest of the day. We reach one of the private rooms and I usher her inside and close the door behind us. We stand for a moment, each waiting for the other to speak.

I break the silence. 'You understand this... has to be kept our secret, Juliette, at least for now.'

'Of course.' She looks at me with new confidence. 'You know how they talk. It would be such a scandal, if not handled properly.'

'I am glad you agree, Juliette.' I put my hand on her arm, which feels warm and soft through her sleeve, and have a sudden memory of her pulling her dress off to reveal the thin cotton shift she wears underneath. I force myself to focus on my words. 'There will be... opportunities. We need to take care.'

Juliette kisses me. The kiss is spontaneous and seals the pact between us. There is no need to say any more and I watch as she slips back to the nursery. I like the thought of sharing a great secret with her. I will make it public when the time is right and in the meantime there will be opportunities.

Chapter Three

Winter of 1423

Strangely patterned clouds drift overhead as I depart on the journey to London. An old rhyme comes to mind: mackerel sky, mackerel sky, never long wet, never long dry. The road glitters with early morning frost as I guide my horse, a well-bred palfrey belonging to the infant king, avoiding ice-covered puddles. With luck, I hope to reach London before my fingers freeze, although they are already tingling under my riding gauntlets.

The queen told me to travel with some of her personal guards, but I chose to ride alone, prepared to take my chances on the road to London, despite the threat of robbery and the fact I am unarmed. I enjoy the sense of freedom, being able to ride as I please. I also wish to keep this meeting with Duke Humphrey as discreet as possible. There is no way of knowing who in the royal household could be informers to the duke's rival, Henry Beaufort, Bishop of Winchester.

In the pocket of my doublet is the handkerchief embroidered with the red dragon. I would laugh if anyone called me superstitious, yet my keepsake gives me comfort, a token of good luck for my safe return. Juliette secretly visits my room whenever she can, always careful not to be seen at my door and always surprising me.

Once she arranged a hot bath, the first I have tried. A great hogshead half-barrel, lined with clean white linen cloths was filled with pans of scalding hot water. Juliette laughed as I managed to climb in without spilling too much on the floor. In spring and summer I am happy to take a dip in the River Thames which snakes its way around the castle. In the winter I cope as best as I can with my bowl and jug. It feels wonderful to bathe in clean water, with Juliette's soap scented with fragrant herbs, and see her admiring glances.

Another time she arrived at my door with a wooden bowl covered with a cloth, which she removed like a conjuror to reveal all kinds of exotic fruits. Some I have never seen before, even in France. Juliette confesses they were a gift from a merchant for the young king, but his governess told her to throw them out in case they made him ill. We shared the fruit as a late night feast, washed down with some fine ale.

We have become close since that first night and know it won't be long before our great secret is out. I still feel the strange longing at the thought of the lonely queen but push such thoughts from my mind. I could not wish for more from any woman than the love I have from Juliette.

In my saddlebag I carry the folded sheet of parchment with the list of all those who have visited the queen. I studied the neatly written names before I left, wondering what use the duke can make of it. I find it hard to imagine anyone using the festivities as an opportunity to influence the queen. There must be a particular person the duke is concerned about and, if that is the case, he can make my job easier by saying who they are.

I pass the time on my long ride by trying to recall what I know about Queen Catherine's brother-in-law, the enigmatic Duke Humphrey of Gloucester. Already one of the richest men in England, he inherited more vast estates, and the income from them, on the death of his elder brother King Henry V. He has more wealth than most people could dream of, but it seems the duke is still relentlessly ambitious.

My horse snorts a protest as I spur it on faster. The winter chill starts to bite and I pull my cloak more tightly around me as the first snowflakes drift from the wintry sky, settling in my horse's mane like tiny diamonds before melting. I have taken a risk by making the journey to London in late January. So far at least I have been spared the misery of rain and the usually muddy roads are still frozen, with thick ice in the deeper ruts.

The sun is descending in the west before the jagged forest of spires and towers of the capital city appear on the horizon. The muddy, dung-strewn roads are busier, with groups of riders on horseback, heavily laden carts drawn by horses and oxen, as well as poorer travellers making the long journey on foot. I scan the skyline, remembering the tallest of the spires is St Paul's, close to the duke's mansion on the banks of the Thames.

As I reach the city gates I am saddened to see a crowd of poor and sick men, women and children gathered to try their luck with travellers, despite the falling snow. A waiting beggar tugs at my cape, asking for charity to feed his starving family. I throw the ragged figure a silver groat as a reward for his nerve and in memory of the starving citizens of Rouen.

The streets of London are a riot of sounds and smells, exciting and dangerous in equal measure. Women call to me from open windows, offering a good time as I ride past. Street vendors try to sell me everything from cups of ale to miracle cures. Piles of rubbish and the stink of open sewers make me ride with more urgency to the cleaner streets of Westminster, where ramshackle wooden buildings are replaced by slate-roofed stone houses.

Duke Humphrey's mansion is not difficult to find. Baynard's Castle is the grandest of all the fine houses overlooking the river like a row of subtleties, finely crafted from sugar at a lavish banquet. I announce myself to the smartly-dressed guards at the high, wrought-iron gates and am not kept waiting long once the duke learns of my arrival.

After stabling my horse I am ushered through a side entrance and escorted up a polished marble stairway to the duke's personal study. The oak panelled room is hung with fine tapestries and a good fire blazes in a hearth decorated with gilded cherubs.

Duke Humphrey stands looking out of the window at the murky, fast-flowing River Thames. Boats with great tan sails drift effortlessly past. Others are rowed upriver against the current by hard-working watermen, all dusted with lightly falling snow. The duke welcomes me and points across the water to the south bank.

'They've built a new bull-baiting theatre—right next to the bear-baiting pit.' He scowls at the thought. 'Savages.'

For once I find some common ground with the duke. 'I visited the bear-baiting once, out of curiosity, my lord.' I look across the river. 'I heard the spectacle was not one to be missed, yet I found the sight of bears being taunted by packs of dogs disturbing.'

Duke Humphrey nods in approval and places a welcoming hand on my shoulder. 'You must be frozen after your ride, Tudor. Come and sit by the fire and tell me the news from Windsor.' He pulls a bell cord and a liveried servant appears. 'Claret—and have a room prepared for my visitor. He will be staying overnight.'

The servant vanishes like a ghost and soon reappears with two finely engraved goblets on a polished silver tray. We watch in silence as he pours generous measures, first for the duke, then for me. The man hands us a goblet each, then silently closes the door as he leaves.

I am surprised at the duke's generosity and how he treats me more like a friend than a servant. 'Thank you, my lord.' I sip the claret and the rich red wine warms me in an instant, taking me back to my time in France. I place the goblet on a table and unfold the parchment with the list of Queen Catherine's visitors, smoothing it out before handing it to the duke.

'I decided to deliver this in person, my lord. You asked me to show discretion.'

Duke Humphrey studies the list, as if looking for a particular name. 'This is everyone?'

'It is, my lord. I have employed a clerk to keep records. He has no knowledge of the purpose, of course.' I hope the duke won't ask if the queen knows of the list, as I have no wish to lie if it can be avoided.

'Good work, Tudor. I knew I could rely on you.'

I feel a flicker of conscience as I take another sip of the duke's fine claret. I could have produced the list without the queen's knowledge, although not without being disloyal to her. I find I am warming to the duke, though. After all, we share the same interest—the well-being of the queen and the infant king.

'It would make my task easier, my lord, if you could tell me who I am on the lookout for and why?' It seems a reasonable question.

The duke sips his claret before answering. 'Edmund Beaufort, for one. Or his uncle, Bishop Henry Beaufort. There is a rumour Bishop Henry is plotting to betroth his young nephew Edmund to the dowager queen.' He scowls again. 'Which of course, I could not possibly support.'

I see the duke hates the Beauforts with a vengeance, yet they are first cousins. Duke Humphrey would be in line for succession to the throne, after his elder brother Duke John of Bedford, the heir apparent, if anything were to happen to the young King Henry. I decide to risk speaking my mind.

'Forgive me, my lord, I understand Bishop Henry Beaufort is the queen's guardian and also appointed guardian of the young king. Is there something else I need to know?'

'Indeed there is, Tudor.' The duke takes another sip of claret and savours the taste. 'My late elder brother bankrupted the crown to finance his war in France. Parliament had taxed the people as severely as it dared, so Henry Beaufort secured loans against the crown jewels— and pledged further loans to the king of twenty-six thousand pounds from his own personal wealth.' He half smiles, yet his eyes are cold. 'And where do you suppose a bishop would find that sort of money?'

'I have no idea, my lord.' Twenty-six thousand pounds is a fortune, even by the standards of the royal family, enough to pay for an entire invading army. 'The money could have come from an inheritance?'

The duke scoffs. 'Henry Beaufort is the bastard son of John of Gaunt, Duke of Lancaster, the second of four illegitimate children. He inherited nothing, which is why he ended up in the church.'

'You suspect foul play?'

'Exactly!' The duke's brow creases in furrows like a freshly ploughed field. 'I suspect the bishop is corruptly abusing his position and, what is worse, my brother John is in league with him.'

I turn the duke's allegation over in my mind as I ride at an ambling gait back to Windsor Castle next morning. I slept soundly after a hearty meal in the duke's well-appointed kitchens, reputed to be the finest in the whole of London, and had been in no hurry to leave. Now the air feels a little warmer in the winter sun. The overnight fall of snow is turning to a muddy slush and spatters in the air, bringing curses from a man walking in the road as my horse trots past.

I decide the journey has been worthwhile. I have met the duke's demands without compromising my loyalty to the queen. Instead, I have proved I put her interests before my own. I have also earned Duke Humphrey's goodwill and trust, which could prove useful in the future.

I had known of the rivalry between the duke and the Beauforts, although I cannot pretend to understand it. The way the duke speaks of Bishop Beaufort anyone would think he is the devil incarnate, but I see how marriage between Edmund Beaufort and Queen Catherine would seal the power of the bishop, who already seems to control the parliament of Westminster.

Apart from his influential uncle, Edmund doesn't seem to have a great deal going for him. As the third son, Edmund has no money and poor prospects. He is now of marriageable age and in search of a worthy heiress. I dismiss a surge of jealousy that the young noble and his uncle plan to marry him to Queen Catherine, if the rumours the duke has heard are true.

Dusk is turning the sky to an ethereal pinkish grey by the time I reach Windsor and make my way to the castle stables. The rain, which started as a light shower an hour before, has become more determined and I am glad of my wide-brimmed hat and riding cape. Made of oiled leather, the cape is long enough to cover my legs and keeps the worst of the rain from soaking me to the skin. My boots are leaking though, and I feel the cold, unpleasant chill as rain trickles inside them.

My mind turns to Juliette. I have only been away for one night and am already looking forward to seeing her again. She will be full of questions about London, so I am glad I can tell her my journey has not been wasted. I must be wary of Duke Humphrey and give him no cause to mistrust me, but now I feel I understand him a little better.

They should be expecting my return, yet no light burns and no one is there to greet me as I arrive back at the stables. Apart from the horses the stables are deserted and I make a mental note to speak to the ostler. He has enough staff to ensure there is always someone there to greet visitors and tend their horses.

I unbuckle and remove the bridle, then unhitch the girth of the heavy wet saddle and lay my saddlebags to one side. I hear the door bang behind me as I brush my horse and comb its mane and tail. I would have liked to wash the horse down but the hour is getting late, so after making sure it has enough feed and water, I spread fresh straw on the cold ground of its stall.

A muffled cough is followed by the scrape of heavy boots and I turn, expecting one of the stable grooms. Instead two swarthy men I have never seen before charge at me, knocking me roughly to the ground. I am cold and tired after the long ride from London and they have surprise on their side. To be ambushed once safely home is the last thing I expected.

'Unhand me!' I struggle to break free from their firm grip.

Anger helps me find new energy and with a curse that reverberates around the stables I kick with all my strength, aiming between the legs of the man to my left. His grip loosens as my rain-soaked riding boot makes him double up with pain. Taking advantage of my freedom, I barge the man to my right against the hard stone wall of the stable, driving the wind from his lungs. Then I punch the man's jaw so hard at least one of his teeth is lost.

I turn to see what has become of the first man in time to see him pull a knife from his belt. The short blade glistens as he charges a second time and I throw myself to the ground, avoiding the savage blow by inches. Both men pile on top of me, one holding my hands while the second ties them behind my back, pulling so tight the rope cuts into my skin. They pull me upright and make me stand, one pinioning each of my arms.

'Do you know who I am?' I struggle to break loose but it is no good, as my hands are tied so tightly they start to feel numb.

A third man appears out of the darkness and I realise he must have watched the fight, waiting for his accomplices to do their work. Lithely built with lank hair and a jagged scar running across his face, he grins, revealing blackened teeth.

'Yes, Mister Tudor... we know who you are.' His voice is rasping, with a northern accent.

He punches me hard in the chest, winding me with the unexpected force of the blow and if it were not for the men holding me I would have collapsed to the ground. They pull me upright again as I try to clear my head. The scarred man grabs my hair and pulls my head back.

'I have a message to deliver to you, Mister Tudor.'

I feel the warmth of the man's foul breath in my face. 'Who are you?' I don't recognise any of them. 'What is this all about?'

'You like asking questions, don't you, Mister Tudor? Well, this is what happens to people who ask too many questions.'

I look from one to the other and see the man with the scarred face is in charge, the other two following his orders. I try to recall if I have seen any of the men before and a tantalising memory hovers somewhere at the back of my mind, then eludes me.

'You won't get away with this. I am a servant of the king.' The threat is my last hope and now my anger is replaced by the cold shock of fear. I am no match for the three thugs and there are no witnesses.

The scarred man gives a rasping laugh and punches me hard in the face. I feel the sting of searing pain and hear a crunch as my nose is broken. I taste the metallic warmth of my own blood as it runs down my face.

'Keep your nose out of things that don't concern you, Mister Tudor, or next time we'll finish the job.' He swings his fist again and punches me hard on the side of the head.

This time the other two thugs let me slip to the stable floor, one of them kicking so hard I hear a crack as my rib breaks. The men are laughing as they leave with no remorse for their actions. As I lie on the cold floor, drifting into unconsciousness, a name floats into my mind. Only one person could be behind this.

Chapter Four

The low-ceilinged basement room that serves as the castle infirmary has several wooden beds for care of the sick and injured. The windows are small and high on the north facing wall, so the infirmary always seems dark, particularly in winter. There is a fireplace, though no one has thought to light a fire, so I wake shivering and disorientated, wondering where I am.

The queen's personal physician, James Somerset, a kindly, absent-minded man with a straggling grey beard, examines my black eyes and bruised face with professional detachment. 'You'll live, Tudor.' He shakes his head, as if the assault is somehow my fault. 'I've done my best with your nose. After the swelling reduces... it should be straight enough. You took quite a beating.'

I don't need to be told. My nose has stopped bleeding, although I feel a deep, dull ache and my head throbs, more than the worst hangover I can ever recall. The sharp pain from my broken rib stabs like a blunted knife with each move I try to make. Somerset has bound my ribs with clean white linen, explaining that he can apply leeches, although there is little else to do. I know many weeks will pass before my injuries heal.

The queen's physician leaves, recommending plenty of rest, and Juliette appears at my bedside, a frown of concern on her face. I am relieved to see her, and am grateful as she places a cool hand on my forehead.

'How do you feel?'

'I've been better.' I manage a weak smile. 'How did I get here?' My voice sounds hoarse. My throat hurts when I try to speak and the constant buzzing in my ears makes it hard to think.

'One of the grooms found you in the stable this morning.' She looks at me with concern in her eyes. 'Who attacked you, Owen? What happened?'

'Three men ambushed me in the stables when I returned. I don't know any of them, although I have a good idea what this is about.' I remember my concern for the young clerk. 'Have you seen Nathaniel?'

Juliette looks confused. 'No. What has he to do with this?'

'The men who attacked me told me to stop asking questions.' I grimace as my head hurts. 'Before I left for London I told Nathaniel to check the stores in the kitchens. I needed Nathaniel to gather evidence before I could do anything, and now I'm worried I've put him in danger.'

I groan and swing my legs over the side of the bed then try to stand. I have to warn the clerk and hope he has the evidence I need. I like the mild-mannered young man and it will rest heavily on my conscience if anything has happened to him.

Juliette gently pushes me back down on the bed. 'You need to rest, Owen.' She pulls a rough woollen blanket over me, glancing at the fire, which has still not been lit. 'I'll see if I can find Nathaniel—and I will have someone sort out that fire, it's freezing in here.'

I am reluctant for her to leave but know she is right. 'Take care, Juliette.' I look down at my blood-stained doublet. 'Can you bring me some clean clothes?'

'Of course, sir.' She turns to go then leans over and kisses the one part of my face not covered in bruises. 'I love you, Owen Tudor,' she whispers.

'Even with a broken nose?'

'Even with a broken nose!'

I wake with a start to find Nathaniel sitting at my bedside, reading a leather-bound book by the flickering light of a candle. A fire blazes in the infirmary grate, filling the room with much-needed warmth and the tang of wood smoke. The corners of the room are filled with shadows and I guess I must have slept through most of the day. My head is still sore but I am relieved to see the young clerk has not suffered the same treatment.

Nathaniel closes his book. 'Juliette said I should let you sleep, sir.' He points to a change of clothes in a neatly folded pile. 'She brought you those.'

'Thank you, Nathaniel.' I rub my eyes, the pain in my nose a dull ache now. 'I'm relieved to see you.'

'Juliette told me what happened I hope the attack wasn't my fault. It was not possible to do as you asked.'

'What do you mean?'

'There are no proper records of what should be in the stores.' Nathaniel shrugs. 'Some deliveries, such as bread and milk, are used right away. Other orders, like cases of wine from France, take months to arrive. The problem is supplies can go missing and we have no way of knowing.'

I sit up, wincing at the pain in my side. 'Did they threaten you?'

'Samuel Cleaver told me to... keep out of his kitchen. He had me thrown out of the stores as soon as he heard I was in there. They didn't hurt me or make any threats.' He looks embarrassed. 'I'm afraid I told them...'

I climb out of bed, more easily this time. 'You told them you were working on my orders?'

Nathaniel nods but says nothing.

'Don't look so down—I would have done the same if I'd been in your position.' I change into the clothes Juliette brought and throw my ruined, blood-stained doublet to the floor. I am pleased to see she has also replaced my sodden riding boots with my best black leather pair, which I pull on, already feeling better.

'We could have Cleaver arrested and locked up, even though we don't have any proof. He obviously has something to hide.'

Nathaniel looks concerned. 'What if we then have to release him?' His forehead creases in a furrowed frown. 'And what about his henchmen? We still need to find the men who... did this to you.' He looks at my bruised face.

'Locking up Samuel Cleaver will only solve half the problem.' I remember the feel of my nose breaking and don't relish the thought of being caught out a second time. They threatened to finish the job and are capable of doing so.

'One of the men had a scar on his face, across the left cheek. Have you seen anyone like that?'

'No. The trouble is...'

I close my eyes for a second and grit my teeth as I try to bear the pain from my cracked rib. 'What were you saying?'

'The trouble is,' Nathaniel continues, 'unless we can find these men, there is a danger they might do it again.'

'I can't do my job if I'm looking over my shoulder all the time.'

'What other option do we have?'

'None I can think of.'

I finish dressing and we walk through the servants' passageway to the offices of the constable. Sir Walter Hungerford is tall and well built, approaching fifty and never seen without his sword of office, worn low on a belt. He greets me like an old friend.

'What the hell have you been up to, Tudor? Fighting again?'

I attempt a smile. 'It was three against one. They ambushed me in the stables last night. That's why I've come to see you.'

Sir Walter tells us to take a seat and closes the door. 'So, what's this all about?'

I am unsure where to start. 'This is my clerk, Nathaniel. I tasked him with making an inventory of the kitchen stores, as I suspected all was not as it should be, my lord.'

'There's always theft from kitchens, Tudor.' There is a patronising tone to his voice. 'Cooks work long hours on low wages, so it doesn't surprise me if they sometimes help themselves. This suggests something else though.'

'We need your help, my lord. We've been warned off by the head cook, Samuel Cleaver, which confirms my suspicions he is up to no good.'

'You want him arrested?'

'I don't have any proof.' I feel another stab of pain from my wounded rib. 'Samuel Cleaver's no fool. He will deny it all.'

'What do you suggest then, Tudor?' Sir Walter sits back in his richly upholstered chair. 'I can't go round arresting people without proper reason.'

'I'm going to let him know he can't get away with having me warned off. I thought as constable and steward of the king's household you should be made aware of this, my lord.'

'Of course. I think it's best if some of my men escort you.'

'One should do. I don't want this to get out of hand, if that can be avoided.' I look at the constable. 'I'd like to deal with this without it coming to the queen's attention. It is, after all, a household matter, my lord.'

Sir Walter shakes his head. 'And how do you propose to explain two black eyes and a broken nose to the queen? You look like a prize fighter from the back streets!'

'I will explain I was set upon by thieves, on my return from London.'

'True enough,' the constable agrees. 'I'll send a good man with you to the stores. I'll also have the captain of the guard tell his men to keep an eye out for you until this business is sorted out.' He shakes his head again. 'This reflects badly on us all here, Tudor. I'll help you if I can.'

I thank him and head for the Great Kitchen, followed by one of the royal guards. I feel a mix of apprehension and anger about confronting Samuel Cleaver, although it gives me peace of mind to know the guard is standing by. Cleaver wouldn't be so stupid as to attack one of the queen's guards. That would be treason, so he could face the death penalty.

The Great Kitchen is a steaming vision of hell when we arrive. I can't understand how anyone would choose to work in such conditions from first light until after the last supper of the evening. Young boys, barely ten years old, are the scullions, apprentices who hope to one day become cooks. They scrub blackened, greasy iron pans and wash clattering piles of pewter platters.

The smell of burning wood and charcoal from ovens and stoves mingles with rich aromas of boiling stews and freshly baked bread. Two young kitchen girls pluck feathers from fat chickens still steaming from the scalding house. A man strains with effort as he turns a whole pig on a roasting spit, his face bright red and running with sweat from the heat of the coals.

There in the middle of it all stands Cleaver, in a linen apron, shouting orders and cursing the poor quality of staff at the top of his voice. He spots us as soon as we set foot in the doorway and scowls as he mops his thick, muscular neck with a cloth. He looks surprised to see me.

'What can I do for you... gentlemen?' Cleaver stresses the last word to make it sound as insincere as possible, and then nods in the direction of the royal-liveried guard at the door. 'What's this all about?' His tone is challenging.

'We need to check the stores.' I note Cleaver's expression of disbelief. 'Routine housekeeping. I want to see how deliveries are recorded and that everything is as it should be.'

My tactic of coming straight to the point seems to have worked. Cleaver looks again at my black eyes and bruised nose, then at the studious Nathaniel. Samuel Cleaver is a man used to having his own way and scowls in annoyance.

'Come with me,' he leads us towards the stores, 'I'll show you.'

We follow him down scrubbed stone steps into the basement. The food store is underground, cool in summer and freezing in winter. This is useful for keeping supplies of food fresh, although not so good for working in. Samuel Cleaver shows us the different rooms within the basement, each designed for a particular need. In the flesh larder brown cured hams and sides of venison hang alongside braces of pheasants and grouse, suspended from iron hooks in the low ceiling.

Next to this is the wet store, where rows of oak barrels contain everything from salted herring to whole cod fish stored in wet seaweed. Freshwater carp and eels, as well as pike, are stored alive in the castle moat until needed. Alongside this is the dry larder for pulses and grain, with great round cheeses taking an entire shelf and giving off a distinctly mouldy odour. The light is poor in the storerooms, although we see there are no thugs waiting in dark corners.

Cleaver turns to me. 'We have enough to feed an army here. If you wish, Master Tudor, you can have your clerk,' he gives a dismissive wave to Nathaniel, 'check the stores against the deliveries, although I can save you the time. You will find everything is accounted for.'

I silently curse, as the head cook has the self-satisfied look of a man who is one step ahead of the game. He had been expecting our visit and made sure there is nothing that can be used as evidence against him. The place looks as if it has been made ready for an inspection.

'Everything does seem to be in order.' I lift the lid on a wooden crate, which proves to contain casks of French red wine, then pull one out to examine it. 'I think we have seen enough... for today.'

Samuel Cleaver's expression changes. 'I'll thank you, Master Tudor, to leave the running of the Great Kitchen to me.'

'I'm sure you are as keen as I am to make sure nothing goes missing, as if I find it has, there will be... consequences.'

The head cook sees us to the door. He mops his shiny head with the cloth he carries and glowers as we leave with the guard following behind.

'Take care, Master Tudor.' Cleaver manages to add a note of threat to the words.

✷ ✷ ✷

I lie awake, trying to think. I am not prepared to turn a blind eye to Samuel Cleaver, as my predecessors seem to have done. Even Sir Walter seems sympathetic towards Cleaver, although he has ordered a man to be posted outside my door. All that achieves is to make it impossible for Juliette to visit. They can't guard me forever, yet I cannot live with the risk of being attacked hanging over me. Nathaniel is right. It will be difficult to prove any theft.

I eventually drift off to sleep, my mind troubled by memories of the man with the scarred face. A knock at my door wakes me and I realise I have overslept, as bright daylight streams through my window. The throbbing ache in my head is reducing, helped by a sour-tasting potion of willow bark Juliette sweetened with a little honey and made me drink. Pulling on my clothes, I open the door to see Nathaniel.

'Good morning, sir.' Nathaniel looks unusually cheerful. 'I've had an idea. The men who attacked you must have told the stable grooms to keep out of the way when you returned from London. Someone should know them.'

'Of course.' I gesture for Nathaniel to enter. 'It could be the only way to find someone prepared to give evidence against Samuel Cleaver.'

Nathaniel sits in one of the leather chairs while I put on my boots. 'We must find out who was supposed to have been on duty in the stables. It shouldn't be too difficult.'

We head back to find the captain of the guard. It doesn't take long before a young stable lad is arrested and locked in a cell in the guard room. He cowers in one corner and looks doubtful about my promise to protect him in return for giving evidence. We know he is the one who should have been on duty in the stables on the evening of the attack, so it is only a matter of time before we make him talk.

I try again. 'Tell me where I can find these three men or you'll be charged with conspiracy to steal from the crown.' I look at the young boy. 'You understand what that will mean?'

'If I help you find them, sir, will I be allowed to keep my job?' He looks desperate. 'It's all I have.'

I feel some sympathy for the stable boy, who was unlucky to be caught up in Cleaver's plans. 'We'll see. Where can we find the men?'

'The man with the scar...' The boy hesitates, frightened of the consequences of helping me or of remaining silent.

'Go on?'

'He warned me to keep away from the stables, sir.'

'You know him?'

'No, sir, but I think I know where he can be found.'

I turn to the captain, who has been watching the questioning with interest. 'Can you send some men with him?'

'Of course,' the captain agrees, 'leave it to me.'

'If I'm any judge he'll talk soon enough.' I watch the stable boy massaging his wrists as the iron handcuffs are removed and hope my instinct is right. I understand how the boy is frightened of the three men and there doesn't seem to be any point in sacking him from his job. 'Good luck and remember—it is as much in your interests as mine that we find these men.'

The stable boy understands only too well. 'I'll do my best, sir.'

I realise I am late for my meeting with the queen, and as I approach her apartments I wonder again about Duke Humphrey's words. Loyalty and trust are complicated things. The duke trusts me, but I have a greater obligation to the queen. I knock on the door and enter. The queen is alone and I see I have kept her waiting.

She is dressed for the winter chill, with a dark, long-sleeved dress and a fur cape over her shoulders. Her hair is hidden by an elaborate French headdress. I don't find it flattering, as her headdress draws attention to her slender neck, making it look even longer. I find myself wondering how she looks with her hair down, over her shoulders.

'Good morning, my lady.'

The queen studies me as if seeing me for the first time. 'I am sorry to hear you were attacked. You should have had an escort from the palace guard. The road to London is notorious for robbers.'

I have already decided to make light of it. 'Fortunately I carried nothing of value, so if they intended to rob me they were disappointed.'

'And the duke? Was he also disappointed?'

'Duke Humphrey seems content with the list of names I gave him.'

'Good. Although I feel his methods are... underhand. If he wishes to know whom I am meeting with, all he needs to do is ask.'

'He is a thorough man. I believe he has your best interests, and those of the young king, at heart in this.'

'It sounds as if he has won you over?'

'They say to keep your friends close—and your enemies closer.'

'Is Duke Humphrey of Gloucester an enemy, or a friend?'

'For now, he is a friend.' I wonder how much to reveal. 'Although you are right, he is no friend of your guardian, Bishop Henry Beaufort.'

The queen looks at me with new respect. 'You have done well to make something from this situation.'

'Thank you, my lady.' I sense something between us has changed and hope she is starting to see me as her trusted man.

The captain of the guard is waiting to see me. 'We think we have two of the men who attacked you, Tudor, although we need you to identify them, if you will?'

'Of course.' I feel as if a weight has been lifted from my shoulders. 'The man with the scar?'

The captain shakes his head. 'No sign of him, I'm afraid.'

'Do you think they'll talk?'

'With a little persuasion.'

I follow the captain to the cells where the two men are held and recognise them immediately, the awful memory of the attack flooding back as I study their scowling faces.

'Your lives will be spared if you confess right now. Tell me where we can find your accomplice—and who put you up to it?' My voice sounds threatening as it echoes in the dark prison.

The men look at each other before one speaks. 'I don't know what you're talking about.' The arrogance in his words surprises me, considering the man's situation.

'What about Samuel Cleaver? Is it worth losing your lives to protect him?'

The men look at each other again and my instinct tells me they are wavering.

'Will you question them for me, Captain?' My voice is raised so the men will hear. 'I'm sure you can persuade them to be more helpful.'

It is enough. The older of the two men speaks. 'I have a family. Will you promise protection if we testify that Cleaver has been helping himself to supplies?'

'You have my word.' I turn to the captain. 'Let's visit Samuel Cleaver right now—before he gets wind of this.'

A dozen guards accompany us on the short walk to the Great Kitchen. I expect Cleaver to confront me like a cornered bull, ready to take as many men down with him as he can. I am wrong. The powerfully built head cook is as keen as we are to keep his arrest private from his inquisitive staff.

Cleaver follows behind the captain, apparently unconcerned about being led to the dungeons. I follow behind with the guards, relieved it has gone so easily. As the guard commander said, such things reflect badly on the security of the queen's household and also the safety of the young king. Bishop Henry Beaufort, as their guardian, can have both me and the captain replaced any time.

'Why have you arrested me?' Cleaver addresses his question to the captain, a note of challenge in his voice.

The captain looks back at Cleaver. 'You'll find out soon enough.'

Cleaver moves with surprising speed for such a heavy man. As soon as we are out of sight of the Great Kitchen he surprises us by sprinting for the trees, with the castle guards in pursuit. The first of the guards to lay hands on him is felled with a powerful punch, then Cleaver grabs the fallen man's halberd and turns to face the others, yelling and swearing for me to come and face him like a man.

The captain has seen enough and nods to the remaining guards, who understand what they have to do. I watch as Cleaver charges the closest guard. The man parries the halberd and Cleaver disappears from view as several guards wrestle him to the ground.

I take a deep breath and turn to the captain. 'We don't have any evidence, although you've seen for yourself how he behaves like a guilty man?'

The captain agrees. 'I will send them all to Newgate Gaol—unless you have other ideas?'

'See he has a fair trial, Captain.'

Chapter Five

Summer of 1428

I made the forty mile journey from Windsor to Hertford Castle, on the banks of the River Lea, with Nathaniel to oversee the arrangements for the queen's summer banquet to be held there. The old motte and bailey castle, with its wide moat and high curtain wall, was built by the Normans and gifted to the queen by King Henry V. It is where they stayed when they first married and, as with Wallingford Castle, Hertford is now to be used by the queen as a summer residence.

We have been kept busy organising repairs and redecoration to the great hall, built for his own use by John of Gaunt and still adorned with the enormous antlers of stags he no doubt hunted in the castle grounds. Nathaniel has worked long hours, checking enough deliveries of food and supplies to feed an army.

Over the past five years Nathaniel has become a loyal friend and my right-hand man, reliable and trusted. He has been in charge of supplies to the queen's household since Samuel Cleaver's downfall and inspects the store rooms each day to check for any discrepancies. We never apprehended the scar-faced man, and the palace guards watched over me for almost a year before I asked them to stop. Even five years later, I sometimes look over my shoulder to see if I am being followed.

Now the queen and young Harry have joined us here, together with most of her remaining household. I have been able to secure a comfortable room for myself above the servants' lodgings. Low, dark wooden beams mean I must take care not to hit my head, but my room is spacious enough to also serve as my office while we are here. Scanning the guest list for the banquet I see the great and the good of England are invited, and one name stands out like a bed bug on white linen.

I tap the name with my finger. 'Edmund Beaufort... I wonder if he's making his move at long last?'

'He was invited at the suggestion of his uncle, Bishop Beaufort.'

'I don't doubt it.' I sit back in my chair and think for a moment.

Edmund Beaufort has visited the queen several times over the past few years, usually in the company of his uncle the bishop. The last time he had been escort to his mother, the Countess of Somerset. They never stay overnight and on each occasion the facts are duly reported to Duke Humphrey, but nothing seems to have come of it. I still feel a strange jealousy at the idea of Beaufort marrying the queen and am secretly pleased to be in a position to do something about it.

'Help me keep an eye on him, Nathaniel.'

Nathaniel doesn't need to consult his list. 'I've been informed he's planning to stay for a week, so I've put him in the lodgings furthest from the royal apartments.'

'Good. I must also mention to Juliette to watch for him.'

Juliette is now the only servant remaining from the queen's French entourage and has become the handmaiden of her bedchamber. As well as increasing her status within the household, this means Juliette is even more invaluable to me, as she is with the queen from the moment she wakes to when she falls asleep. Little can happen in the queen's household now without Juliette learning of it.

'Would you like to deliver this list to Duke Humphrey in London?' I already know the answer. He enjoys his occasional visits to the city, particularly in the summer, and seems to like the importance of visiting Baynard's Castle. On his last visit he spent a whole afternoon in the duke's library with one of the finest collections of rare books in the country.

'I would—and I will also take the opportunity to meet with some of our suppliers while I am there.'

I thank Nathaniel and leave to see how the king has settled into his newly refurbished lodgings. Harry will be seven years old in December and has grown into a likeable boy, with a lively imagination and an endless curiosity. He seems to think of me more like a favourite uncle than his servant, although Queen Catherine has instructed all the household staff to call him 'Your Grace'. It is important they remember he is the king.

Dame Alice Boteler has served as the king's governess for the past four years. In place of Juliette and the nursery maids, his nurse, Joanna Astley, cares for the king through each night. Dame Alice is kindly enough towards me, although we did not have the best start when she first arrived. She told me her task is to teach the young king good manners and courtesy, as his previous nursery maids had not done so. Dame Alice also has the consent of council to chastise the king as she sees necessary.

I resent her criticism of the way Harry has been raised by Queen Catherine and Juliette, although I must admit that, at times, the young king is quite demanding. Today the king is trying on a new outfit to wear at his public appearances, a dark red doublet trimmed with gold braid and a velvet hat with a gold coronet around the brim. As he sees me he raises a miniature sceptre in greeting.

'Good day, Master Tudor.' His voice is still reedy, although he is growing stronger and beginning to look as if he might one day become a true king.

'Good day, Your Grace.' I bow to the king, playing along with him. 'Dame Alice.' I bow to the governess, who curtseys in reply. 'Is there another public appearance planned?' I like to know everything that concerns the king or his mother.

Dame Alice shakes her head. 'We need to be ready, as the Duke of Gloucester rarely provides notice of when he wishes the king to be seen by the people.'

I know how the duke can descend on us unannounced. It is his way of doing things. Over the past five years Duke Humphrey had been through a difficult time, having married an heiress, Countess Jacqueline of Hainault, and then failed to secure her titles and lands that he considered his by right.

The duke even led an army of mercenaries across the English Channel to take Countess Jacqueline's inheritance by force, yet returned empty handed, having abandoned his wife in Mons and returned with his young mistress, Lady Eleanor Cobham. At least the duke seems to be settling down and putting his energies into the welfare of the young king.

I watch as Dame Alice makes Harry parade up and down the room in his new outfit, pretending to wave royally to cheering crowds on each side. It is hard to reconcile the child I see with my memory of his father King Henry V, rallying the army at a siege, a warrior king.

'Is there any word about when the Earl of Warwick is to become the king's tutor, Dame Alice?'

She looks up at me sharply, as if the subject is not to be discussed, and then her attitude softens a little. 'My understanding, Master Tudor, is that parliament has given approval for Sir Richard to take up his duties in the autumn... before the king's seventh birthday.'

I knew the day would come, as Sir Richard Beauchamp, the Earl of Warwick, was named in the late king's will as his infant son's governor and tutor. The earl has only been an occasional visitor, as he is Captain of Calais, although he sees it as his duty to visit the young king whenever he returns to England.

I have allowed myself to settle too comfortably into the routine of the queen's household and grown out of touch with events in Westminster. Dame Alice is well connected and is regularly visited by members of her family who wished to see the young king. Her understanding is almost certainly correct.

Dame Alice crosses the room and lowers her voice. 'I also heard the Earl of Warwick is to become master of the royal household.' She watches my reaction. 'Where would that leave you, Master Tudor?'

'I am sure, Dame Alice, that the earl has more important matters to concern himself with than such things as ordering fresh flowers for the queen, keeping up supplies of mutton or ensuring clean linen for summer banquets.'

I sound more confident than I feel. There cannot be two masters of the household and I know the freedom I have enjoyed could end with the earl's arrival. At least I am forewarned, for which I am grateful to Dame Alice. I decide to spend more time on my visits to the king from now on, as I need Dame Alice's support.

'I shall look forward to assisting the earl.' I try to sound conciliatory. 'And we are all most grateful to you, Dame

Alice, for the excellent way you are preparing the king for what lies ahead.'

Dame Alice blushes at the compliment. 'Thank you, Master Tudor.' She glances across at the king, who is throwing his sceptre up in the air. He tries to catch it and fails, laughing as it clatters to the floor. 'This work seems easy enough to most, although it does have its challenges.'

That night when Juliette steals into my low-ceilinged room, slips out of her dress and lays by my side in the darkness, I find myself reflecting on our future. It is as if an invisible barrier, like a heavy iron portcullis, has descended, stopping our lives moving forward. For five years, she has waited for me to agree the time is right to marry. Tongues have wagged and people gossiped. It was difficult for us both in the early years, yet now we think little of it.

I know she hoped to conceive a child. It has been the way of women to tip the balance, but when no child came, doubts began to form in my mind. There is no way of knowing which of us is at fault or if it is simply not God's will. I lay awake at her side, wondering how long the life we know can continue.

My easy relationship with Juliette has not been the same since the attack in the stables. The guards keeping watch over me meant she could no longer come and go as she pleased. It kept us apart at nights for almost a year and, although we see each other every day, an unspoken distance has slowly grown between us.

Now I have a new concern as I reflect on my conversation with the king's governess, Dame Alice Boteler. I would never admit to being ambitious and have been content in my work, but the Earl of Warwick will make me a servant again. Everything will change, including the way the king thinks of me—and perhaps even how the queen sees me as her trusted right-hand man.

That is what troubles me most. After five years, the queen has yet to soften her attitude towards me. I see her every day at meal times, meetings about visitors, banquets and all the other household matters. Sometimes I catch a glimpse of the woman I have fallen in love with, although she never confides her secrets to me and is as untouchable as ever.

I put my arms around Juliette and pull her closer. It has been a good summer and, although the hour is late, there is still enough light to see she is still awake. I like the feel of her soft warmth pressing against me and am never happier than when I lay still and listen to her gentle breathing, even though my thoughts now are of the queen.

I turn onto my side to look into Juliette's eyes. 'Nathaniel showed me the list of guests for the summer banquet. Edmund Beaufort is staying here for a week.'

'Do you think he is going to try his hand with the queen?' The thought clearly intrigues Juliette. 'I've never heard her even mention Edmund Beaufort. How exciting!'

I sit up. 'What?'

Juliette's eyes twinkle with amusement at my indignation. 'I think it's about time.' She strokes a hand down my chest and laughs as she feels me tense. 'The queen should stop being a widow—and start living again.'

'Edmund Beaufort has no money, no prospects...'

'Queen Catherine has more than enough money.'

'He is six years younger than her.'

'Perhaps that is a good thing?' Juliette giggles and sees how it infuriates me. 'If I didn't know better, Owen Tudor, I would think you are jealous of Edmund Beaufort.'

I lie back, knowing Juliette is right. I don't need to worry about what may or may not happen between the queen and

Edmund Beaufort. There are plenty of others who will do that. I drift off to sleep imagining what Duke Humphrey will say when he reads Nathaniel's list of guests.

The royal banquet at Hertford Castle marks the high point of summer and also the beginning of the end of my daily routine. The king will soon be old enough to no longer need his mother's care and the Earl of Warwick will take charge of his household. It remains to be decided what will become of Queen Catherine's household; although I think it unlikely she will be allowed to stay with her son.

Dressed in the king's royal livery I watch as the guests arrive, the cream of England's nobility, chattering like magpies and greeting each other with over-loud exclamations. The lords wear brightly coloured sashes and swords glittering with gold and silver ornament. The ladies have furs and fashionable headdresses with exotic feathers and necklaces of rubies and diamonds. I think each guest wears jewels worth more than I will earn in a year.

The banquet is one of the grandest I have seen and has taken weeks of preparation. The old kitchens at Hertford are stretched to the limit, as the banquet demands vast quantities of food and drink, more than enough to feed a small army. The cost of candles, tapers and table linen has severely stretched the household budget.

I strain to hear over the noise as the names of newly arriving guests are announced by the doorman. I am beginning to make my way through the throng of nobles when I hear the latest arrivals are Duke Humphrey and Duchess Eleanor of Gloucester. The duke has been busy, divorcing his first wife, Countess Jacqueline. He has now married his former mistress, and the beautiful new duchess is already the centre of attention.

Slim, attractive and at least ten years younger than the duke, Duchess Eleanor wears a crimson silk dress with long sleeves. I smile as I see her basking in the attention and am surprised when she notices and smiles back at me, an unexpected connection, when to everyone else I seem to be invisible.

Edmund Beaufort arrives late, together with his purple-robed uncle, Bishop Henry Beaufort. Edmund is tall and his handsome, clean-shaven face makes him seem younger than his twenty-two years. Fashionably dressed in black velvet, he has an ostrich feather in his hat and wears an impressive dress-sword at his belt. In no time at all he is surrounded by ladies and begins flattering them in his cultured voice.

The Duke of Gloucester has also noted the new arrivals. His smile looks as if it takes real effort and his dark eyes are glowering. It seems the bishop is the more skilled of the two at concealing his true feelings. He loudly congratulates the duke on his recent marriage, without a trace of irony, at the same time managing to communicate his disapproval to everyone within earshot.

Their sparring is interrupted by a fanfare of trumpets to announce the arrival of the king and his mother, the queen dowager. Young Harry is dressed in yet another extravagant outfit, this time with a perfectly fitting gold coronet which flashes with rubies and diamonds. In his right hand the young king carries his sceptre while he clings to the arm of Queen Catherine with his left.

The queen glides through the guests like an elegant swan in shimmering white silk and lace, with a necklace of diamonds which catch the light as she moves. She seems happy for the first time in ages and younger than her twenty-eight years. In keeping with tradition, Queen Catherine leads the little king to the top table. Each of the guests file into their appointed place, while the queen's minstrels play tunefully from the high gallery.

'What do you think?'

I turn to see Juliette has found her way to my side, a fashionable lace headdress in place of the headscarf she always wears. She is attractive in a well-fitting blue dress I have never seen before. Apart from her lack of jewellery, I realise Juliette could pass for one of the noble ladies.

'You look... beautiful, Juliette.'

'Thank you, Master Tudor.' Juliette scans the guests, who have fallen silent and are sitting with bowed heads as Bishop Beaufort, stands and begins a ponderous Latin grace. After the bishop finishes she lowers her voice so only I can hear.

'Which one is Edmund Beaufort?'

'He is to the right of the bishop.' I have watched Edmund Beaufort since he arrived, and see that after Henry Beaufort introduces him, Queen Catherine pays him no further attention.

We watch as a procession of liveried servants enter carrying silver platters piled high with choice meats, which they take to each guest in turn, waiting while they help themselves from each platter, picking out tasty morsels with their fingers, the sign of good manners.

As well as cuts of beef, veal, pork, mutton and venison from Windsor Great Park, the guests are served with rare salmon, fresh river trout, eels and crayfish. The centrepiece of the banquet is a whole roasted peacock, served dressed in its own iridescent blue feathers, plucked and replaced after the bird had been cooked, its beak and feet gilded in gold leaf.

I made sure that even the wine goblets used by the guests are in order, with the queen and top table drinking from gold plate, the next most important using polished silver and the lesser nobles provided with pewter. Servants are ready with flagons of wine as soon as any goblets are empty, so before long the buzz of polite conversation has taken on a raucous undertone.

The bishop calls them to order and the queen makes a short speech, thanking everyone for attending. Then there is a fanfare of trumpets and four page boys enter, carrying a model of Hertford Castle over a foot high, made entirely from sugar and complete with a miniature Royal Standard flying from the top. It is placed before the queen and the guests applaud as the young king smashes many days of hard work to pieces.

'An omen, you think?'

Juliette is dismissive. 'Don't be so superstitious, Owen Tudor.'

'It's my Welsh background, you see. It's in my blood to be superstitious.'

Juliette looks to see if I am joking. 'I asked the queen where she hopes to move to after the king is of age.'

Again, she has surprised me. 'When was this?'

'This morning... when I was dressing her.' Juliette glances around and lowers her voice. 'She said she thinking of making Wallingford Castle her main residence.'

I am relieved and concerned at the same time. 'Has the queen been told when this might happen?'

Juliette gives an almost imperceptible shake of her head. 'I imagine it will be when the king is seven, in December.'

I watch as the banqueting guests become even more rowdy. Several of the younger lords, already looking the worse for drink, argue loudly about the merits of hunting stags or boars. It is time for Juliette to follow the queen back to her apartments to change for the evening entertainments.

Later that night I lay awake, thinking back over the events of the long day. I have been kept even busier than usual, overseeing the clearing up after the banquet. The entertainments, music and dancing went on longer than planned, due to the late summer evening and because most of the guests were quite drunk. It seems they have consumed almost the entire contents of the castle's wine cellar between them.

I feel tired but content I have done my work well, and Queen Catherine thanked me for my help in making the day a success. I recall how happily she laughed as she danced with young Edmund Beaufort—but then she danced with several of the younger nobles present. There was nothing wrong with that. I also saw Duke Humphrey watching the two of them together. There doesn't seem to be anything the duke can do about it, despite his evident disapproval.

I drift off to a troubled sleep, wondering if the queen will choose to take me with her as keeper of her new household in Wallingford or wherever it will be once the king reaches his seventh birthday. I find a little comfort from the knowledge that Duke Humphrey will support the idea, as he will still want a watch kept over the queen.

Juliette comes to visit my dreams. It is hard to see her in the darkness as she climbs into my bed and lays close, her fingers stroking the hair of my chest. She straddles me and loosens her long hair from its restraints. I can see her more clearly now, completely naked as her golden hair glistens in the moonlight from the window. Except that Juliette has dark hair. The woman who leans down and kisses me so passionately in my dream is Catherine.

Chapter Six

It is Juliette who innocently sets the chain of events in motion, little knowing where her words will eventually lead. She mentions to me that Edmund Beaufort has been to visit the queen, at night, in her private apartments. No one would have known except for Juliette. She always helps the queen prepare for her bed, yet that evening, the queen says she will not be needed. She tells me as she closed the door she heard a man ask a question. She recognised his cultured voice and also overheard the queen's happy reply.

The next day Edmund Beaufort decides to stay a little longer at Hertford. One week becomes two, and then he announces he will accompany the queen when we all return to Windsor. The young noble's attention seems to be having a good effect on Queen Catherine, transforming her into a younger and happier version of her former self.

I grit my teeth when I watch the queen and her young lover take long walks together in the castle gardens and riding in the grounds. I am envious when I see how well Edmund Beaufort plays with Harry, teaching the young king how to make a silver coin appear as if by magic and showing him how to fish for trout in the river, to the great consternation of Dame Alice Boteler.

Juliette is not the only one to notice how Catherine is falling for the young noble's relentless flattery. It is also impossible for her not to mention it, as I ask her each day. After the third day, I make a difficult decision and summon Nathaniel to take a letter to Duke Humphrey. This time it is not a list of names; the note is simply an observation that it seems Edmund Beaufort is becoming close to the queen.

I plainly hear my disloyalty as Nathaniel reads back the words I have dictated, although I tell myself my actions are in the interests of the queen. If I don't act soon I fear it will be too late to do anything. Over the past week Catherine has become a changed woman. Her conduct with Edmund Beaufort is always correct in front of her staff and servants, yet I know she is secretly in love with her young admirer— and now Beaufort is making clandestine midnight visits to the queen's bedchamber.

The first sign of the consequences of my letter is when Duke Humphrey arrives, as usual unannounced, and has a stormy meeting with the queen. He gives a curt nod as he leaves with a satisfied expression. After the duke has gone the queen summons me. Edmund Beaufort has left for London soon after the duke and the queen is not in good spirits. In my heart I already know the reason. The duke has somehow banned Edmund Beaufort from seeing her.

The queen is not alone in her room when I arrive, as the young king sits on the floor by the window, playing with a row of wooden toy soldiers. They are brightly painted in the livery of the royal guard and he is setting them up in rows and knocking them all down again. I can't help wondering if Harry's new tutor, Sir Richard Beauchamp, has any idea of the work he will need to do before the boy is even close to the warrior king his father had once been.

Harry greets me as I enter. 'Good day, Tudor.'

I bow to the young king. 'Good day, Your Grace.'

The queen speaks with sadness in her voice. 'Duke Humphrey has finally shown his hand.'

'In what way, my lady?'

'He came to tell me he has persuaded parliament... to agree I cannot marry without the king's permission.'

I glance across at Harry, who is lining up his soldiers in rows and taking no interest in his mother's conversation. 'When he comes of age?'

The queen raises her voice. 'Ten years from now!' She struggles to compose herself. 'And in the meantime...'

'You must have the duke's consent?' I see from her expression that my guess is right.

'Have I not been a widow long enough?' She sounds on the brink of tears.

'I don't see what the duke can do if you choose to marry without his consent?'

Queen Catherine looks at me wide eyed. 'Any man who marries me without consent will forfeit his lands and title.'

I understand. The duke has found a way to deter even Edmund Beaufort. Bishop Beaufort has been out-manipulated. Although I doubt the politically astute bishop will let the matter rest, it seems Duke Humphrey has shown he can still rally the support of parliament.

The young king knocks his soldiers to the floor again and runs over to Catherine. 'Can I go outside, Mother?'

Queen Catherine stares out of the window. 'You must come in if it starts to rain, Harry.' She turns to me. 'Please will you escort the king to Dame Alice? I am tired and need to think.'

I take the young king by the hand and with a bow to the queen lead him from the room. I have never seen her cry before and have mixed feelings. Perhaps Juliette had been right and it is time for the queen to start living her life again. Edmund Beaufort might not have been the ideal suitor but he made her happy.

I look down at Harry walking at my side and realise the queen's happiness is not Duke Humphrey's concern. The duke is keen to protect his place in the line of succession and at the same time, deliver a blow to the power and ambitions of his rivals, the Beauforts. This is something Duke Humphrey would have been planning for some time, yet my letter probably strengthened the duke's resolve.

✦ ✦ ✦

As I feared, the arrival of Sir Richard Beauchamp in Windsor changes everything. The earl is tall and assertive and well used to having his own way. Even though he is approaching fifty and his beard is silvery grey, he looks younger. He had been master of the Horse for King Henry V and was once the leading tournament jouster in England.

It was Sir Richard who led the English forces against Owain Glyndŵr's army and forced the Welsh to run for the hills. It was said he captured the Welsh banner when he routed the Welsh forces and displayed it as a trophy in the hall of his castle in Warwick. Owain Glyndŵr barely escaped with his life, although he has never been seen since.

The earl had a distinguished career fighting the French, so it is easy to see why he has been chosen to make a man of the young king. As soon as he arrives, Sir Richard calls the household staff to assemble in the great hall and announces that, forthwith, Windsor Castle will be the king's main household, of which he will be the master. The queen's household is to prepare to move to Wallingford Castle, which will be the queen's main residence.

I feel their eyes on me and bite my lip, trying to appear confident as Sir Richard's clerk reads out the names of those who will remain in the reduced household of the queen. My name is first on the earl's list. I thank God and silently promise to serve the queen, for as long as she needs me, wherever she decides to live out her days.

Juliette's name is not on the list. She puts her hand to her mouth as the clerk announces she will continue in the household of the king, as an assistant to Dame Alice. I assumed that, as the queen's personal handmaiden, Juliette will remain in her household. She stands with the other women of the household and looks across to where I stand with the men, her face a shocked expression of disbelief.

I am not paying attention as the earl's clerk reads out the rest of the names on his list, as a question occurs to me. The queen must have agreed the list with Sir Richard, so is it her way of ensuring she has a trusted person close to her son or is there another reason? Queen Catherine might be holding Juliette responsible for revealing her night-time liaisons with Edmund Beaufort. I see Juliette looking across at me and wonder if she has reached the same conclusion.

She seeks me out after the meeting is over and the household servants begin to return to their duties.

'What will we do?' She studies my face, as if trying to read my feelings.

'I didn't see this coming, Juliette. Has the queen said anything to you about how she plans to keep an eye on Harry?'

'No... although she was concerned the Earl of Warwick would be too harsh on him.'

'That could be the reason you've be chosen to stay with Harry.'

'Not because of Edmund?'

I put my finger to her lips to stop her saying any more. 'We must never speak of that again.'

Juliette seems as if she is about to cry. 'The queen wishes to stay with the king's household for as long as she can.' Juliette puts her hand on my arm, apparently no longer caring who sees. 'It will give us time...'

I know what she is hoping. 'I will ask the queen...'

This time it is Juliette who puts her finger to my lips. 'Let us choose our moment?'

'You are right. The queen has enough to worry about.'

I am right, for Sir Richard wastes no time in imposing his new regime on the young king. He decides Harry is too old for toy soldiers and orders them to be burned. Instead, the earl starts teaching him to use a sword, pitting him against young nobles of his own age. Unfortunately they have more experience, with predictable consequences. By the end of the first week, Harry has blood-stained bandages on both his hands and a cut on one cheek that refuses to heal and looks likely to leave a scar.

The queen is upset when she sees her son's fencing wounds and sends for me. I find her alone in her apartment, the first time we have been alone together since the earl's arrival in Windsor.

'It seems I am powerless to do anything about it.' She looks at me with sad eyes. 'I wrote to Bishop Beaufort, as he is the king's official guardian.' She shakes her head in despair. 'He replied reminding me it was my husband's wish for the Earl of Warwick to be Harry's tutor, as stated in the late king's will.'

I have known Harry since his first steps and feel responsible for his safety. 'I understand Sir Richard is to start preparing him to ride in the joust this afternoon. I could find an excuse to see it is done without unnecessary risk?'

Catherine places her hand on mine. 'Would you do that for me?'

My body tingles with the warmth of her hand. Concern for her son has made her break the rule that keeps the safe distance between us, the first time she has touched me. As we stand there for a moment I look into her eyes and see the sadness diminish as something unspoken passes between us.

'You know I will do anything for you, my lady.' My words seem to have new significance, which is not lost on Catherine.

'Thank you.' She removes her hand, almost reluctantly.

I feel strangely elated as I visit the tiltyard to see how her son will cope with the earl's dangerous training. I have seen the young king being fitted for a steel breastplate and helmet and am concerned about how Sir Richard intends to make a man of him. I have no idea how I can keep my promise to the queen, but I can't stand by and watch Harry be injured.

The young king is already mounted on one of the smaller horses, instead of the timid highland pony he prefers. It looks as if he is already learning to control the horse and Sir Richard proves a skilled and patient tutor as he shouts words of encouragement. Once he is satisfied the king can stay seated in the specially made jousting saddle, Sir Richard hands him a long wooden lance. It is light and barely half the length of a proper jousting lance, yet I can see Harry is struggling to ride while holding it.

At the end of the tiltyard is the quatrain, a target used for training jousters. A painted shield is fixed to one end of a rotating pole, with a weighted sack suspended from the other. The aim is to strike the shield with the tip of the lance while avoiding being hit on the back with the heavy sack as it swings around.

One of the stable lads speaks in a hushed tone as the young king trots his horse down the tiltyard. 'God help him, the poor bugger.'

Another of those watching is concerned. 'He's not yet seven years old, is he?'

The small horse gathers speed and we watch as the lance begins to overbalance the young king in the saddle. I am no jouster, but know it is considered poor technique for riders to steady their feet in stirrups, which are kept long.

'He'll be lucky to reach the end of the tiltyard, never mind hit the bloody target!' It is the stable lad again.

We watch as Sir Richard shouts for Harry to hold the lance high. It is too awkward for him and he forgets to keep control of his horse, which starts to veer off course. We can see what is going to happen, yet no one moves to stop it. I cannot resist shouting as well.

'Sit straight, Your Grace!'

The young king glances up, recognising my voice and managing to recover his seat in the nick of time. I am rewarded with a frown from Sir Richard and wonder if the earl wants Harry to take a fall, to teach him a lesson.

'Lean back into your saddle, Your Grace!' Sir Richard shouts to the young king, as he approaches the quatrain.

Harry leans back, the end of his lance wavering in the air as he rides. Then there is a cheer from the small crowd as his lance glances the edge of the black shield, fortunately not with enough force to swing the heavy sack of wet sand around.

Harry is still in the saddle as he brings his horse to a halt in front of the stables. For the first time I have an insight into a father's pride in his son. The late king would have been pleased to see his son do so well on his first attempt. I also realise Sir Richard knows exactly what he is doing. Although the horse is small, he has chosen well.

As I make my way back towards the castle I find myself wishing I have a son of my own. I am twenty-eight now, old enough to have had several sons if I had not been so indecisive. I resolve to discuss the future with Juliette that evening. Glancing up at the autumnal sky I wonder how much longer we will remain at Windsor before the queen's household moves to Wallingford.

Juliette lies on the comfortable pallet bed in my room and watches as I work at my desk in the last of the evening light. Nathaniel has been given the challenge of listing everything the queen will need when her household leaves Windsor Castle. His list fills many pages of yellow parchment.

'Are you going to be long?'

I turn and sit back in my chair, rubbing my tired eyes. 'This will keep. I can finish it in the morning.'

Juliette watches as I pull my shirt over my head and pour cold water from the jug into my bowl and splash some over my face. I smooth back my hair and sit on the end of the bed and pull off my heavy boots, then finish undressing and climb under the woollen blankets where she is waiting.

She still wears her thin cotton shift and is propped up on the pillow with the look I know means she wants to talk. For once I am ready to. Seeing how quickly Harry is growing has made me think about how the years are passing.

Juliette takes my hand in hers. 'I find it strange, not seeing the queen so often.'

I understand, as Juliette came to England with Catherine and has spent almost every waking hour with her since she became her personal handmaiden. 'Everyone is finding it difficult, even the queen. Sir Richard doesn't even like Harry spending time with her.' I shake my head. 'It's as if he thinks she will somehow undo all his good work.'

Juliette looks thoughtful. 'The two households are growing apart. Sir Richard seems to be encouraging it.' There is a hint of bitterness in her voice when she mentions the earl, ever since his clerk had not read out her name on the list of the queen's household.

'I have to keep things together as well as I can.' I take her in my arms and hold her close to me. 'Everyone wants to know when the queen is going to leave.'

'It's all they talk about.' There is a note of sadness in her voice.

I brush a strand of auburn hair from her face. 'The truth is… nobody has told her when we have to leave this place. They are so preoccupied with Harry—it's as if they've forgotten about his mother.'

'We always knew it would be like this.' Juliette sits up again. 'We need to decide what we are going to do.'

'What do you mean?'

'You know what I mean? I'm talking about you and me.'

I don't reply. Earlier I had decided to ask her to marry me; now I feel the familiar reluctance to make such a commitment. My thoughts are instead on how I felt when the queen put her hand on mine. It wasn't accidental. She had been reaching out for me and I hadn't misunderstood what passed between us in that moment.

'Say something, Owen.'

I cannot do it. We would have been happy enough, wherever the queen took us. It would have meant Juliette persuading the queen to take her back as a maid, although it shouldn't be too difficult, with her being one of the few French servants still in the household.

'What am I supposed to think if you say nothing?' Her voice is raised and she looks close to tears.

I know I can't remain silent for a moment longer. 'I'm sorry, Juliette.'

'Sorry?' She sounds exasperated. 'I would have followed you anywhere. You know that?' She wipes a tear as it runs down her face. 'Is this because we haven't had a child?'

I don't reply. I will never find anyone else as perfect for me as Juliette. She loves me unconditionally and has always tolerated my failure to commit to her.

'Say something—or I am giving up on you!' She sobs.

'I'm not saying goodbye, Juliette.'

'It's her, isn't it?' She glowers at me. 'Tell me you're not in love with Catherine?'

I try to find words to deny my feelings, yet they will not come.

'I knew it.' Her voice is bitter and she turns away from me, still sobbing.

I feel her whole body jerking with each sob. I have let her down, but cannot deny the thrill I feel to know that, after so many years of secret longing, Catherine, the Queen of England, has reached out for me.

Chapter Seven

Winter of 1428

The relentless, bone-chilling cold is made harder by the absence of Juliette. Although I often see her and she is always courteous, I am pained by the sadness in her eyes. On New Year's Eve I join the congregation in the Chapel Royal for the midnight mass and pray on my knees for guidance. As I look towards the altar I see Queen Catherine turn her head and glance back at me. Our eyes meet only for a second but it is enough.

After six months of uncertainty at Windsor, the consent of parliament is finally obtained for Queen Catherine to remove her household to Wallingford Castle. Although even further from London, Wallingford can be reached by boat on the River Thames and is a comfortable day's ride from her son. This is some comfort to the queen, as the young king will often visit and she can return to Windsor whenever she pleases.

The sprawling castle at Wallingford had a small fortune spent on it by successive owners, yet has most recently been used as a prison fortress. I arrive with a small army of carpenters and craftsmen, cleaners and restorers, to make it a palace fit for the queen. I see this move to Wallingford as a fresh start. I miss Juliette's company, although we parted on good terms and I hope not too many months will pass before I hear she has found another.

The old castle is spacious, having been expanded and extended many times from the original motte and bailey. The high tower on the top of the motte, dominating the skyline for miles around, will fly the Royal Standard when the queen is in residence. The kitchen, with its red-tiled, pointed chimney is next to the great hall and the royal apartments face out over the river. Two curtain-walled outer baileys add protection and the peaceful cloisters of the priory of St Nicholas offer somewhere to escape the noise and bustle within the castle grounds.

I ride around the perimeter wall of the great castle, accompanied by Nathaniel, who takes notes of the things needing repair and ideas for improvements. On the riverside are rows of willow traps, full of wriggling eels. A weir provides water for the castle mill, which grinds flour for the bakery, as well as for the people of Wallingford. We watch at the busy quayside as trading boats from as far as London unload supplies for the royal household.

The castle is far from luxurious, and little thought had been given to the servants' accommodation in the past. As I found during my summer visits, servants and household staff are expected to sleep wherever they can. For those who work in the kitchens this means a warm pallet close to the ovens. Some even choose to sleep in the stables with the horses. There is no obvious place for me to stay.

While overseeing the refurbishment of the queen's apartments I discover chambers which might have once been lodgings for Queen Isabella's ladies-in-waiting. I make one of these my study, as it has an adjacent room where I can sleep at night. It is not as well appointed as my room in Windsor but has a mullioned window with good views out over the river. This is useful as I can observe anyone crossing the bridge approaching the main gate. My new room at Wallingford also has the advantage of being close to Queen Catherine's apartments, connected by a narrow corridor.

By the time the queen arrives at Wallingford the refurbishment of her apartments is complete, as well as the wing for use by the young king and members of his household who travel with him. It is agreed that the king will visit for the summer months, so I arrange for the old tiltyard to be renewed and made ready for use.

Wallingford is more than simply a change of location, as the queen's new household is more relaxed and informal than at Windsor, particularly under the strict regime of the Earl of Warwick. The queen seems happier for the first time since Edmund Beaufort left and even Duke Humphrey seems more interested in his career at Westminster than who is coming and going at Wallingford.

On a bright spring morning I am invited to ride with the queen and her ladies as they explore the Berkshire countryside. We are accompanied by the elderly Constable of Wallingford Castle, Thomas Chaucer, and escorted by four of his mounted soldiers. I like Chaucer, although I am aware the constable is a first cousin of Bishop Beaufort and undoubtedly the bishop's spy in the queen's new home.

A portly man in his sixties, with the leathery, weather-beaten face of someone who spends a great deal of time outdoors, Thomas Chaucer is the only son of the renowned poet and philosopher Geoffrey Chaucer and has been constable at Wallingford Castle for many years. He has a ready wit and an endless knowledge of the history of the castle and the local area. Most importantly for me he has been helpful with the difficult task of removing tenants to make room for the queen's household.

I ride behind the queen and her ladies-in-waiting, enjoying the feel of the sun on my back after the long winter. Wallingford is more rural and quieter than Windsor and we meet no one as we ride alongside the riverbank and down a lane leading to open meadow pasture. The only sounds that morning are the calls of distant woodpigeons and the leisurely clip-clop of our horses' hooves on the old cobbled road.

Thomas Chaucer rides at my side and is in a talkative mood, keen to share his tales of serving with the king in France.

I encourage him with a question I know he will appreciate. 'You fought at the battle of Agincourt, Constable?'

'I took twelve men-at-arms and thirty-seven of my best archers to Agincourt, in the service of King Henry.' He glances across at me. 'Were you there, Tudor?'

'I was fourteen. They said I was too young to fight.' I look across at the old constable. 'Was it as tough as I've heard?'

Chaucer sits back in his saddle as he reminisces. 'Lost half my men. I nearly lost my horse!'

'I served Sir Walter Hungerford, first as a page and later as his squire, with the king's archers at the siege of Rouen.'

Chaucer seems impressed. 'Of course—I know Sir Walter well. He's done well for himself, as he is Baron Hungerford now.' He smiles. 'Who'd have thought he would become Treasurer of England?'

'He was most generous to me. It's thanks to him I am here today.'

Before the constable can reply, a colourful cock pheasant is startled from the hedge with a screech and a rapid whirring of wings. Its sudden appearance frightens the queen's horse, which rears up, throwing her to the ground. One of the queen's ladies-in-waiting shrieks with alarm and I dismount and rush to Queen Catherine's assistance. I can see she has fallen badly.

'Someone hold the queen's horse!' I take Catherine's gloved hand. 'Where are you hurt, my lady?'

She doesn't answer and her eyes look dazed. Fearing the worst I turn to Thomas Chaucer.

'Can you send men for a wagon or the queen's carriage? We need her physician. She won't be able to ride back to the castle.'

Thomas Chaucer shouts to two of the guards and they ride off. He dismounts and takes the bridle of my horse, as well as the queen's.

Picking up the queen in my arms I carry her to the grassy bank, then turn to her ladies-in-waiting who watch with shocked expressions. 'I'm afraid the queen has fainted, but thank God, her injuries don't look serious.'

I am watching when Catherine's eyes flutter open and begin to focus on my face. 'How do you feel, my lady?'

'My head hurts—and my ankle.' Her voice is soft.

I smooth her forehead gently with my hand and feel her relax a little. Before I realise what is happening my touch becomes a caress and I see how she looks into my eyes. It is the same look I saw when she glanced back at me in the chapel at Windsor.

Thomas Chaucer seems to feel he is in some way responsible for her accident. 'I'm sorry Your Highness, the hedgerows are full of pheasants—they can be quite excitable at this time of year. I should have ordered a man to ride ahead to flush them out.'

'A pheasant, of all things!' She manages a weak smile. 'It's not your fault, Constable. My mare is skittish about things like that. I should have controlled her better.'

Chaucer still holds the bridle of the queen's grey mare and pats its neck. 'She seems to have calmed down, Your Highness.'

We hadn't ridden far from the castle and the carriage soon appears in the distance. I am concerned the queen will have difficulty climbing into it when it arrives.

'Could you try to stand, my lady?' I help her, offering her my arm for support. 'I think the only way to get you safely into the carriage is for me to lift you.'

Catherine puts her arm around my neck to steady herself and for a second I hold her close, surprised at how light she feels, and then carry her to the waiting carriage. Thomas Chaucer leads the queen's horse by the bridle and once the carriage has been turned around we head back to the castle.

I wait outside the queen's apartments while she is seen by her physician, James Somerset, who eventually emerges and says the queen wishes to see me. She is sitting in a chair by the window overlooking the river and turns when she hears me enter. A swelling on her forehead is noticeable now, but she smiles when she sees it is me.

'How are you feeling, my lady?' I return her smile, noting there are no ladies-in–waiting in her chamber now and we are alone.

'My head aches... and my ankle is a little swollen.' She stretches out her leg and looks down at her foot. 'Somerset has told me he will prepare a poultice of herbs.' She wrinkles her nose at the thought. 'He says I will find it difficult to walk for a few days.'

'You had a lucky escape, my lady.' I think she is fortunate not to suffer far worse injuries.

'It all happened so quickly. I wanted to thank you, Owen, for helping me.'

'I only did what anyone would have done.'

'I am glad you were there this morning.'

I see the look in her eyes. Again, an unspoken bond passes between us and on an impulse I take her slender hand in mine, the greatest risk I have taken yet. If I have misread her it could cost my job and I might never see her again.

'I thought... it was going to be a lot worse for you.'

She doesn't pull her hand away or reproach me. Instead she gives my hand a gentle squeeze. It tells me all I need to know. I look down at her small hand, her long fingers with their gold rings set with rubies and diamonds. It feels warm and soft, a hand that has never known hard work. Catherine's fingernails are perfectly manicured by her maid. A memory of something Juliette said flickers through my mind and I push the thought away.

'I need to get back on a horse as soon as I can.'

'They do say that you should get back in the saddle if you take a fall.'

'Does the same apply to lovers, do you think?' Her voice sounds suggestive.

I feel her caress the back of my hand with her thumb, a subtle gesture. Even if anyone is watching they would not notice, yet it sends a clear message. Emboldened, I decide to take another risk before the moment passes.

'Edmund Beaufort?'

Catherine sighs. 'He was a breath of fresh air when I needed it. I believed I was in love with him... yet he was too easily frightened off by Gloucester.'

'And now you need... to get back in the saddle?'

She doesn't reply and I hold my breath, wondering if I have gone too far, then she leans across and kisses me softly on the cheek. It is completely unexpected.

'I love you, Catherine.' My voice is almost a whisper. Although there is no danger of us being overheard, my future hangs in the balance.

'I have known, for a long time, Owen,' she smiles, 'your poorly kept secret.'

I hold her close and tenderly kiss her on the lips, something I dreamed of for many years. It feels so natural I can't believe she has made me wait for so long.

The harbingers arrive first, with their banners and proclamations, the advance party of the young king, who is to stay for the summer and prepare for his coronation. Sir Richard Beauchamp is making no compromises with his responsibilities as master of the king's household, which numbers almost two hundred, including several young nobles, royal wards of a similar age, who are being educated with him, his first royal court.

This is more than double the household of the queen and Nathaniel is kept busy allocating lodgings for this great influx of people, planning how they will all be fed and ordering long lists of extra supplies. There are so many we have to create a tented area in the outer ward. With more than sixty additional horses, a new stable is hastily built against the inner curtain wall, along with more temporary accommodation for visitors and servants.

The earl has also sent a message. I am required to personally inspect everything from the stables to the refurbished tiltyard and the cleanliness of the castle kitchens. I privately curse Sir Richard, as I have been happy since the queen moved to Wallingford. It seems we will now be returning to the old regime of Windsor Castle and I must become a servant again.

The preparations have barely been completed when there is a fanfare of trumpeters and the clatter of many hooves on the cobbles as the young king rides through the gates of Wallingford. Ahead of him ride Sir Richard's entourage of knights and the esquires of the body he has recruited to provide more training for the king. Harry follows, with the earl at his side, followed by fifty men of the royal guard resplendent in full livery. It has only been four months, yet Catherine hardly recognises her son. Sir Richard has dressed him as a young knight for his triumphal entrance and he seems to have a new confidence, although he is still not eight years old.

Harry dismounts expertly, despite the long sword he wears, and proudly marches to where Catherine waits. 'Good day, Mother.' He bows, from the waist as he has been taught.

Catherine smiles. 'Welcome to Wallingford Castle.'

Harry hugs his mother. He notices Sir Richard frowning behind him, clearly displeased at how easily the young king has forgotten how he must behave.

Catherine looks up at the earl. 'And welcome to you also, Sir Richard.'

The earl dismounts, removes his hat and bows to Catherine. 'I am at your service, my lady.'

That evening Queen Catherine hosts a welcome banquet in the great hall, her son the guest of honour. The queen makes a grand entrance with Harry at her side, his armour replaced with a tunic of burgundy velvet. She wears a new dress of azure silk, made for the occasion, with a tall, conical hat in the English fashion. Catherine blushes when I privately tell her I have never seen her look more beautiful.

Sir Richard proposes a toast. 'To the King of England... and King of France!'

Catherine leans across to the earl and lowers her voice. 'King of France?'

A crease of annoyance furrows the earl's brow. 'Henry's father would have been crowned King of France long ago, my lady. We must arrange young Henry's coronation and then he must travel to France.'

'Is it safe for him in France?'

'Of course.' Sir Richard looks surprised Catherine would even ask such a question. 'You understand the dowager queen does not attend the coronation of her husband's successor, my lady?' There is a condescending tone to his voice.

'I understand quite well, Sir Richard.' She smiles at him, yet her eyes are cold.

'It is important that the king understands the country. I would be grateful, my lady, if you will help him practice his formal French in preparation for the visit.'

After they have eaten, the trestle tables are cleared from the centre of the great hall for dancing. The musicians are a great success and a good quantity of wine and ale is drunk. The young king looks tired from his long ride and Catherine bids him goodnight, announcing that she is also ready to retire for the night. I follow her at a discreet distance until we are alone.

'I was standing behind you and heard the earl's words.'

Catherine pulls off her uncomfortable headdress. 'I suspect the earl is acting on orders from my brother-in-law, Duke John of Bedford.' She shakes her plaited hair loose. 'He has always been obsessed with securing the French crown. He persuaded my father... to grant it to my husband and now he wants my son to claim it.'

'What of your brother, Charles?'

'I had a message from him. He wanted to let me know he is to be crowned King of France on the seventeenth of July.'

'That's barely a month away.'

'Sir Richard knows full well—he puts me in an impossible position.' Her neck flushes red at the knowledge of her powerlessness.

'Life is a balance of holding on and letting go. You must let him go.' I place my hands on the queen's shoulders. 'And I will stay here with you.'

Catherine puts both arms around me and pulls me close, resting her head on my chest. 'I am glad to have at least one friend who cares what becomes of me.'

I embrace her. We have both drunk more than a little wine and I feel the warmth of her body pressing against mine. I meant it when I told her I'd never seen her looking more beautiful. The fresh country air and sunshine have turned her pale skin to gold and, until now, she has seemed happier.

Sounds of music and dancing drift through the castle. We hear the crash of something breaking, followed by laughter. It seems the celebrations will continue long into the night. I should return to the great hall to oversee the servants of the queen's household. I have trained them well, although by tradition they are allowed to use up whatever has been left after the banquet. If that includes drink there is no telling what they might get up to.

I reluctantly pull away. 'I must go, before they find the keys to your wine cellar.'

Catherine holds on to me. 'Don't leave.' It is a command, not a request.

She takes my hand and leads me into her private bedchamber, pausing to slide the iron bolt on the inside of the door across. I have secretly longed for this moment and designed the layout of the queen's apartments to provide her with the greatest privacy, as far away from the guest lodgings as possible.

'What about your handmaiden?' Catherine has yet to find anyone as good as Juliette. The latest of her maids is a local girl, one of the staff at Wallingford Castle when we arrived.

She is in awe of the queen and rarely speaks unless she has to.

'She can enjoy the dancing. I told her she would not be needed until the morning.'

'So... who will help you undress, my lady?'

Catherine smiles mischievously. 'I rather hoped it would be you, Owen Tudor.'

She pulls off her stiff, uncomfortable headdress, flinging it to the floor, and looks at me with a challenge in her eyes. I say nothing but carefully liberate her tightly coiled hair. It cascades over her shoulders in blonde waves, making her look young and innocent, less like a queen, more like the woman I long for and love so deeply.

I take her in my arms and kiss her, feeling her respond with surprising passion, her hands caressing my back, softly at first, then pulling me close to kiss more deeply. Ours is the kiss only lovers know, and we are as one as we forget the world.

It takes only a moment to loosen the bindings of her dress and I follow her example, casting each of her expensive garments carelessly to the floor until she stands before me, beautiful and naked. Her pale skin turns to gold in the flickering candlelight and she looks almost too perfect to be real.

I lead her to the bed and she lays back to watch as I take off my boots and undress, enjoying the way her eyes devour every inch of my body before I lay at her side. We look into each other's faces for a moment and our special, unspoken communication means there is no need to talk. We kiss again, more slowly this time, more sensually. My mouth moves to her soft breast and I gasp as I feel her delicate fingers stroking me.

'I need you, Owen Tudor,' she whispers.

We have become lovers, after all those years of denial and longing, Catherine of Valois, the most beautiful woman in England and France, is mine.

I wake with a start, confused for a moment by the unfamiliar surroundings, before I remember I am in the servant's lodgings at Westminster Palace. I have been dreaming again of that first night in the queen's apartments. I remember every moment of her passion, her complete abandonment to me. There had been no shyness, no awkward moments. It felt as if we were always meant to be together, that we were always lovers.

With an effort, my thoughts return to the reason I am in London. Plans for Harry's coronation as King of England after his eighth birthday have been brought forward, following news of Charles VII of Valois' coronation as the French king in Reims Cathedral in July. Henry Beaufort makes a rare visit to Wallingford Castle to announce the chosen date of the sixth of November. He dresses in scarlet robes and hat, having secured his long-held wish to become a cardinal, yet his time in France has aged him.

Duke Humphrey visits soon afterwards, demanding to know every detail of what the bishop has said. I am happy enough to oblige, although it seems they would both do well to forget their political differences. I also note that Duke Humphrey asks me to reveal nothing about who else has visited the queen, as if she has ceased to be of importance to him.

I rub my eyes and study the small patch of autumnal sky I can see from the high, cobweb-encrusted window. It looks like it will be a dry morning, a good omen, as there were heavy rain showers on the journey to Windsor Castle, where I stayed overnight before continuing to London.

I wonder how Catherine is. She had no involvement in the planning of her son's coronation ceremony, yet tells me that suits her, as long as they do not expect too much of Harry. We have always known the ceremony will be in Westminster Abbey, and Catherine has secured me a good vantage-point as a royal usher, helping the great and the good of England to find their places in the crowded aisles.

It means I am present at the dress rehearsal in the abbey the previous evening and have time to visit the magnificent tomb of King Henry V. I stand before it in silence for a moment, marvelling at the craftsmanship of the effigy in the king's likeness, and wonder what the late king would have to say about his wife now being her servant's lover. The thought seems irreverent in the hallowed cloisters of Westminster Abbey.

On the great day I dress in my fine livery and share bread and cheese in the servants' kitchen. There is a buzz of anticipation, with many people coming and going and shouting orders. I spare a thought for the young king, who has spent the eve of his coronation in the Tower of London, where, in keeping with tradition, he has created more than thirty new knights.

I am kept busy in the crowded aisles of the abbey, as some guests complain they are too far away while others try to use their rank to demand a better seat. Then a distant cheer from the waiting crowd is followed by a shrill fanfare of trumpets, announcing the arrival of the king's procession. Harry has travelled through the city from the Tower, riding a white horse and led by the Earl of Warwick as his guardian and governor.

The trumpeters sound again and then the choir sing the *Te Deum*, the surreal, unearthly sound reverberating around the towering abbey and making the hairs stand up on my arms. The formal ceremony in the abbey is mercifully short.

Cardinal Henry Beaufort has altered the traditional coronation ceremony to include French practices, as his intention is to show this is only the first part of a fuller coronation, which must be completed in France.

The young king looks small, surrounded by bishops who seem grander in their high-pointed ceremonial mitres. Henry Beaufort sits to the king's right and Duke Humphrey to his left. I fix the scene in my mind so I can describe it to Catherine on my return. Archbishop Henry Chichele, who crowned Catherine and presided over Harry's christening, anoints the young king with holy oil from the golden eagle and ampulla. Harry looks serious as the heavy gold crown of St Edward the Confessor is placed firmly on his head.

After the ceremony, a splendid feast is held in Westminster Hall. The first course is venison and ham painted with gold, beef and mutton, cygnets and herons, with a great pike served in the mouth of a golden lion. The second course of whole pigs, roasted and glazed, is followed by the grand birds, crane and bittern, partridges and peacocks.

Next a whole antelope is served, with a golden crown around his neck on a chain of gold. The final course is of smaller birds, egrets, curlews, snipes and larks. Carp and crabs are served with a cold meat pie in the shape of the royal arms in red and gold. The centrepiece is now a figurine of the Virgin Mary, holding the infant Christ.

The sun is a blindingly dark orange, low on the horizon, as I return to my lodgings. I am pleased for Harry that this ordeal at least is over. The weather has remained fine and the coronation has attracted the largest crowds seen in London for years. I share a room with soldiers who had been holding back the crowds. One of them tells me he saw a woman crushed to death and a number of cut-purses had their ears cut off as punishment.

Chapter Eight

It is a relief to be back at Wallingford Castle after the extravagances of the coronation, yet Catherine confides to me that she has been unable to sleep, fearing for the safety of her son when he travels to Paris. Her brother Charles has a new champion in France in the unlikely form of a young woman named Joan, who has somehow become a heroine of the people.

The woman they call the Maid of Orleans has rallied the French army. It seems she hears the voice of God and has ended the English siege of the strategically important city of Orleans. Catherine's brother-in-law John, Duke of Bedford, finds his position as Regent of France threatened—and the uneasy truce with Duke Philip of Burgundy is wavering.

I do my best to reassure Catherine, but in my heart I know she is right to be concerned, as the timing could hardly be worse. Her brother Charles has now been crowned, so there is a real risk that making a great show of crowning Harry King of France could lead to war. Paris is no longer safe for the English and the young king is an obvious target for the French.

An opportunity to raise these concerns comes when Catherine is invited to visit Duke Humphrey's London mansion. I contrive to accompany the duke on his early morning ride along the Thames embankment, where the air is cold enough to show the hot breath of our horses. I see my chance to mention our reservations about the second coronation once we are out of earshot of the guards.

The duke is candid. 'My brother believes the claim to the French crown can be strengthened by this coronation.' He frowns at the thought. 'It must go ahead though, even if the siege of Paris is imminent. To turn back now would be disastrous, so I've persuaded parliament that strong military intervention is the only answer. We've started recruiting five thousand additional men to support those already there.'

'I worry for the young king, my lord.'

'The nobility of England are vying with each other to support the king. You need to understand, Tudor, the prospect of the coronation in France is an opportunity for people like Cardinal Beaufort to grow even richer.' His tone becomes patronising as he warms to his theme. 'Soldiers have to be paid, and men like Beaufort rub their hands together at the prospect of even more loans to the crown.'

'What of the queen's brother Charles, my lord?'

'What of him? He was lucky at Orleans. You've served in France, Tudor. The French are a fickle lot. My brother will show them it takes more than a young woman dressed in a man's armour to stop him.'

Duke Humphrey urges his horse into a brisk trot and I must do the same to keep up. Sometimes it is easy to see the resemblance of the duke to his elder brother, King Henry V. They have the same contempt for the French, even when it is obvious they have met their match. I only saw Duke John of Bedford from a distance and never spoke to him, yet I can imagine the duke will stop at nothing to see Harry crowned in France, regardless of the cost.

Late that evening I wait until we are alone in the duke's well-appointed guest apartments and repeat every word he has said to Catherine. She listens with a mother's concern for her son.

'I don't trust Duke Humphrey—or his brother John!'

'Why not?' The sudden hardness in Catherine's tone surprises me. Her French accent has returned, as it does when she is annoyed.

'Duke John of Bedford is the heir apparent. If anything were to happen to Harry...' Her words tail off, as she contemplates the thought of her son being put in danger.

I take her protectively into my arms. 'I told you, the duke promised five thousand men to protect your son. You mustn't worry, they will keep him safe.'

'I still don't want him to go. Does he have to be drawn into a fight... against my own brother?'

'I am afraid it seems you have no choice.'

Catherine crosses to the window, with its splendid view of the River Thames, still bustling with boats despite the late hour. 'I am tired of being treated like I have no mind of my own, with no opinions, as if I am of no consequence.' She turns to face me. 'I do have a choice—and I don't think even Duke Humphrey cares what I do any more. Did he ask you if I have had any visitors?'

'No. He seemed more interested in talking about himself.'

'You see?' Catherine holds both of my hands in hers and looks into my eyes. 'He thinks he has made it impossible for me to marry. What if I marry someone who has no lands for him to confiscate?'

I feel a cold sense of foreboding. 'What do you mean?'

Catherine laughs at my innocence. 'If I were to marry you, what could they do?'

'Well, they could have me hanged at Tyburn. Publicly flogged?'

'Not while I still have breath left in me they won't!'

There is new fire in her eyes and I realise she is serious. 'Would you marry me?' I hold my breath, waiting for her answer.

'Are you asking me, Owen Tudor?'

I take her hand. 'I love you, Catherine, as deeply as a man can love a woman.' I kiss her softly on the lips and pull her closer so I can look into her beautiful blue eyes. 'I will always love you, until the end of my days, as God is my witness. Will you be my wife, Catherine?'

'I will.' She hugs me so hard the old wound to my rib begins to hurt, and then whispers in my ear, as if we are likely to be overheard. 'I love you, Owen. We must marry in secret, so by the time they find out it will be too late.'

'We cannot stay in Wallingford.' My head is buzzing as I start thinking about the practical consequences. 'It will be best if we find somewhere safe, as I dare not think what will happen when word gets out.'

'Find us somewhere,' she smiles, 'if anyone can do it, you can.'

'What do you think Duke Humphrey will say when he learns what we've done?'

Catherine laughs, her eyes shining with happiness. 'Duke Humphrey and the cardinal—and all those who would have me locked away and forgotten—can say whatever they wish!'

Everything changes from that moment and all the things which were so important become irrelevant. The only person I dare to take into my confidence is Nathaniel. The former clerk is now responsible for the finances of the queen's household and the two of us have become close friends over the years. I need Nathaniel's help if our plan is to have any chance of success and arrange to meet in my study at Wallingford.

I see he knows me well enough to guess I am about to say something important. Once again I worry I am putting Nathaniel in danger by involving him, but this time I have no choice.

I take a deep breath. 'Catherine has agreed to marry me.' Even as I say the words the idea sounds absurdly reckless.

Nathaniel raises his eyebrows in surprise. 'I must congratulate you... although I don't see how they will ever allow such a thing.'

'That is why I'm telling you first. They will never allow it, so it has to be done in secret—and kept secret until it's too late for them to stop us.'

Nathaniel sits back in his chair and strokes his new beard which makes him look older. Eventually he speaks. 'We need to find someone prepared to conduct the service.'

'It doesn't have to be a priest, although I know Catherine will want the marriage to be blessed, even if it has to be done in secret.'

Nathaniel agrees. 'It will help if they have influence at the Council of Westminster, someone whose word will not be questioned.'

'Such as a bishop?' I see the sense of Nathaniel's suggestion.

'A bishop would be ideal, if you can find one who does not feel obliged to inform Cardinal Beaufort.'

'Bishop Philip Morgan of Ely is a Welshman, wealthy enough not to need Cardinal Beaufort's support—and influential enough not to worry about upsetting Duke Humphrey. I could ask Catherine to write to him, requesting his help.' I have never spoken to Bishop Morgan but he has known Catherine since before she came to England and would not betray her trust.

'I'll be happy to deliver the letter to the bishop in person, if that would help?'

'I think it best if nothing is written down about this, at least for now. Will you travel to see the bishop and see if you can persuade him to visit the queen here?'

'You are right. It is a risk to even tell Bishop Morgan what you are planning—yet I don't see we have any choice.'

I feel a sense of foreboding again. 'Do you believe in destiny, Nathaniel?'

'You believe it is your destiny to marry Queen Catherine?'

'I've always believed some things are meant to happen—and if this marriage is, then nothing we do will stop it.'

Bishop Morgan arrives the following week and has a private meeting with Catherine. A large man with a florid face and a deep Welsh accent, he suffers with poor eyesight and has learned to become a skilled listener. This proved invaluable in his diplomatic work, as the bishop served as Chancellor of Normandy and supported the peace negotiations.

Catherine confides to me later that Bishop Morgan tried his best to persuade her to see sense. He warned that the consequences could be serious for her and worse for me, yet realises she is determined and has offered his full support. The marriage will, he says, teach humility to those who are too quick to dismiss the mother of the king.

That evening the three of us meet in the queen's apartments to discuss the arrangements. Catherine introduces me to the bishop, who is greatly interested in my Welsh ancestry.

'I served as rector of Aberedowy as a young man.' The bishop has a wistful look in his eye. 'If I hadn't gone into the church I could have been with your father, Tudor, fighting the English.'

'My father was steward to the Bishop of Bangor. I remember little of that, as I was only seven when I came to London.'

The bishop smiles. 'And now you wish to marry Queen Catherine. Can you confirm to me that you are free to do so?'

'I can, Bishop Morgan, and I am grateful that you agreed to travel here.'

The bishop turns to Catherine. 'There are many who would not agree, my lady, although I see no obstacle to this marriage—and I am happy to officiate at your wedding. We can hold it in the chapel here in Wallingford. It seems as good a place as any.'

'Thank you, Bishop. There is one person we trust to be a witness, yet we still need to find a second. The problem is... we suspect the Constable of Wallingford, Thomas Chaucer, might be an agent for Cardinal Beaufort—and we can't be sure who else to trust.'

The bishop looks unsurprised. 'I will ask my good friend William Grey, the Bishop of London, to act as our second witness. It may be helpful if the validity of the marriage is ever challenged.'

'Do you think it will be challenged, Bishop?' I am concerned at how quickly our plan could unravel.

'Of course—although you must understand that it is consummation which truly seals a legally binding marriage. Let us imagine you were to have another child, soon after you are married.' He pauses to allow us to think about what he is saying. 'There would be little point in their challenging that, would there?' There is a twinkle in his eye when he sees our reaction.

Catherine brightens as she understands his point. 'Any children of my marriage will be members of the royal family.'

I have always wished for a son and can see the logic of what the bishop is saying. Even Duke Humphrey will hesitate to accuse the king's mother of having a child outside a legal marriage, particularly with his somewhat questionable past in that regard.

The bishop continues. 'You will find William Grey is both discreet and sympathetic. He has little time for Cardinal Beaufort's politics or the way he conducts himself as Bishop of Winchester. William may even agree that you can stay at his palace until all this blows over. He lives in London now and his country residence would be the perfect place to escape the attention of those in Westminster.'

Catherine is interested. 'Where is his country palace, Bishop?'

'It's a manor house in a village called Much Hadam, in Hertfordshire.' He gives me a knowing look. 'Out of sight is out of mind, Tudor, remember that. They will have their hands full with this coronation in France and will be too busy to go searching for the mother of the king.'

After some discussion we decide the service will be held at midnight in the castle chapel. I am relieved to learn that Thomas Chaucer has been called away on business in London, and doubt anyone will wonder who is burning church candles at such a late hour. Nathaniel has agreed to act as a witness and also to keep a watch on the door to prevent the ceremony being interrupted.

Our second witness, Bishop Grey, has arrived from London earlier in the day and spent a long time in a meeting with Queen Catherine and Bishop Morgan. He is elderly, but his mind is sharp. Bishop Grey is content to agree the plan to allow us sanctuary at his country manor, although he cautions that his tenure as Bishop of London is to end after a year. After that we might need to make alternative arrangements, depending on the reaction at Westminster if the marriage is discovered.

We all agree it will be best for our plan to be kept secret for as long as possible. Catherine's main concern is how we can keep it from everyone when she visits her son in Windsor. There will be little privacy in the king's busy household and it seems almost certain someone will find out, particularly if she is with child.

The castle chapel is ancient with small leaded windows set high in the walls. I shiver in the cold night air, hardly able to believe what is happening, and pace nervously in the dark hallway of the chapel. I repeatedly ask Nathaniel if he can see anyone approaching and start to wonder if something has gone wrong when Catherine arrives, a beautiful silk gown under her dark riding cloak.

Bishop Morgan has rehearsed the simple ceremony with us both in the privacy of the queen's apartment and recites the formal wording from memory.

'Owen Tudor, wilt though have this woman to thy wedded wife, wilt thou love her and honour her, keep her and guard her, in health and in sickness, as a husband should a wife and forsaking all others on account of her, keep thee only unto her, so long as ye both shall live?'

I am ready. 'I will.'

The bishop continues. 'Queen Catherine, wilt though have this man to thy wedded husband, wilt thou love him, honour him, keep him in health and in sickness, as a wife should a husband and forsaking all others on account of him, keep thee only unto him, for so long as ye both shall live?'

Catherine replies. 'I will.' Her voice is clear and confident in the still night air.

Now I answer. 'I receive you as mine, so that you become my wife and I your husband, to have and to hold from this day forward, for better, for worse, for richer, for poorer, in sickness and in health, till death do us part and thereto I plight thee my troth.'

Catherine responds and it seems time stands still. I look at Catherine and see not a queen but the confident woman who loves me, and who I love so deeply in return. I take the gold ring, which Catherine has chosen from her jewellery, and place it on her finger. The bishop gives us his blessing and it is done. I kiss my new bride and a Welsh servant has married a queen.

We thank the bishops for their kindness and loyalty to the queen, and Catherine presents Nathaniel with a gold crucifix as a token of her gratitude. Moving silently back through the silent castle grounds, I finally close and bolt the door of Catherine's bedchamber, to spend our first night together as husband and wife.

✷ ✷ ✷

The house at Much Hadam is on the edge of a quiet village some forty miles north of London. Although officially the palace of the Bishops of London, it is more of a manor house than any of the palaces I have lived in. The main feature is a high-ceilinged timber hall, over a hundred years old. The decoration is simple, as befitting its religious function. The rooms are spacious and the furniture practical.

My concern is Catherine will think it too plain after the luxury she has known, but I needn't have worried, as she finds our new home at Much Hadam offers her the freedom she always longed for. The one thing that troubles her is Bishop Morgan's suggestion about how she can explain her sudden disappearance. Before leaving Wallingford the bishops joined us for a toast in the queen's apartments and the talk soon turned to this problem.

Bishop Grey raised the question. 'What are you going to tell the rest of the household?'

The question hangs in the air and I glance at Catherine. We haven't discussed it, although we can hardly expect to slip away without anyone noticing. There are always visitors calling at the castle to see the queen and the bishop is right, we must decide what is to become of the household staff.

Catherine answers. 'We need time. There must be some way to answer any questions before it's too late for them to challenge our marriage.'

Bishop Morgan nods to Catherine. 'You don't need anyone's permission to travel around the country. For now, all you need to say is that you wish a change from Wallingford. You don't have to tell anyone where you've gone.'

'They will think it strange if I travel alone—and they will wonder where Owen has gone.'

A thought occurs to me. 'I will tell Nathaniel to keep the queen's household busy. I can say I'm going to the coronation in France. That will buy plenty of time.'

Catherine looks uncertain. 'What will they say if someone like Duke Humphrey insists on knowing where I am?'

Bishop Grey answers. 'I understand you will not like this, my lady, although it will stop any questions if it were suggested there is a problem with your health?'

'To say I am ill?' Catherine frowns at the thought.

Bishop Grey looks flustered. 'In a manner of speaking, my lady. I was thinking of your father. It could be suggested that you have... shown early signs of his problems.'

'You mean to suggest I am losing my mind?' Her French accent returns and her face is flushed.

Bishop Morgan intervenes. 'You said the constable here, Thomas Chaucer, is a first cousin of Henry Beaufort and possibly watching your household for the Cardinal?'

I see where this is leading. 'I could explain to him, in strict confidence, why the queen has to be taken away from public view for a while—and ask for his co-operation in keeping this secret for as long as possible?'

The bishop nods again. 'He will no doubt inform his cousin, Henry Beaufort—who in turn will ensure no questions are asked.' He looks at Catherine. 'You will need to consent to this, of course.'

Catherine stares out of the window. I follow the direction of her gaze and see how the ancient leaded-glass distorts the view of the river, blurring the edges between where the water ends and the land begins. I remember how they locked her father away for his own safety and to hide his torment from the people. Catherine once confided to me that even her mother acted as if he was dead. No questions were asked as no one wanted to hear the King of France had gone mad. It was plausible that his daughter could inherit something of his ways.

'I agree,' she says, her voice so soft it can hardly be heard.

I know her well enough to see she already regrets her consent. I am the only one who knows her secret. Sometimes she wakes and has to struggle to recall her own name or where she is. The day could come when she will not be able to remember anything. The possibility she truly does have something of her father's madness troubles me, and for her it could become a paralysing fear.

Chapter Nine

Spring of 1431

The powerful longbow creaks as I heave it back to full stretch and sight down the arrow. My arm strains with the effort of holding it perfectly still. I realise I am holding my breath and remember to breathe out. With a familiar swish that takes me instantly back to my youth, I loose the arrow and grin like a boy as it strikes satisfyingly deep into the centre of the makeshift straw target.

One of the unexpected aspects of life at Much Hadam Palace is that I have plenty of time to improve my skill with archery. That is part of the problem. Before my marriage to Catherine I worked hard, in a position of trust and responsibility, making sure the queen's household ran smoothly. Now I see myself as a kept man, living off my wife's allowance, with only maids, cooks and gardeners to worry about. Even they have little need of me, for as servants of Bishop Grey they ran his palace well enough on their own.

The village is little more than a hamlet, so the parish church of St Andrew's, said to have been built by men returning from the Crusades, is the focal point. When Bishop William Grey visits he explains that the grandeur of the village church, with its unusually long nave, is because of the adjacent official summer palace. The ancient door has iron hinges with fleur-de-lis, a sign of its Norman past, and the spire is a tall, traditional Hertfordshire spike, visible for miles around.

I am grateful for how well everything has worked out. Catherine's wealth and allowances are more than enough for us to live in comfort for the rest of our lives. Bishop Grey doesn't even require payment of rent, as the palace is owned by the church commissioners. It has all become a little too easy. I am lucky beyond my wildest dreams, yet find myself longing for the day when we can live openly as husband and wife, rather than hiding away in secret.

To show my gratitude and keep myself busy I cut down the young trees which have self-seeded in the churchyard, clear ivy from the walls, and restore headstones which have fallen. I find a rickety wooden ladder in the crypt of the church and climb high onto the roof to repair slates which became dislodged in the winter storms. It is satisfying work and I feel I am contributing to the local community, as well as keeping myself gainfully occupied.

The villagers I meet are friendly and assume I am in the bishop's employment, doing the work on his orders. It surprises me how easily we have fitted into our simple life in the country after the luxury of Windsor Castle or even the hustle and bustle of life at Wallingford.

Nathaniel rides to visit us and reports that all is quiet at Wallingford Castle. It seems our plan has worked. No unexpected visitors have called and no awkward questions have been asked. He brings a bundle of letters and messages for the queen, including one from Harry in Windsor. Catherine is able to reply to them all without revealing she is no longer in residence there—or almost nine months pregnant with her second child.

I worry that, instead of glowing with health, Catherine spends so much time in her bed. I know almost nothing about childbirth so must rely on the judgement of the village midwife. A cheerful, buxom woman with unruly ginger hair, as far as I am aware she neither knows or cares about our identity and seems reassuringly unconcerned about Catherine.

'She needs to rest, sir.'

I search the woman's deeply lined face for clues to what she thinks. 'Is it normal for my wife to look so pale?'

The midwife must see my concern. 'Your wife has not slept well for many nights, sir, so it is best she stays in her bed.'

'Can you tell how much longer we have to wait?'

'The baby will come soon enough, one day, two at the most. I will stay here and have everything ready.'

I feel a little reassured. 'You must tell me what I need to do.'

'Some say husbands should keep away, but I know better.' She gives me a conspiratorial look. 'You sit with your wife, sir. She will be glad to see you.'

I try to let Catherine sleep for as long as she wants, then take the midwife's advice and go to see her. Catherine is curled up on her side, a thin coverlet over her, her swollen stomach clasped in both hands. I pull a chair to her bedside and take her hand.

'How are you feeling?'

She looks up at me with drowsy eyes. 'I can feel the baby moving.' She places the flat of my hand on her bulge. 'The child kicks hard. It must be a boy!'

I can feel a strange movement. 'Is it bad luck to talk about names before the baby is born?'

'No.' Catherine laughs. 'Although I didn't have any choice with Henry.'

'Well, this time you can choose.'

'Truly?'

'Of course,' I stroke her forehead, 'I will name the next one.'

'In that case... if it is a boy I would like to call him Edmund.'

I sit back in the chair. 'Edmund?'

'You don't mind?'

'Of course not.' I hope she misses the lie and remember my jealousy at how happy she had been with Edmund Beaufort. 'What if it is a girl?'

'What was your mother's name?'

'Margaret.' A distant memory comes back to me. 'My father called her Meg when I was a child—although her proper name was Margaret.'

'Margaret it is then,' says Catherine decisively. 'We will name her after your mother.'

'Thank you,' I feel strangely emotional, 'that would mean a lot to me.'

The end of the taper in my hand shakes as I light another candle. I can't recall when I had last been so nervous. The midwife closes the door on me, shutting me out of women's business. All I can do is wait and pray and pace up and down. Unable to help I try not to think about the stories I've heard about what can go wrong.

I always wanted a son but have given little thought to what it could mean to be a father. It seemed unthinkable when Bishop Morgan first suggested a child would make it impossible for even Duke Humphrey to challenge the validity of our marriage.

I hear Catherine calling out to God, followed by a worrying silence, and am about to knock on the door when I hear the cry of a new born baby. Unable to contain myself any longer I push the door open a little and peer inside, not sure what to expect.

Catherine is propped up in bed holding a pink bundle to her breast and smiles as she sees me. 'It's a boy, Owen. We have a perfectly healthy boy.'

The midwife wraps the baby tightly in clean linen and I look down at my son.

'Edmund.'

Catherine looks at us both proudly. 'Edmund Tudor.'

✻ ✻ ✻

Nathaniel's expression of surprise makes me grin like a fool when I ride through the gates of Wallingford Castle alone. 'Good to see you, old friend, it has been a while!'

Nathaniel shakes my hand. 'Good to see you too, Owen. What brings you back to Wallingford?'

'We need to talk, in private. Catherine wishes to visit her son in Windsor.'

Nathaniel sends for something for me to eat while I leave my horse at the stables and then follow him to the royal apartments. I find it strange to discover my room in Wallingford is exactly as I left it. Out of habit I check Catherine's apartment and find the furniture covered with dust sheets, as if she is expected to return at any time. A serving girl arrives from the kitchens, carrying a platter of bread and beef with a flagon of beer and two pewter tankards.

I wait until the staring girl has gone, then close the door and ask Nathaniel to take a seat. 'Catherine is missing Harry and wants to visit him in Windsor.'

Nathaniel watches as I pour us both a tankard from the flagon of ale. 'Does she plan to tell him about you—about his half-brother?'

I take a drink before answering and pull a face at the bitter taste. 'That's the thing, Nathaniel. She wants to tell him and I've no idea how Harry will take it.'

Nathaniel drinks some of his ale while I tear a chunk of bread, still warm from the oven, and bite into it hungrily.

'You think he is too much under the influence of his tutor, Sir Richard Beauchamp?'

'I do. He could have me thrown in the Tower—we simply don't know.'

'What about young Edmund?'

'Catherine has asked the midwife to care for him while we visit Windsor.' I smile as I remember. 'I thought it a step too far for her to turn up carrying a baby.' I take my knife and cut myself a thick slice of beef. I've hardly eaten all day and it tastes good. 'As far as anyone is concerned, Catherine has recovered her health and there is no reason to suspect she has a second child.'

I study my friend, one of the few people I can trust and rely on. Nathaniel looks like a noble now, with his neatly trimmed beard. He has invested in good clothes and wears fine leather boots and a fashionable black felt hat. It is hard to remember the man in front of me as the studious clerk I once knew.

He takes another drink while I wolf down the rest of the bread and beef. 'I can arrange the visit to the king, although I wonder... if it is a good idea.'

'We will need to bring the usual retinue of servants and a royal escort.'

'That's easy enough to organise, but what about the queen? Is she coming here?'

'No, we will travel by St Albans. You can wait there with the retinue while I ride ahead and collect Catherine from Much Hadam.'

'You haven't decided if you will tell the king?'

Nathaniel's question is one I have discussed many times with Catherine, once almost arguing about it. 'We will have to see, Nathaniel. I am considering telling Sir Richard, if I have the chance.'

Nathaniel's eyebrows rise in surprise. 'What if he reacts badly?'

'I think Sir Richard will agree that Catherine can see Harry when she wishes, and we can only do it with his support. It is a risk—but we can't hide for the rest of our lives.'

Harry is taller and it seems the training has finally had effect, as there is something more regal about his manner. The earl has dressed him in an ermine-trimmed robe for the meeting and he wears a gold coronet unselfconsciously. Instead of running to embrace his mother he bows to her formally and waits while she curtsies in return before speaking.

'It is good to see you, Mother.'

Catherine smiles. Her son is playing the part as he has been instructed. 'And you, how you have grown.'

I am watching Sir Richard who stands behind the king with another knight I've not seen before at his side. Both wear their swords on low slung belts, fighting weapons, which have probably seen use in battle. I see the earl is studying Catherine, as if trying to detect anything unusual. Someone must have told him she suffered with her father's problems, and I guess it could have been Cardinal Beaufort.

Most importantly, I realise that the earl and the knight, who must be the king's full-time bodyguard, seem disinterested in me. Standing well back from Catherine, for once I find it useful to become an invisible servant again. It comforts me to know the bishops have kept their silence. No one knows our secret, for now, at least.

Harry sees me though. 'Good day, Tudor.' There is a welcoming note in the young king's voice. 'You must ride with me while you are here—and see how I have improved my skill at the joust.'

I bow to him. 'It will be a great honour, Your Highness.'

Sir Richard notices me at last. 'I need to talk with you, Tudor.' He looks at Harry. 'We will leave the king to spend a little time with his mother.'

'Of course, my lord.'

I follow the earl down long, familiar corridors, rehearsing in my mind what I need to say. It crosses my mind that these could be my last moments as a free man, if God wills it. Sir Richard takes me to the room he uses for his study and keeps me standing while he sits behind a large oak desk cluttered with papers.

'So tell me, Tudor, is the queen dowager ill?'

I look at the earl. An honest man, although unpredictable, Sir Richard's long grey hair is receding and his face is deep with the lines which show he has not chosen an easy life, despite his considerable wealth.

'Queen Catherine is well, my lord, yet there is something I have to tell you.'

'What is it?' He doesn't sound the least bit interested in what I have to say.

'She has remarried, my lord. To me—and we have a child now.' I blurt it out, my carefully rehearsed speech forgotten.

The earl stares at me in disbelief and slumps back in his chair as he calculates the significance of the news. 'Who knows of this?'

'We kept it secret, until now.' It is only half a lie.

'The child... was born in wedlock?'

'He was, my lord.'

'And you have witnesses to the marriage?'

'We do, my lord. Two bishops.'

The earl studies me with new curiosity. 'You know the consequences of this, Tudor?'

He still hasn't invited me to sit and I stand straight, trying to sound more confident than I feel. 'I wanted you to be the first to know, Sir Richard, as we need your advice before we inform the king.'

The earl sits up and it is clear their tactic has worked. 'The queen dowager is not informing him right now?'

'No, my lord, we thought it best...'

'I don't want him told until after he returns from the coronation in France, is that understood? He has made good progress and something like this could be upsetting.' The earl stands and walks to the window. He seems deep in thought, then turns to face me. 'I appreciate your discretion, Tudor, but you know what people will say?'

I don't answer as I know well enough.

The earl regards me with steel-grey eyes. 'They will say you abused your position, took advantage of the queen— seduced her.' He shakes his head at the thought. 'I doubt the Duke of Gloucester will take kindly to this, Tudor. He'll have your head on a spike!'

Now I regret ever agreeing to leave our peaceful sanctuary at Much Hadam. I made the long journey so Catherine can see her son and now I can't be sure if I will even be allowed to leave. The earl can have me arrested and will not be unduly concerned about the queen dowager's wishes.

'I will have to worry about that when the time comes, my lord. It is the queen dowager who needs your help and support.'

The earl crosses over to an elaborately carved cabinet. 'I don't know whether to curse you or thank you, Tudor.' He pulls open the door to reveal a collection of wine casks and silver goblets. He fills two goblets from one of the casks.

'By God, you seem to have outsmarted us all. I don't like that—but I appreciate your honesty.' He hands one goblet to me and raises his own. 'Congratulations, Tudor. I have decided your intentions are honourable.'

I raise my goblet in the air. 'To the King of England and of France.'

'To the King.'

★ ★ ★

Bishop Philip Morgan fills his chair to overflowing with his portly figure as his deep voice rises to the high, hammer-beamed roof of the great hall at Much Hadham palace. He has been invited for dinner and says a long Latin grace before we can eat. When he finishes I fill the bishop's goblet with sweet, amber-coloured mead.

'What news from London, Bishop?'

The bishop tastes the rich mead and nods in approval. 'The rows between Duke Humphrey and Cardinal Beaufort have reached a new level. They divide the council with their accusations.' He pauses as if recalling some incident. 'I regret to say their self-interest is to the detriment of the country.'

'Perhaps it will keep them too busy to concern themselves with us?'

'God willing.' He makes the sign of the cross absent-mindedly on his chest. 'That and, of course, the coronation in France.'

'You are to travel to France, Bishop Morgan?' Catherine sounds concerned.

'I am.' He frowns. 'You know the girl Joan was put on trial?'

Catherine answers. 'We heard.'

'Duke John of Bedford has colluded with Cardinal Beaufort. They wish her dead before the coronation.'

'She is to be executed?' Catherine's French accent returns.

'I regret to say... she is.' He looks saddened at the prospect.

'Has she been found guilty of witchcraft?' I think it unlikely.

'Witchcraft, heresy—and dressing like a man. Her crime is to believe she hears voices telling her she is chosen by God to lead the French army to victory.'

'No good will come of this. Duke John of Bedford will make a martyr of her.' Catherine must be thinking of her brother.

The bishop nods in agreement. 'The whole thing is a sad business. I understand that she is only nineteen years old.'

The maid brings their first course, a fine glazed ham, carved into slices and served on trenchers of bread. I see the bishop's goblet is already empty and refill it with mead. Bishop Morgan mentioned a liking for it once and Nathaniel makes sure we have a cask when he visits.

'You said that Bishop Grey's tenure is coming to an end?'

The bishop finishes his mouthful of ham before replying. 'Robert Fitzhugh is to become the new Bishop of London. I knew his father, Baron Fitzhugh. A good man, I worked with him on the Treaty of Troyes.'

Catherine remembers him. 'I travelled with Baron Fitzhugh from France. He helped escort the late king's body back to Westminster Abbey—and now he too is dead.'

'Does this mean that we need to move from here, if Bishop Grey's tenure is ending?' I have mixed feelings at the thought, as I am comfortable at Much Hadham and it is where my son was born.

The bishop lays down his knife and looks at us both. 'That depends. Robert Fitzhugh's appointment is supported by Cardinal Henry Beaufort.'

'So we cannot rely on him to keep silent?'

Bishop Morgan shrugs his shoulders. 'All I am saying is... we can't be certain. William Grey is a trusted friend, while Robert Fitzhugh is young and ambitious.'

Catherine looks around the great hall which has become their home. 'I don't want to be too far from Windsor. Now we have taken Sir Richard into our confidence it should be easier to visit Harry.'

Bishop Morgan drains his goblet of mead. 'I am to join the king in France for his coronation visit—and this is not envisaged as an expedition of short duration. John Stafford, Bishop of Bath and Wells and Bishop William Alnwick of Norwich are to accompany me. I expect it could be some time before I am able to return, so you are welcome to stay at the manor of the Bishops of Ely in Hatfield. My house is not as grand as this,' he waves at the high ceiling self-deprecatingly, 'although it has the advantage that no one will expect to find you there.'

Chapter Ten

We become guests of Bishop Morgan in late summer and find he has been modest about his manor house in Hatfield, Hertfordshire. Some seven miles west of Hertford Castle, the village is known as 'Bishop's Hatfield' because of the imposing palace of the Bishops of Ely, and his house at Hatfield has great chimneys of red brick, extensive, well-maintained gardens and at least twenty full-time servants and staff.

On the outskirts of St Albans, Hatfield also has the advantage of being closer to Windsor Castle, although young Harry is in Calais, with the Earl of Warwick and Bishop Morgan, preparing for his coronation. He is not expected to return for at least six months and his formal letters, rarely revealing more than he is in good health, are delivered from Wallingford by Nathaniel.

Nathaniel stays overnight at our spacious new home, before returning with Catherine's letter of reply. He also acts as my deputy at Wallingford, keeping the servants and staff of the queen's household under the illusion that she could return at any time. On his last visit he also brought an innocent looking letter from Cardinal Beaufort, also now in France, enquiring after the queen dowager's health. Catherine drafts what she hopes is a reassuring reply, although we guess it will not be the last of the matter.

I was content at Much Hadham but never felt completely at ease, as we always knew it was a temporary home. Bishop Morgan has tenure for life as Bishop of Ely, so we are welcome to remain at his home in Hatfield for as long as we wish. Catherine seems more content now and delights in taking personal care of Edmund, rather than having to hand him over to nursemaids, as she had with Harry.

The bishop's servants are used to visitors staying and have no reason to guess their newest tenants are the Queen Dowager of England and her second husband—or that the noisy infant is a half-brother to the king. Catherine is grateful for help from one of the palace maidservants, a local woman named Briony. She has been in the service of the bishops of Ely since she was a girl and soon becomes Catherine's personal chambermaid and companion.

A few years younger than Catherine and always talkative, with an engaging sense of humour, Briony was born in Hatfield, so her local knowledge is useful to us. She explains that each Wednesday the town square becomes a bustling market place and people travel from all around the area to buy and sell all kinds of goods and livestock and share news and local gossip.

Briony is the only one of the Hatfield servants trusted with the secret of Catherine's true identity. She finds it hard to believe she is the maidservant to a queen, yet she understands the need for secrecy. As well as helping Catherine care for little Edmund, Briony has a new role; to help stop rumours among the other members of their household.

In the village of Much Hadham it had been almost impossible for Catherine to take a walk without being noticed. Hatfield is quite different, a busy market town, with new people passing through on their way to London or north to York. For the first time in her life Catherine is able to come and go as she pleases without drawing attention. Briony helps her to dress so she blends in with the local women and they often visit the bustling market together.

Catherine enjoys exploring the ramshackle market stalls, which spring up in noisy profusion once a week. It is possible to buy everything from freshly baked bread and live chickens to the practical boots worn by country people. Cooking pans in all shapes and sizes are sold alongside candlesticks and spurs, woollen cloth, silk and linen. Cartloads of dry rushes for hall floors are heaped next to bales of wool and planks of wood.

Farmers bring wagons laden with sacks of corn, wheat and barley, millers offer bags of flour and blacksmiths shoe horses. Catherine's favourite corner of the market is where she can find fresh garden produce, apples and sweet pears, vegetables, garlic and herbs. Sometimes there are even spicerers at the Hatfield market, selling exotic cinnamon, cloves and many different types of sugar.

Traders shout for Catherine's attention, offering free samples and passing ribald comments when they think she is out of earshot. Briony knows many of them by their first names and is happy to teach Catherine the art of bartering—never paying the price which is asked.

Edmund grows into a strong and healthy child, with his mother's bright blue eyes and golden hair. Briony carries him when they visit the market and Edmund squeals with delight when she holds him high to see the assortment of goats, sheep and pigs herded into pens, some newly slaughtered and hanging by their back legs, dripping bright red blood.

Drovers with barking dogs bring great herds of black cattle from as far away as Wales to Hatfield, to sell on livestock market days. With so many animals in a confined space it is inevitable that some will escape, causing chaos as market stall holders shout to each other as they try to catch them.

I enjoy talking with the Welsh drovers, who bring great flocks of sheep from the hills of Wales. It is the first chance I have to practise speaking Welsh since I was a boy and it makes me feel nostalgic to visit the places I remember from my youth. A plan forms in my mind to seek sanctuary at Beaumaris on the island of Ynys Môn if we ever find life too hard in England.

As the first of May approaches Briony pleads with us to take part in the annual May Fayre, an old tradition to welcome the summer. She sees we need persuading, 'It's the best of all the country fairs—people travel from miles around and musicians play while the women dance around the maypole.' Briony turns to me. 'You will have to go into the forest with the men and help choose the best tree—it's all part of the tradition.' She turns to Catherine. 'And you, my lady, must dress in white linen and dance with me!'

Catherine smiles at Briony's enthusiasm. 'It is a long time since I have danced.'

Briony encourages her. 'That's all the more reason for you to take part, my lady.'

'I think I will,' Catherine agrees. 'And you, Owen, can help the men.'

As the day approaches, I find myself helping to carry a long, straight tree from the woods. Great care is taken in choosing the tree as there is local pride in competing with neighbouring villages for Hatfield to have the best and tallest maypole. The bark of the tree is stripped and women decorate it with brightly coloured ribbons before the men erect it in the middle of the market square.

A crowd gathers to see the dancing and Briony and Catherine wear white dresses with garlands of flowers. Musicians start playing to riotous cheers from the crowd while the youngest girls dance in an inner circle around the maypole. Catherine and Briony join the older women in the outer circle. Each holds a ribbon, attached to the maypole and during the dancing the ribbons become completely intertwined and plaited.

A good deal of ale is drunk at the May Fayre and dancing around the maypole is followed by mummers performing amusing plays, jugglers, acrobats and more singing and dancing. I take part in an archery tournament, coming a respectable second to the local champion and win a hogshead of wine, which I promptly share with the other competitors.

It is an idyllic life for us all, with only one dark cloud on the horizon. Catherine is anxious about Harry and longs for him to return safely to Windsor. At last Nathaniel arrives with a letter from the young king. Catherine hastily breaks the royal seal and reads the letter with increasing concern.

'Harry has travelled from Calais to the castle in Rouen. He says it was a long journey by road with a large company of men-at-arms. He is staying with his uncle John, Duke of Bedford and a large company of guests, including many French and English nobles and important councillors.' Catherine looks up at me. 'He also writes that Joan of Arc was burned at the stake in the market place. He did not see it but says he heard the cheering crowds.'

I place my hand on her arm to reassure her. 'Harry is growing fast, Catherine. I'm sure the Earl of Warwick will ensure he is well guarded—and remember Bishop Morgan is also there with him.'

Catherine looks concerned as she reads her son's letter a second time. She sees from the neat hand it has been dictated to his scribe, yet the phrasing reveals the words as his own. She can only imagine what it must be like for him, surrounded by men like Duke John, who are prepared to do whatever it takes to see him crowned King of France.

'It seems to me he is being used by his uncle John to bolster the confidence of the English army. There is no need for Harry to spend so long in France, particularly while Paris is still under threat.'

I recall Duke Humphrey's words. 'You are right, Catherine. Almost everyone involved has some kind of self-interest. There is nothing we can do about it.'

'I know—but that doesn't stop me worrying about him.'

Nathaniel waits to tell us his news. 'I had a visitor at Wallingford Castle last week, a wine merchant from London. He claims to be interested in supplying us but was asking too many questions.'

'What sort of questions?' I have been expecting our long absence to eventually come to notice and am glad we have Nathaniel to help deal with such things.

Nathaniel looks at Catherine. 'He was asking if he could see you, my lady.'

Catherine is surprised. 'What reason did he give? I would not normally see a wine merchant.'

'That's what I told him. He said he'd been sent by the Duke of Gloucester, who enquires after your health.'

'First Cardinal Beaufort—and now Duke Humphrey.' I sense that word about our clandestine marriage has somehow leaked out, although at least it seems no one knows we are at Hatfield.

Late that night I am awake and restless at Catherine's side. 'It is only a matter of time before we are discovered by Duke Humphrey. Nathaniel says the duke is running the country while everyone is away in France.'

Catherine studies my face in the darkness. 'You are worried about what he could do?'

'I am. He has the money to pay for spies to find us, so I would prefer to be honest with him, rather than hide as if what we have done is something to be ashamed of. Do you think I should ride to London and try to explain?'

Catherine sits up. 'No! The risk is too great. What will I do if he has you arrested?'

'It is a risk we have to take, Catherine.'

'In that case, I should tell you my news.'

Now I sit up. 'What news?'

'I am with child again, Owen. We are going to have another baby.'

I embrace her. 'Do you think this time it will be a girl?'

Catherine laughs. 'It will be good to have a daughter.' She hugs me tightly, holding me down as if to stop me escaping. 'I can't have you locked up in the Tower of London. I'm going to need you here.'

'What do you propose we do about the Duke of Gloucester?'

'I have an idea about that. In the morning I shall write a letter to Duke Humphrey, thanking him for his concern over my health and asking him to grant me a favour.' She watches to see my reaction.

'What favour?' Now I am curious.

'I will ask him to reward one of my most loyal servants, a man named Owen Tudor, who has faithfully supported me through my most difficult times.' She smiles. 'I will request that the duke petitions parliament to grant you the rights of an Englishman, for your service to the dowager queen.'

'Do you think he will consider it?'

'How can he refuse a request from me?'

'Duke Humphrey will see it as a way of further strengthening his hold over you.'

'I haven't forgotten you are still his spy in my household, Owen Tudor...'

'You would do well to remember that, Dowager Queen Catherine.'

I stay awake long after she has fallen asleep in my arms, my mind a whirl of ideas and possibilities. With the rights of an Englishman I would be able to own land and property. There could even be the chance of a knighthood if the king eventually accepts me as Catherine's husband. Catherine's request is important for me, for as well as Edmund, our family will soon be increased by one more.

As summer turns to autumn I find I am less worried about the imminent birth of our second child. Catherine seems more at ease with herself, even visiting the weekly market with Briony. I persuade the midwife from Much Hadham to come and stay at Hatfield as Catherine's time draws near and Briony agrees to act as her assistant.

It is a straightforward birth, early in the morning and all over quickly, yet not the daughter we hope for. The midwife holds the new born baby for me to see. It is another boy, already wailing with his strong lungs, shattering the tranquillity of the bishop's palace.

'What shall we name him, Catherine?' We have not discussed names for boys.

'We could call him Owen, after you?'

'I always liked the name Jasper.'

'Jasper? Wherever did you hear of anyone called Jasper?'

I hold the baby in my arms. 'Jasper was the name of one of the three wise men.'

'Jasper Tudor. I think you are going to be a man after my own heart.'

Catherine sits up in bed and watches the two of us. 'I think I could become used to the name Jasper. At least it is one people will remember.'

★ ★ ★

The last letter received by Catherine from her son in France is short and factual, confirming he is well and thanking her for his tenth birthday present, a gold ring set with a ruby, which Bishop Morgan agreed to deliver for her. Harry wrote that he was about to leave the abbey of St Denis, where he has been staying after the long journey, to make the short ride into Paris for his coronation. Riding with him are the Dukes of Bedford and York, the Earl of Warwick and others in a large company.

There are no further letters from Harry, although Catherine does receive a reassuring letter from Bishop Morgan that the king has finally been crowned by his great-uncle, Cardinal Beaufort. Bishop Morgan adds that the cardinal insisted on singing the Mass, much to the annoyance of the Bishop of Notre Dame, whose cathedral is used for the ceremony. Afterwards there is a great feast, although the bishop observed that the French people were unsurprisingly reticent in their celebrations.

Catherine hands the bishop's letter to me. 'Harry will return to Calais by way of Rouen and Abbeville and sail back to England in February.'

'Would you like to be there to greet him when he returns?'

'I would, Owen.' She brightens at the thought. 'It has been such a long time since I last saw him.'

'It will be good for you to be seen in London, although I'm not sure the people are ready to see these two!' I look at Edmund and Jasper playing together on a rug in front of the hearth.

'I will give thanks to God when my eldest son is safe in England.' Catherine looks concerned. 'I pray he never returns to France, as there is nothing but danger there for him.'

Briony agrees to act as nursemaid for the boys while we travel to London. It is late February and the roads are too icy for a carriage, so we make the twenty mile journey to Westminster on horseback. Luckily the rain holds off until we arrive. Catherine is found lodgings in the Palace of Westminster, while I must find a space in the servants' quarters, the first time we have slept apart since the visit to Windsor Castle.

Harry is met on his return to London by members of all the London guilds, resplendent in their formal robes. I find it hard to see him through the high-spirited crowds which fill every space in the narrow streets, then I hear the sound of trumpets and a great cheer. The serious young king rides a white horse and is wearing a gold coronet. Harry seems more than his ten years and I feel I am looking at a stranger.

Sir Richard Beauchamp rides at the king's side wearing full armour which shines in the sunlight. Cardinal Beaufort in his scarlet robes rides behind, followed by an endless procession of mounted knights and men-at-arms in the colourful royal livery. The clatter of hooves and pounding of marching feet on the cobbled streets remind me this is a real, victorious army, as well as a show for the people of London.

By the time the procession reaches Westminster Abbey the crowds are straining for sight of the young king. I remember a woman was crushed to death at the first coronation and am glad to escape through the servants' passageway. I have not seen Catherine since the previous day and wish I could be at her side, but it is important to keep my distance and play the role of her servant.

Having no wish to listen to Cardinal Beaufort bless the king in the abbey, I make my way through to Westminster Hall, where an army of servants are preparing for yet another coronation feast. There is seating for well over three hundred guests, with endless rows of trestle tables being covered with white linen and a high canopy of cloth of gold over the chair where Harry will be seated.

It is the sight of the golden canopy, more than all the marching knights and soldiers, that makes me realise how special and important Catherine's eldest son has become. The boy I once knew so well has become a young man. I am stepfather to the first ever King of England and of France, who could become the greatest king in history.

Chapter Eleven

Summer of 1432

The return of Bishop Morgan from France marks a new phase in our lives, as the bishop agrees to move in to the wing at Hatfield House we have reserved for him. It suits us all, for Bishop Morgan is growing old and his presence at Hatfield makes it easier for us to deal with visitors.

To my surprise Duke Humphrey honours Catherine's request and obtains the consent of parliament for me to have the rights of an Englishman. The parchment scroll, with the grand seal of parliament, is delivered by Nathaniel and we study it closely. I have been allowed to own land and property in England but there are conditions, as a codicil has been added barring me from holding a crown office in any city or English town.

The codicil troubles me. 'Do you think this suggests the duke has suspicions about us?'

'If Duke Humphrey suspects you he would never have agreed to my request, and by proposing this to parliament the duke has shown his support for you, Owen.'

'Thank you for asking the duke to do this.' I know there is something I can do for Catherine in return. 'My promise to Sir Richard Beauchamp was you would not tell Harry until after he was crowned in France. We have honoured that promise, so perhaps now is the time to be honest with him?'

'I want to tell Harry about you.' Catherine smiles. 'Then there will be no need for secrecy and we can live wherever we choose.'

Nathaniel has been listening to the discussion in silence. 'It is almost summer. Could we invite the king to visit you at Wallingford Castle, as he did before the coronation? It would be easier to find the right moment at Wallingford than at Windsor.'

'What about Edmund and Jasper?' Catherine sounds anxious. 'It will be impossible for them to remain unnoticed at Wallingford and I'm not happy to leave them here. They are still too young to be left for so long.'

'I will ride to Windsor and speak with Sir Richard.' I smile as I recall our last meeting. 'He is a good man, with considerable influence. If Sir Richard agrees the time is right, we will all travel to Windsor to see your son.'

Catherine looks surprised. 'Edmund and Jasper as well?'

'Why not? They are his half-brothers.'

Nathaniel accompanies me on the thirty-five mile ride to Windsor, as it is on his route back to Wallingford. We leave at first light in bright sunshine and I am in good spirits, with a fine new sword, as well as a sharp dagger with an ornate handle, at my belt. Presents from Catherine, they are crafted from fine German steel and show I am to be taken seriously.

I ride a powerful black Welsh Cob I bought at the Hatfield horse fair and anyone seeing us on the road could mistake me for a knight, although Nathaniel no longer looks like my squire. He dresses more like a London merchant, in a fine hat and velvet cape, and has become prosperous through his business dealings. He also wears a sword on a low belt and claims he knows how to use it.

I find myself wondering if the young king will reward me with a title, as I like the thought of resurrecting one of the lost lordships of Wales. It would be good if we can find a place where no one cares I had once been Catherine's servant and our boys can grow up to marry noble ladies and be proud of their Welsh heritage.

Before we leave Hatfield Catherine has one more surprise for me, although it is a poorly kept secret. We are to have another child. If it is a boy we will name him Owen. I smile as I remember how Catherine protested that one Owen Tudor in the house is more than enough. She has not forgotten her promise, for if the child is a girl she will be named Margaret, after my mother.

I turn to Nathaniel as we approach the village of Abbot's Langley. 'We should rest the horses here a while and find somewhere to eat.'

'There is an inn at the crossroads,' Nathaniel points ahead. 'I've stopped here before.'

We tie up our horses and push open the door. Although the day is sunny, the inn is dark inside and smells of stale beer and wood smoke. Black-painted beams support the low ceiling and we duck to avoid hitting our heads. A group of men argue and curse as they play a game of cards. I find a quiet table while Nathaniel orders a jug of ale and some trenchers of bread and ham.

'I was wondering, Nathaniel, what your plans are?'

'Plans for what?'

'The future—after our news becomes public.'

Before Nathaniel can answer our jug of ale and two pewter tankards are placed on the table. The man who serves us turns to go and I catch a glimpse of his face. Even in the gloom of the inn I recognise him immediately. He is older, his lank hair thinning and grey, but I will never forget the scar. I am about to challenge the man then stop myself.

It seems he hasn't recognised me, which gives me an advantage.

I watch as he returns to the kitchen. 'That was one of the men who attacked me, Nathaniel, in the stables all that time ago at Windsor.'

'Are you certain?'

'Yes. I always wondered if I'd see him again. As far as I know his accomplices ended up in jail—or were hanged. This one was never found.'

'So there's nothing we can do?'

'Not really. Too much time has passed.'

'You won't tackle him on your own, when you return?'

I pour us both a tankard of ale. 'You worry about me?'

'I do, Owen.'

'I may have a word with the captain of the guard at Windsor, if I have the time.'

The man returns with a platter of bread and several thick slices of cured ham, with a chunk of cheese, but doesn't show any sign of recognising me. We finish our meal, keeping watch for the man, then I slip out of the door while Nathaniel pays.

Nathaniel echoes my own thoughts as we ride towards Windsor. 'I'd like to know what happened to Samuel Cleaver.'

'Me too. I'd almost forgotten about him—until now.'

At last the distinctive silhouette of Windsor Castle appears on the horizon and it is time for us to part.

'Take care to avoid Abbot's Langley on the way back.' Nathaniel waves and spurs his horse, as he hopes to reach Wallingford before nightfall, a further thirty-mile ride in the late summer evening.

I arrive at Windsor and stable my horse, then ask if I can see Sir Richard. The earl is busy but agrees to see me later that afternoon, so I find myself with time on my hands and decide to visit the captain of the guard. He is surprised to see me and greets me warmly.

'Owen Tudor—and wearing a sword at last!'

'Good to see you again, Captain. I've come about Samuel Cleaver, you remember him?'

The captain did. 'He was charged and locked up in Newgate Gaol. I heard he somehow managed to escape while waiting to be sentenced.'

'I thought it's impossible to escape from Newgate?'

The captain shakes his head. 'Cleaver had an accomplice. They wounded one of the guards but he was able to describe the man. It was the one we never caught.'

'I saw him, at the inn in Abbot's Langley. He works there.'

'You are sure it is the same man?'

'Of course, I will never forget him.'

'I can let you have a couple of men if you want to go after him?'

'I'll let you know, Captain. It depends on the outcome of my meeting with Sir Richard.'

I thank the captain and make my way back down the long corridors to wait. As I turn a corner I almost bump into Juliette. She looks slim and attractive in a fashionable burgundy dress with long sleeves and a lace headdress that suits her. I stand there staring at her for a moment, my mind full of memories.

Juliette speaks first. 'Owen! I was wondering what had become of you.' She looks at me in silence for a moment, as if overwhelmed by memories. 'You look well. What brings you to Windsor?'

'I have a meeting with the Earl of Warwick.' I am surprised at how Juliette has become even more beautiful as she has grown older.

'Where have you been?' There is accusation in her question.

I don't wish to lie to her, so close to being able to reveal our secret.

'I am still with Queen Catherine's household.' It is the truth.

She reaches out and places a hand on my arm. 'I have missed you, Owen.'

I feel the warmth of her hand, but must not allow her false hope. 'Did you return to France for the king's coronation?' I try to keep my tone business-like, as if I'm talking to any of the king's staff and not my former lover.

Juliette seems to sense my coolness and removes her hand. 'Yes. We were away for most of the year.' All trace of her pleasure at the sight of me is gone.

'And have you... found someone else?' I have no right to ask, but am still deeply concerned about how I have treated her, after she trusted me with her love.

'Who could take your place?'

I can't answer and see the sadness in her eyes, the woman I could have married so long ago. I made my choice, although I have not forgotten how special our time together had been.

'Would you ever come back to me, Owen?' There is sudden hope in her voice and I wish I could tell her the truth about my marriage to Catherine, about Edmund and Jasper and our life now in Hatfield.

'I am sorry, Juliette. You should find someone more worthy, while you can.'

Our brief exchange troubles me as I head for my meeting with Earl Warwick. Although I left Hatfield in a positive mood, the sight of the scar-faced man, then seeing Juliette, brings back more painful memories than I would have wished for.

The earl keeps me waiting before inviting me into his study. A map of France is spread out on his desk and marked with coloured lines to show the extent of English territory. Last time I saw the earl was in London, dressed in full armour at the head of the king's royal procession. Sir Richard wears a plain tunic now, over a faded linen shirt. He looks older and regards me with poorly disguised suspicion, his eyes going to the fine sword and dagger at my belt.

'Come with me, Tudor, there's something you should see.'

The earl leads me out through the rear doors to a courtyard where the men-at-arms practice swordsmanship. As we approach I can hear the clang of swords on armour and the occasional deep-voiced call of encouragement. We enter the yard and see a knight in full armour sparring with one of the royal guards.

The guard swings his broadsword at the head of the knight, who parries the blow to a cheer from the men-at-arms gathered to watch. With a bone-jarring clang the knight delivers a well-timed blow to his opponent's helmet using the weighted pommel of his sword. The guardsman seems concussed for a moment, and then raises both hands as a sign of surrender. Then the knight raises his visor and I see it is unmistakably Harry, although I would never have recognised him.

'I presume you want me to say it's time to tell the king what you've been up to, Tudor.' The earl keeps his voice low.

It is not the welcome I expected. 'We have honoured our promise to you, my lord.'

The earl nods. 'You have, and for that at least I am grateful.' He looks at me as if he wishes things could be different. 'I am going to ask you to delay a little longer.'

'Why, my lord?'

The earl glances at the men-at arms gathered around the king. 'Not here. Come back to my study.'

We walk back down the corridor in silence, then reach Sir Richard's study and he ushers me inside and closes the door.

'It is not because of the king—although he could do without all this.' The earl looks serious. 'John, Duke of Bedford has succumbed to the same illness that finished his brother. I understand he does not have long to live.'

'Why does that mean we have to keep our secret?' I find it had to see how the Duke of Bedford has any significance for me.

'Don't be a fool, Tudor. You know Duke Humphrey will have you arrested as soon as he learns of your disloyalty? If Duke John dies, which he surely will, Humphrey will be the heir apparent. It would be the worst possible time for you to give him a way to discredit the king.'

'How would the truth discredit him?' I am confused. 'We were properly married and King Henry's half-brothers were born within wedlock.'

'Let me spell it out for you, Tudor. First you will be locked up in the tower. Then rumours will spread that Queen Catherine was unable to control herself and lay with her servants. Your witnesses will be silenced, one way or another.' He gives me a scathing look. 'Any records of your marriage will be destroyed. Put quite simply, I don't want the truth, as you insist on calling it, to be known until the king is of age.'

'Sixteen? Catherine will never agree.'

The earl stands and opens the door. 'You had best make sure she does, Tudor. And remember—watch your back.'

★ ★ ★

The warning signs are there, although I don't want to acknowledge them. Catherine is even more upset than I expected at the news she must not tell Harry about his brothers until he comes of age. It means another five years of secrecy and subterfuge. She becomes obsessed with the idea something will happen to the baby she carries.

She wakes me in the middle of the night, her face pale and her eyes wide in the dim moonlight through the window. 'I've had a bad dream, Owen. I saw my own funeral, in Westminster Abbey.'

'It's only a dream.' I smooth her brow, then run my hand over her rounded curves. 'Not long now before there's one more in our family.'

Catherine is still reliving her dream. 'There was a little effigy next to mine. It was a boy... he looked like you.'

'It's natural for you to worry when the child is so close.'

'I worry something will happen to me before I can explain to Harry.' She has concern in her eyes. 'I must tell him, before it's too late.'

'You will, Catherine, as soon as this baby is born.' I hug her closer. 'And it is going to be the easiest birth of all of them.'

Catherine agrees. 'We were lucky with Edmund and Jasper, they're both growing into strong healthy boys.'

'So forget your silly dreams?'

'There is something I want to tell you, Owen.'

'What's that?' I suspect I already know the answer.

'Sometimes my dreams seem... real. I find it hard to remember what I've dreamed and what has really happened.'

'I think we all do that a little.'

'No, you don't understand. I sometimes... forget who I am.'

I put my arms around her protectively. 'That's not surprising. We've been pretending you are an ordinary woman for a long time now. Even I have to remind myself you are the mother of the king.'

When I wake to find the bed next to me empty I suppose Catherine has risen early. I lie there alone, listening to the summer birdsong and thinking about the conversation we had in the middle of the night. Catherine's baby is close to being due and it is only natural she should worry.

As I dress I decide to make a special effort to help her from now on. We never discuss her father's madness or how difficult it must have been for her to witness as a child. I am unsure if to do so will make her nightmares worse or help her come to terms with her past.

The bishop's cook, a cheerful woman named Mary, is making bread in the kitchen. There are plenty of bakers in Hatfield, although Mary likes to make fresh loaves every day and regularly tells me there is nothing to compare with the smell of baking bread. She looks up and smiles when she sees me.

'Good morning, sir.'

I watch her kneading and turning the soft dough on the old oak table. 'Good morning, Mary. Have you seen my wife?'

Mary stops her kneading and looks at me as if unsure what to say. 'I have sir... I thought it strange she was going riding—in her condition, if you know what I mean?'

'She was riding?'

'Not on a horse, sir. I saw her leaving the stables in the wagon when I came to light the ovens early this morning.'

I glance at the ovens, now almost ready for the bread. 'Thank you, Mary.'

I am worried now as it is not a good idea for Catherine to ride in the old wagon with the baby due. We used it to carry our luggage to Much Hadham, and when Edmund was born he was brought to Hatfield on the wagon. Well built, with a rain canopy supported by wooden hoops. It is only used occasionally now for carrying supplies. Briony and Catherine sewed cushions, padded with wool, for the boys to rest on, but the wagon is uncomfortable to ride any distance on the poor local roads.

In the stables I find the wagon and both the horses we use to pull it are missing. I curse the time I have wasted since she left, and saddling my Welsh Cob, canter to the crossroads. The town is to the left but it is not a market day and the road looks deserted. Ahead is the road to London and I can see a few riders in the far distance but no sight of our distinctive wagon.

That only leaves the lane which skirts the bishop's land to the west and runs down to the River Lea. The ride along the bank of the river is a favourite of Catherine's although I think it unlikely she would take the carriage far as the roads are deeply rutted.

Our last conversation returns to my thoughts. If Catherine woke not knowing who she was, she could be anywhere. I ride back to the stables and go in search of Briony. She is not in her room, which reassures me a little as I hope it means she is with Catherine. At a loss to know what to do, I ask the cook to explain to Catherine if she returns that I have ridden to Windsor in search of her. The realisation she might have gone to see the king has been at the back of my mind since I first learned she is missing.

The road becomes busier as the morning draws on. Once I think I can see the wagon in the far distance, and then find it is a different one as I ride closer. I can ride faster than the slow wagon, but Catherine left early. I continue as fast as I can, only stopping once to water my horse, yet by the time I reach Windsor it is late afternoon.

There is no Royal Standard flying, which suggests that the king is not in residence. A guard informs me the king is in Westminster and has been there for some time. I thank the guard but now have a new problem. Westminster is a good day's ride from Windsor and Catherine might have left the wagon in preference for a riverboat, if she is even trying to see her son. I have ridden too far to turn back, so decide to find a pallet in the servants' quarters and ride to London at first light.

The London road is busy with carts and wagons, as well as horses riding alone and in pairs, although I don't see Catherine's wagon all day. I have not slept well the previous night and woke with tell-tale welts where bed bugs have feasted on my blood. The bites soon begin to itch annoyingly, which does nothing to improve my mood.

By the time I arrive at the Palace of Westminster I am wondering if the journey has been a waste of time. Unlike Windsor, where I am known by many of the servants and staff, I find it impossible to gain access until I claim to have an urgent message to deliver to the Earl of Warwick. The soldiers on the gate look at my fine clothes and sword and ask me to wait.

A page boy eventually arrives to take me to see Sir Richard. I allow my horse to be led to the stables and follow the page with mixed feelings. I am right to be concerned for as soon as I see the earl it is obvious he is not in a good mood.

'I've been expecting you, Tudor.'

'Is Queen Catherine here, my Lord?' I silently pray for good news as I wait for his answer.

'The queen dowager arrived here demanding to see the king. As you know, she was in no condition to have risked such a long journey.'

'Is she alright?'

'No thanks to you, Tudor.' He glowers. 'I thought you agreed to stop her telling the king until he is of age?'

I thank God Catherine is safe. 'I thought she had respected your request, my lord, but she left without my knowledge.' I see the earl looks annoyed but not angry. 'Has she told the king?'

'She has not seen the king.' He softens a little. 'The journey here brought on the birth of her child.'

'Where is she now, my lord?' The news is a shock.

The earl points towards the towering spire of Westminster Abbey. 'This is no business for the king's physician. She is being cared for in the abbot's infirmary.'

I find Catherine sleeping, her face as white as a fresh linen sheet. One of the abbey monks is seated at her side, his head bowed in prayer. I cross over to Catherine and kiss her tenderly on the cheek. Her skin feels cold and she stirs and says something, but I can't make out her words. There is no sign of Briony or our child. There should be a baby, snuggled in the bed next to her or perhaps in a basket.

I turn to the monk. 'Where is the baby?'

The monk looks at me, as if wondering what I mean, then makes the sign of the cross as he understands. 'The child is given to God.'

'It was a boy?' Somehow I have known for months.

Catherine murmurs something and I lean over her and strain to understand her words.

'I named him Owen, after you.'

I kneel in prayer in the privacy of the chapel of St Paul, to the side of the aisle of Westminster Abbey. Candles flicker in the silence as I pray for Catherine, that God is merciful and spares her. I say a prayer for the mortal soul of my youngest son, Owen, who is taken before I even see him. I pray for my boys, Edmund and Jasper, that they will have as rich and rewarding a life as mine.

Chapter Twelve

Autumn of 1436

Catherine is never quite the same as the woman I fell in love with. A year has passed since that fateful day in Westminster, yet its shadow lingers over our lives. On a good day, Catherine is as bright and happy as ever, reminding me of the beautiful young queen I would lie awake dreaming of. Then a dark depression drifts over her and she becomes distant and forgetful. I find her most difficult when she insists her youngest son, Owen, still lives.

'I gave him to the monks.' She looks shocked that I don't believe her. 'He is alive, I saw him when he was born. He has your dark hair.'

I recall the words of the monk who prayed at her bedside. 'He was given to God.'

Catherine is adamant. 'He lives, Owen.' Her eyes flash with anger and she grips my hand so hard it hurts. 'Don't you want to see him? Our son is waiting with the monks of Westminster Abbey for us to visit him.'

'I'm sorry, Catherine. You have to understand. Our son is dead.'

Catherine stares at me in wide-eyed disbelief. 'Why would you lie to me about such a thing?'

I hold her close until her anger passes. 'We have two good strong sons. Let us put the past behind us and talk about our future.'

Edmund and Jasper bring a new happiness to me. I like being a father and am determined to do everything I can to give them the best start in life. I buy them each a pony from the horse fair and teach them to ride. I spend hours in the woodshed crafting them little bows of yew. We set up a straw target in the courtyard and after many failed attempts they learn to shoot an arrow straight and true.

In the evening, before they go to bed, the boys beg me to tell them stories. I tell them my real name is Owain ap Maredydd ap Tudur. Flickering candlelight casts grotesque, dancing shadows as I tell them of the last true Welsh prince, Owain Glyndŵr, and the great adventures of the Welsh rebellion against the English. I see their wide eyes when I explain how their grandfather, Maredydd, escaped with me to London when he was forced to flee his homeland.

I also tell them how their half-brother, Harry, is King of England and of France and will one day make them knights of the realm with noble titles. Catherine still insists that she wishes to see her eldest son but now I have taken precautions. The wagon is secured with iron chains. Briony is almost dismissed for her failure to prevent Catherine from leaving the house is let off with a warning. She is needed all the more now another baby is on the way.

It comforts Catherine to feel a child kick in her belly again and she insists this time it will be a girl. After four boys she knows it is her time. She is so certain God will not refuse her prayers she sews miniature dresses with Briony in anticipation. At nights she asks me to place my hand over the baby and I laugh as I feel it move inside her.

'Her name will be Margaret, after your mother.' She repeats the words so often I know they will come true, even though she has taken to her bed again, and is now too weak to climb down the stairs.

I caress her brow. 'You must eat, Catherine.' I secretly worry at how her bones show through her pale skin, a painful reminder of her frailty.

'Later, Owen. I will eat later.' Catherine refuses whatever the cook makes to tempt her.

'You have to eat—for the baby to grow strong.' My persistence is rewarded by Catherine tasting a spoonful of warm mutton soup. It is a start.

She looks up at me with ice-blue eyes. 'I wish to pay for prayers to be said for Bishop Morgan, every day.' Her voice sounds weak, barely more than a whisper.

'I will ask Nathaniel to see to it.'

'Will we attend his funeral?'

'Bishop Morgan was laid to rest in the chapel of Charterhouse, in London. You were not well enough to make the journey.'

I don't tell her that had been almost a year before. It happens more often now and I am growing used to Catherine forgetting things. Bishop Morgan had been more than a friend to us both. He risked his reputation, his livelihood and perhaps even his freedom for us. We will always remember his kindness and generosity but now he is gone and will be missed.

A flicker of concern appears on Catherine's face as the consequences of the bishop's death dawn on her. 'This means our time in the bishop's house is at an end?'

'It will take some time for them to appoint his successor, but yes, Catherine, it is time for us to leave.' I feel the nagging uncertainty about our future return.

Catherine looks around the room which holds so many memories. 'Where will we go?'

I take her hand. 'I will find us somewhere safe, Catherine. There is no need for you to worry.'

I fish with the spoon in the bowl of warm soup and find a tasty morsel of well-cooked mutton, which I offer to her. She takes it as a child would and opens her mouth for more. I cannot share my secret with Catherine until she is stronger. On his last visit Nathaniel told me Duke Humphrey had called at Wallingford Castle with a score of armed men, looking for the queen. It seems he knows our secret, as he demanded answers when he questioned the servants of her household. Although it is clear the duke doesn't know where we are living, I fear it is only a matter of time before he discovers our hiding place.

Nathaniel rides through the night from Wallingford Castle. The first I know of his arrival is when I am woken by his hammering on the door until it is answered by a worried servant.

'I must speak with Master Tudor.' He shouts as he barges past the servant. 'It is most urgent.'

I pull my clothes on as fast as I can and find he is already at the top of the grand staircase. 'What's happened?' I guess the answer from his exhausted and dishevelled appearance.

'Duke Humphrey's men are on their way here.' Nathaniel shakes his head. 'They are going to arrest you, Owen. I came as soon as I knew.'

'Thank you, Nathaniel.' I glance back to my room where Catherine is still sleeping. 'How long do we have?'

Nathaniel frowns. 'They could be here any time. The thing is...'

'What is it?' I know Nathaniel well and see the concern on his face.

'I heard that Duke Humphrey has taken this personally. He has sworn to bring you to account.'

'I can't leave Catherine, Nathaniel. She is in no condition to travel—and the boys...'

'I will stay here with you, if you wish.' Nathaniel's hand drops to the hilt of his sword. 'Queen Catherine is as safe here as anywhere else, as are Edmund and Jasper.'

'I've put you in danger too many times, Nathaniel. You know it will be hard for you if things go badly?'

Nathaniel nods. 'I understand—and I've made my decision.'

As dawn breaks Duke Humphrey's men swarm into the bishop's courtyard like a pack of hunting dogs. The man commanding them places guards on all entrances to the house. I am expecting them and open the door, stepping out into the courtyard to face the young officer.

'What is the meaning of this?'

The officer hesitates before replying. 'I have orders from the Lord Protector of England. You are Owen Tudor?'

'I am.'

'Duke Humphrey has ordered me to take you into custody, to answer before the king's council.'

'I must remain here to care for Queen Catherine. She is with child and unwell.'

The officer seems unsurprised. 'The duke is aware of the queen's condition, Master Tudor. My orders are that the queen dowager is to be admitted to the Abbey of St Saviour, in Bermondsey, to be cared for there by the nuns until her child is born.'

'Queen Catherine is unfit to travel to London. I can't allow it!' I raise my voice and see several of the guards move closer, ready for the command to arrest me.

The officer holds his ground. 'I am authorised to use force if necessary, Master Tudor.'

'What about my sons?'

'The sons of the queen dowager are to be taken into the care of Katherine de la Pole, the Abbess of Barking, for religious education.'

I curse my decision to remain at Hatfield when we could have all escaped to Wales, although I know in my heart that even there I could be hunted down and arrested. The duke seems to know everything about us and I wonder if he has an informer in the bishop's staff and servants. I have no choice other than to surrender to the king's men.

Catherine's shrill voice breaks through my deliberations. 'You will not arrest him. As the king's mother, I order you to unhand him!'

I am as surprised as the young officer and we both turn to look at Catherine. She is already wearing her hooded travelling cloak, her arm steadied by Briony, dressed ready for a journey. Catherine looks pale but her voice sounds clear and confident. The officer takes a pace back as if unsure of his position, and his men look to him for orders.

'I will have to be advised by the Duke of Gloucester.' He gives me an uncertain glance then turns to his men. 'In the meantime Master Tudor will accompany the queen dowager to Bermondsey Abbey.'

The first sign of a grey dawn is showing on the horizon as we leave. Catherine rides in the wagon ahead of me and Nathaniel is at my side. Behind us follow the soldiers of the duke, acting as an unnecessary armed escort. They have made no effort to take my sword, for now at least.

I bite my lip and try to hide my concern as I say farewell to Edmund and Jasper. They stand together in their best clothes, looking confused and worried. They were hurriedly woken from their beds and dressed to the sounds of men shouting orders. Servants were running up and down stairs, carrying bundles of our clothes and possessions to load the waiting wagons. Edmund clutches his little yew bow, while Jasper keeps a firm grip on his treasured wooden practice sword.

I feel immensely proud of my sons. 'You are going on an adventure, and I will come for you after the baby is born.' I take my purse from my belt and hand them five gold nobles each. They look at the small fortune and seem to know what it means.

'Be brave, boys.' I tell them. 'Remember you are Tudors.'

I expect Catherine to protest as her sons are taken by the soldiers, but it is as if her defence of me has taken all her energy. She kisses them both and tells them to be good boys, then watches impassively, raising one hand in the air as they ride away. I am concerned about her now, as I recognise the signs.

It takes most of the day for our procession of wagons and riders to reach the old abbey south of the Thames at Southwark, stopping in Barnet at mid-day to rest and water the horses. Catherine looks dazed and nearly loses her footing as the sisters of the abbey help her from the uncomfortable wagon. As they lead her away I realise there is nothing I can do to help her now.

Nathaniel persuades a young priest to let us share his small room, now crammed with as many of my possessions as we could bring from the bishop's house. It is not much to show for a lifetime. My old longbow stands next to a bundle of my clothing on top of a locked wooden chest. Only Nathaniel knows it contains my life savings in gold nobles and silver groats, as well as Catherine's silver and gilt cups. Concealed in old sacks under papers the secret hoard also includes my precious charter from parliament, confirming my rights as an Englishman.

The priest, Thomas Lewis, is a talkative, clean-shaven man with a lilting Welsh accent. Thomas listens sympathetically to my story and explains that he works as a chaplain alongside the abbey sisters, helping pilgrims and the poor. I am pleased to learn the priest is a Welsh speaker. Originally from the North Wales town of Flint, Thomas has many stories of his travels around Wales and is good company.

We take a meal of pottage in the abbey refectory, washed down with sweet mead, and sleep under rough wool blankets on straw pallets, tired after a challenging day. I wake early and go in search of Catherine, finding her in a side room of the infirmary. The winter sun shines through tall, stained-glass windows, creating colourful patterns of light and shade on the well-scrubbed stone floor.

Catherine is awake and propped up in her bed on a cushion, with Briony seated in a chair at her side. She looks better than she has for a long time and smiles when I lean over and kiss her on the cheek.

'How are you feeling?'

She regards me with red-rimmed eyes and glances at Briony. 'The sisters said Briony couldn't stay with me—but I insisted.' Her voice sounds a little stronger again.

'We could not stay at the bishop's house any longer, Catherine.' I look around her sparsely furnished room, taking in the wooden crucifix on the wall above her and the leather-bound Latin prayer book beside her bed. 'This is a good place to have some rest until the baby is born.'

A flicker of concern crosses her face. 'Edmund and Jasper... where did they take them?'

'They are safe.' I try a smile, although it is not how I feel as I miss my sons and worry about them. 'I will bring Edmund and Jasper to see you when the baby is born.'

A week turns into a month and I settle into a routine of visiting Catherine, passing the rest of my days helping the young Welsh priest, Thomas Lewis, deal with the many travellers and poor who come to the Abbey of St Saviour.

As the chill of winter approaches Catherine becomes obsessed by the idea she will never see her sons again. She repeatedly asks me to bring them to see her, even though I patiently explain it is not possible.

One morning I find her dictating her last will and testament to one of the nuns. Catherine's preoccupation with her own death is unsettling. She describes vivid dreams where she sees her funeral, with me leading mourners down the long aisle of Westminster Abbey. Thomas Lewis tries to put my troubled mind at rest, pointing out it is natural for her to be concerned as she reaches full term, although I know it is a bad omen.

As the New Year approaches I worry about Catherine's health. Her cheeks are hollow and her once lustrous hair is thinning, although she has yet to reach her fortieth year. Her bright blue eyes still show the vitality I found so attractive, yet her lapses of memory become more frequent. Sometimes she stares as if seeing me for the first time.

Her latest wish is for me to bring Harry to see her. She pleads with me, saying the touch of a king can heal the sick. I have not dared set foot outside the sanctuary of the abbey grounds, and am not convinced the king would find it easy to see his mother in such a condition. I take her hand in mine and tell her I love her. I promise as soon as the baby is born we will present her to her half-brother Harry.

I kneel in the abbey chapel for the New Year's Eve service and pray for my wife. I also say a prayer for our unborn child and wonder what lies ahead for us all as the bells clang high in their tower to mark the dawn of a new year. Too concerned for Catherine to enjoy any celebration, I retire to my bed and escape into dreams of happier times.

I wake to feel someone shaking me and calling out my name, then recognise Briony's worried face in the near darkness. Her long, dark hair, normally plaited under her headdress, straggles lank and loose over her shoulders. There are red spots of blood on her linen apron. The waiting is over.

'The baby?'

Briony nods. 'You have a daughter.'

My mind is filled with urgent questions. 'How is Catherine?'

Briony shakes her head and tries to suppress a sob. I glance at my sleeping friends and lead her out into the abbey cloisters. There has been a heavy frost overnight and I shiver in my nightshirt as I wait for Briony to compose herself and tell me what I don't want to hear.

Briony dries her eyes. 'I'm sorry. Catherine is weak.' Briony glances towards the infirmary as if she doesn't want to return. 'She is asking for you.'

'Let me have a moment and I'll come with you.'

I dress without waking the snoring figures in the room and follow Briony in the dark to the infirmary, now lit with a dozen tallow candles, which give off a flickering yellow light. Catherine is awake, cradling our new daughter in her arms.

She looks up as I enter. 'Owen.' Her voice sounds weak. 'Have you brought my sons to see me?'

'No, Catherine. The hour is late. They are sleeping.'

I pull up a chair to sit at her bedside and glance at Briony, who withdraws to leave us alone together. The baby is tightly wrapped in clean white linen and its eyes are closed. All I can see is a tiny pale face and a wisp of dark hair. For a second I wonder if our daughter is still alive, then she screws up her face and gives a little cough.

I reach across and she opens her eyes as I caress her hair. I feel a powerful sense of relief, followed by a deep sense of foreboding. My instinct tells me there is something wrong. I remember how our sons were so full of life from the moment they were born, yet our daughter seems so delicate, with the same sickly pallor as her mother.

Catherine forces a smile. 'Margaret...'

'After my mother.' I smile back at her. 'How are you feeling?'

'I need to rest... but I am glad that now the worst is over.'

I kiss her on the forehead. Her brow is feverish. 'You must sleep, Catherine. Briony will take care of our daughter.'

There are beads of sweat on Catherine's forehead, so I cross the room to where a jug and bowl stand on a table and pour a little of the icy water onto a piece of clean linen. When I place the dampened cloth on her brow she closes her eyes with the soothing pleasure of it.

'I love you, Catherine, with all my heart, and pray to God you will soon be well.'

She doesn't answer.

In the three days after our daughter's birth I watch her become a shadow of the woman I first met all those years ago in Windsor. The nuns tell me there is little they can do for her but pray, so I ask Nathaniel to deliver an urgent message to the king, asking him to send his best physicians. They have yet to arrive and in my heart I fear it will be too late.

'Owen...'

Her voice is so soft I have to lean over her and strain to hear. 'I'm here, Catherine.'

'Please tell my sons... I love them dearly.'

'I will.'

I take her frail hand in mine as I have done so often to comfort her in the past. The familiar gold rings on her thin fingers feel loose. Someone has manicured her nails, each one perfectly trimmed. I guess it must have been Briony. I give her hand a comforting squeeze, which she always returns. It is our way of reassuring each other everything is alright. Catherine doesn't squeeze my hand and I look into her ice-blue eyes. They are wide open but I know I have lost her. I hold her in my arms for one last time and weep.

Chapter Thirteen

I find I am looking forward to the challenge of the long ride ahead, as it offers a way of dealing with my grief at the double loss of my wife and only daughter, who has not lived for a week. The baby cried plaintively for her mother, using the last ounce of strength in her tiny lungs to wail in protest at being left. Briony did all she could, staying up all night to care for her, yet the child simply wouldn't feed.

The island of Ynys Môn is almost three hundred miles north-west of Southwark, but I feel an ancient connection with the place of my birth and have nowhere else to go. Thomas and Nathaniel understand why I cannot stay for Catherine's funeral. It is almost certain I will be arrested if I do, with an increased risk of being captured on the roads leading out of the city if I delay my departure any longer.

My saddlebags are hastily packed with half my fortune of gold and silver, entrusting Nathaniel with the safe keeping of my remaining possessions. I wear my sword with pride, my gift from Catherine and a sign to the world that I am a free man, with the rights of an Englishman to travel as I please.

I ride hard all day and spend an uncomfortable night in a hayloft before continuing at first light. As I reach the outskirts of the town of Northampton I hear the urgent rumble of hooves on the hard ground behind me and turn to see a troop of the king's soldiers approaching.

A commanding voice calls out. 'You there! Halt!'

I consider trying to outrun them but the landscape is bleak and open, with no cover in any direction. I turn my Welsh Cob in the road and wait for them to approach.

Their captain addresses me again. 'Are you Owen Tudor, formerly of the royal household?'

'I am.' There didn't seem to be any point in denying it.

'You are summoned by the messengers of the council to appear before the king.' He glances at the armed soldiers to each side of him, as if to warn them to be ready for trouble. 'My orders are to bring you to the Palace of Westminster.'

I sense the young captain is unsure of his ground. 'Are those the king's orders, Captain?'

'They are the orders of the Duke of Gloucester, who acts in the name of the king.'

I know there is no chance of escape. 'I will come with you if I have the word of the Duke of Gloucester that I can explain myself to the king.'

'The duke is in London.' The captain seems confused as to how he can grant my request.

'I will ride with you to London and then you must secure the duke's word—in writing.'

The captain seems relieved to have a way out and leads me back towards London while his men follow behind. As we approach Westminster I am increasingly concerned about walking into a trap. The king will be of age on the sixth of December, after which time the duke will no longer be able to act in his name. In the meantime, I have to find a way to force Duke Humphrey to provide me with his surety of safe conduct.

The solution appears before me as we approach the towering Palace of Westminster. My guards are tired from the long ride and their captain rides a little way ahead. As we pass a water-filled horse trough I slip from the saddle while my horse drinks his fill. I unbuckle my precious saddlebags and run with them until my lungs are burning in my chest. I can hear men shouting behind me as I dart into the servants' passage and through into the sanctuary of Westminster Abbey.

Seeking sanctuary is not a simple matter, as the right to grant sanctuary is at the discretion of the abbot. I do my best to explain my situation to one of the older monks, who listens carefully, then asks me to be seated while the matter is considered. After an agonising wait I am granted an audience with the Abbot of Westminster.

Abbot Richard Harweden is simply dressed in black Benedictine robes, although around his neck he wears a crucifix on a heavy gold chain which belies his humble appearance. He listens impassively while I repeat my story, interrupting only when I say how my youngest son died in the abbey infirmary during childbirth.

'Your son lives. He will become a postulant when he is of age. Until that time he is being raised as a member of our community of St Benedict.'

'I was led to believe he was dead?' The news is almost too difficult to comprehend.

'I regret you were misinformed. The queen dowager was not in any condition to care for him and gave her consent for your son to join our order.'

Now I see why Catherine had been so insistent and feel a stab of regret at how I had been so quick to doubt her. 'I didn't know.' A thought occurs to me. 'Is he here now?'

Abbot Harweden inclines his head. 'He is not, although he will return here when he is older.'

'I would like to see him, Your Grace, when it is possible.'

The abbot studies me appraisingly. 'I will grant you sanctuary while you wait for the letter of safe conduct, Master Tudor. May God be with you.'

'And with you, Your Grace.'

I find my way to the scriptorium, where rows of monks copy Latin texts. One of them agrees to let me write a message to Nathaniel, and I briefly explain that I am safe but Fortune's Wheel has turned against me. I give the monk a silver groat in return for his promise to deliver it to Nathaniel at Bermondsey Abbey. Then all I can do is wait and pray.

I soon begin to tire of the austere life in sanctuary and risk a visit to a nearby tavern. Although I wear a hooded cape I am recognised in the street by a man of the king's guard, who tries to arrest me. I escape down an alleyway and run to Westminster Abbey as fast as I can, lucky to reach my sanctuary before the guard can catch me, but it is a reminder of the dangers London now holds for me.

A week later Nathaniel and Thomas visit with news that Catherine is to be buried here in the abbey. I realise I will be able to be present at the service after all, although I decide to take the precaution of cutting my hair short and shaving my beard, dressing in the plain robes of a monk to reduce the chances of being recognised again. I watch Catherine's funeral from a distance with the other postulate monks and no one gives me a second glance. Even the monks seem to have forgotten the reason for my being with them.

I find it convenient to escape from my grief into the strict Benedictine routine. Waking at midnight, the monks leave their beds in the dormitory for Matins followed by Lauds, before returning to sleep until daybreak, when Prime is sung. After a light breakfast of bread and watery ale, I join in the chantry masses for the souls of those who are buried in Westminster Abbey. Each day I pray for Catherine's soul. Sometimes tears run down my face as I listen to the poignant singing of the masses and think of her. I miss my wife and pray that our sons Edmund and Jasper are safe and well. I also pray for the soul of a baby daughter I never had the chance to know.

At nine the first mass is celebrated at the high altar in the presbytery, followed by prayers and what are called announcements, where duties and penances are assigned. I help with my share of the cleaning and polishing, a small price to pay for my food and lodgings, although both are frugal and I notice my ribs are beginning to show after the poor monastic diet.

Shortly before noon the bell rings for dinner and I join the monks to wash in the laver, where there is clean water and towels to dry our hands. After dinner the afternoon is marked by the services of none at two o'clock and vespers at four, each taking about half an hour. After a light, plain meal, followed by the singing of compline, I retire to sleep.

December dawns and the day of the king's sixteenth birthday finally arrives. I request an audience with the king to explain my situation. After an anxious wait I receive word that he has agreed but our meeting is to be in front of the royal council, which includes Duke Humphrey as well as Cardinal Beaufort. I know that both, as advisors to the king, will take the opportunity to poison young Harry's mind against me, but I have no option now and my only wish is to be allowed to continue on my way to Wales.

I stand before the great council dressed in a plain black doublet and wearing my fine sword and dagger for the first time since I sought sanctuary. It feels strange after living for so long as a monk but I wear them as a reminder to those who would sit in judgement of me that I have been granted the rights of an Englishman.

King Henry sits between his senior advisors, stony-faced Duke Humphrey to the left and Cardinal Beaufort, in scarlet robes, to his right. Henry looks pale and the gold coronet he wears seems heavy on his head. He stares impassively at me without any sign of recognition, confirming my fear it will not be easy to persuade him my intentions were honourable.

Duke Humphrey speaks first. 'Owen Tudor... you are called here to account for your conduct as a member of the late queen dowager's household.' His voice is cold. 'It is your right to make a statement before the council makes its judgement on you.'

I address the king. 'I am, Your Highness, your loyal liege man.' I glance at the duke, then at Cardinal Beaufort. 'Whatever anyone has told you, I swear I have always served and protected the late Queen Catherine, your mother, with honesty, loyalty and integrity.'

My words echo from the ceiling of the great council chamber. Duke Humphrey leans across and speaks to the king in a low voice I can't hear, although I see how Henry nods in understanding. The other members of the council, bishops and nobles, seem to regard me with new interest following my statement.

Cardinal Beaufort gives me a dispassionate stare. 'If you are as innocent and loyal as you claim, Tudor...' He pauses for effect. 'Why is it you felt the need to seek sanctuary with the monks of Westminster Abbey?'

I am prepared for the question. 'The Duke of Gloucester's men came to the late Bishop Morgan's house to arrest me, Your Grace.' I turn to Duke Humphrey now. 'Queen Catherine told his men she wished for me to accompany her to the Abbey of St Saviour, which I did. After her death, I decided to return to my homeland and was arrested again and brought to London, where I sought sanctuary only until the king reached his majority.'

The conviction in my answer seems to silence any further questioners, so I take the opportunity to address the king again.

'Your Highness, I humbly ask you to grant me your consent to return to Wales, where I will live out my life.'

The young king speaks for the first time. 'You are the father of my half-brothers, Tudor. If it is your wish to leave England...'

Duke Humphrey leans forward. 'The matter is to be debated by the council, Your Highness.'

Now Archbishop Henry Chichele speaks. 'The king does not need the consent of council in this matter, unless he wishes it.'

I remember Archbishop Chichele had been a favourite advisor to Henry's father and is the leading expert on legal procedures of the council. It is one of the first opportunities for the young king to exercise his royal prerogative. He has undoubtedly been warned by his guardian, Cardinal Beaufort, of the consequences of allowing Duke Humphrey to control him after he reached his majority.

In a confident young voice, the king orders me to be released, a free man. I cannot miss the glower of annoyance on Duke Humphrey's face and recall the words of Sir Richard Beauchamp. I know from now on I had better watch my back, for I am free but I have made a dangerous enemy.

I am pleased and surprised to find Nathaniel and Thomas waiting for me outside the council chamber, dressed in riding clothes as if for a long journey. 'How did you know I would be released?'

Nathaniel looks serious. 'We didn't—but we should never have let you travel alone, so we want to come with you this time.'

'You will ride with me to Wales?'

Thomas nods. 'I've served my time at the abbey and miss my homeland. I will see if I can find a parish closer to my home in need of a priest.'

'I will be glad of your company.' I glance towards the doorway. 'We must leave before they change their minds.'

Nathaniel has brought me a sturdy horse to replace the Welsh Cob I had to abandon in the street. I run an approving hand over its flank and tie on the saddlebags I'd recovered from my sanctuary in Westminster. Nathaniel and Thomas have divided the rest of my fortune between their saddlebags and each carries a heavy purse of gold and silver hidden under their clothing.

They ride each side of me as we head out of the dirt and noise of the city into the open countryside. The muddy road has frozen hard overnight and puddles glisten with thin ice. The harsh, rattling call of a magpie breaks the silence, sounding to me like an ill omen. I pull my thick felt hat over my ears to protect them from the frost and shiver, despite my warm woollen cloak.

Nathaniel notices me looking over my shoulder. 'You think we're being followed?'

'I hope we are not—but I wouldn't put it past Duke Humphrey to take the law into his own hands. The only way to stay safe is to ride as far from London as we can.'

'What about Edmund and Jasper?'

'They are safe in the care of the Abbess of Barking. I will have to wait a little before I can visit them.' I pray it is true that my sons are now with Katherine de la Pole. 'Have you had any reply to the letters I sent?'

Nathaniel shakes his head. 'No. Perhaps the duke refused them permission to reply?'

'I expect you are right. I shall take some small comfort from the fact my letters were not returned.'

Thomas is concerned as he listens to our exchange. 'Will we be safe when we reach the Welsh border?'

'Not really, Thomas. The king said I was a free man, yet I expect they've already come up with reasons to arrest me again.'

'You have the king's pardon!'

I take one last glance behind us before answering. 'I sensed we were being followed—and we are.'

This time a group of riders can clearly be seen approaching. They ride too fast for ordinary travellers and even from a distance I can tell they are trained soldiers, riding in pairs with one man leading in the front. Winter sunshine flashes from polished breastplates and now we can see they carry long halberds, the weapon of the king's men.

Nathaniel turns in his saddle. 'Should we try to make a run for it?'

'There's no point now they've seen us. Let's find out what they want.'

We wait until the soldiers reach us and I count twenty men, noting they do not wear the duke's livery. Their commander, a well-dressed man a little older than me, rides up and studies the three of us with a scowl of distaste. He wears his sword ready for use and everything about him suggests years of military experience.

'You cost a good captain his job, Tudor, by escaping last time.' He frowns. 'I am not going to allow you to do it a second time, by God!'

'And you are, sir?'

'Lord Beaumont, acting in the name of the king.'

'I have the king's permission to travel to Wales, my lord.'

Lord Beaumont doesn't answer. He nods to his waiting men, who take my sword and dagger, then my precious saddlebags. Nathaniel begins to protest but I shake my head to silence him, as there are too many soldiers. I know what will happen to my silver and gilt cups and plates but I still have my purse, hidden inside my doublet. Even if we have the chance to escape I am certain I will lose all the valuables I have managed to bring from Hatfield.

Last time I had been allowed to keep my sword, as I wasn't officially under arrest. This is different. My sword and dagger are my most precious possessions and I wonder if it is worth trying to protest that the king's wishes are being so blatantly ignored.

I study Lord Beaumont, trying to judge his resolve. 'What's the meaning of this, my lord?'

'I am instructed by the council to take you to Newgate, where you will be held pending trial.'

'What trial, my lord? I have been acquitted by the order of the king himself. My travelling companions are innocent of any crime, so why are they also being detained by your men?'

Lord Beaumont scowls. 'Follow me.' He turns and leads us back the way they came. 'You will ride with us—and if you try anything you will be dragged behind a horse. Do you understand?'

I look across at Nathaniel and Thomas. We understand.

Chapter Fourteen

Winter of 1438

The worst thing about Newgate Gaol is the foul odour permeating the old stones of the building. I taste the taint of death and despair with every breath. The gaol is run by private gaolers known as 'keepers', cruel men, hardened by their work and keen to profit from their charges in any way they can. The other inmates range from those awaiting trial to the most hardened criminals in London, condemned to hang on the gallows at Tyburn.

The shouts and demonic howls of other inmates echo down narrow, dark corridors, keeping me awake at night. One of my neighbours seems to have lost his mind and bangs his empty food dish against the iron grill of his door, loudly protesting his innocence for hours at a time. Clang! Clang! Clang! Clang! The man stops for a moment and I hold my breath, waiting for the racket to continue. It invariably does, at all hours of the day and night. I know it will drive me mad, but there is no point in complaining as no one cares.

My cell is ten feet square with a small, north facing window, too high to see through, yet the source of freezing drafts on cold winter nights. Alone, with only a straw mattress and an old iron bucket, I draw comfort from the thought that my friends have probably been released and are doing what they can to have me released.

There is nothing for me to do other than reflect on the sad turn events have taken. I try to take stock of my life and thank God I have two strong and healthy sons, who give me all I need to live for. I miss them and pray they are old enough not to have their minds turned against me. I miss my Catherine and force an image of her frail body from my mind, trying instead to recall her youthful beauty at our first meeting.

I must presume all my possessions are now stolen or confiscated by Lord Beaumont's men. All I have to show for thirty-eight years is what I managed to hide from the cursory search when I was arrested. I peer through the small holes in the door grill, trying to see down the corridor. A brown rat scuttles busily alongside the wall and out of my limited field of view. There is no sign of my keepers.

Two of them share responsibility for the corridor where my cell is located. They both insist on being called 'master', although there the similarity ends. Master Griffin, the eldest, is surly and rarely speaks unless he has to. He has the dull, dead eyes of a man who has resigned himself to a miserable existence and carries an iron-studded truncheon. I am certain the old keeper would not hesitate to use it if I give him the opportunity.

Master Briggs cannot be more different. He enjoys scheming and taunts his charges with threats and promises he has no intention of keeping. I try to keep on good terms with them both, as my life could depend on it. I once saw Griffin spit in one of the other prisoner's food and know he is capable of worse. At least Master Briggs sometimes brings me a cold eel pie or scrap of ham in return for an extortive payment to supplement my diet of grainy pottage.

I remember one other thing of value I still have and search for the secret pocket where it is hidden. The square of white linen is faded now, creased where it is folded over. I smooth it out and feel a surge of painful memory as I study the red dragon, so carefully sewn. It has failed as my good-luck charm but I hold the square of fabric to my face and feel an unexpected longing for Juliette. She truly loved me yet I turned my back on her for Catherine. I wonder if she is married now or ever thinks of me.

At first I expect to hear what charges are brought against me but several long weeks pass and still no news comes. Then at last the heavy iron bolts on my door scrape and I hear the rattle of the key in the lock. The door bangs open to reveal Thomas Lewis. My first thought is relief that my long wait is finally at an end.

Then I realise what the grim-faced, unkempt appearance of my friend means. Always clean-shaven, Thomas is almost unrecognisable with his dark growth of beard. It is clear from the way he looks at me that he has suffered in his captivity.

I embrace him. 'It's good to see a friendly face. What happened to you?'

Thomas crosses to the rusty iron grill in the door and looks through to see the keeper has gone. 'We are in what they call the wards.' He looks around the tiny cell. 'Not as grand as this but at least we have company. Petty thieves and cut-purses.'

'I paid one of the keepers here to find out about you and Nathaniel.' I smile ruefully as I remember. 'He took my money and forgot his promise.' I look at Thomas. 'How is Nathaniel?'

'I won't lie to you, Owen. Nathaniel was beaten quite badly. They took all his money. Everything.'

'Is he hurt?'

'No bones broken—a black eye and some nasty bruises.'

'And you? I hoped you would have been released by now, Thomas.'

'I've been working as a chaplain, hearing confessions and tending to the sick. It's not very different from what I was doing before—and it means I can visit you.'

'You are only here because of me, Thomas. I'm sorry.'

'We knew the risks—and we've come up with a plan. Before his money was stolen Nathaniel paid to write a letter to Duke Humphrey, pleading our case.'

'The duke will be in no mood to do me any favours, Thomas. He can hold us for as long as he wishes.'

'There was a reply.'

'What did the duke say?'

'We have to await the deliberations of the council.' Thomas frowns. 'We fear they will keep us here indefinitely, so we have a new plan. We can't wait much longer, Owen. Men are dying in this disease-ridden place.'

I curse. 'What else can we do?'

'Nathaniel told me about Samuel Carver.'

'The man with the scar helped Carver escape from here once.'

'Nathaniel thinks they will only help us if someone were to persuade them in person.' His words hang in the air.

'Who?' I cannot think of anyone at all.

'Someone we can trust, completely.' Thomas looks uncomfortable. 'We sent a note to Briony, asking her to visit me here.'

'Briony?' I think back to her nervousness when the baby was born.

'She is working in the abbey infirmary and visited me last week.'

'I would rather not involve Briony.'

'We have few options, Owen. Who else could we ask? Most of the people Nathaniel knows in London are honest merchants—none we could ask to help us escape.'

'There are risks. This could put her in danger.'

'Briony is resourceful. All we asked her to do is deliver a message to the man in the inn at Abbot's Langley.'

Carver proved it is possible to escape from Newgate—but he is a ruthless man with no scruples. Now I have unwittingly put Briony in danger. Far too late, I wish we had made more of an effort to escape when we could. The duke must have learned from his mistake, which is why he sent Lord Beaumont in person to arrest us. I know my friends are right but it pains me to know I must rely on men who should be in Newgate.

'Do you have any money left, Thomas?'

'It was taken from me by Lord Beaumont's men when we were arrested.'

I feel for my purse, hidden under my doublet. 'I've had to pay the keepers but still have most of the gold and a few silver coins.'

'Good. I told Briony to promise five gold nobles once we are freed. We started to worry when Nathaniel was robbed, so were counting on you still having gold in your purse.'

I am already thinking about returning to Ynys Môn. 'Lord Beaumont will take it personally if we escape. They will be covering every road into Wales. We'll have to hide somewhere during the day and travel only at night.'

'Nathaniel has an idea.' Thomas looks through the door grill again, as they both know the keeper could return at any moment. 'We are close to the Thames. He thinks we should take a boat and head up the river towards Wallingford.'

We hear the sound of heavy boots outside and the keeper arrives to escort Thomas back. Thomas makes the sign of the cross and raises his voice so he can he overheard. 'God be with you.'

I know this is for the benefit of my gaoler. 'And with you, Chaplain.'

After Thomas has gone I lie back on my uncomfortable straw mattress, my head buzzing as I think about the possibility of being a free man again. My neighbouring prisoner resumes his habit of banging on his cell door. The sound echoing down the corridor had driven me to distraction before but now it hardly bothers me. My friends have achieved so much while I have done so little, and I resolve to make it up to them when I can.

I sleep with my boots on, ready and waiting for news for three weeks before I hear the furtive scrape of a key in my lock. I know the keepers' routine and feel my heart race as I guess it must be my rescuers at such an early hour. The bolts slide slowly to reduce the noise and the heavy door swings open.

Thomas is waiting and beckons to me. 'Come quickly! We need to get out before they notice we're missing.'

We run down the corridor and pass through a side door into a dingy, high-walled courtyard topped with spiked iron railings. I see the crude rope ladder dangling over the wall and climb to the top, then over the railing and drop to the ground on the other side. I almost collide with Nathaniel, who is waiting in the near darkness with the scar-faced man.

Nathaniel looks relieved to see me with Thomas following close behind. 'I was starting to worry.' He glances towards the river. 'We must be quick—a boatman is waiting.'

I take a last look back at the brooding, silent gaol then we run towards the river. My breath freezes in the air, but I am oblivious to the cold in the excitement of the escape. We dart down an alleyway and soon reach the Thames, where the boatman waits with a lantern. A dog barks somewhere in the darkness, startling me. I hand my purse to Nathaniel, who counts out payment for the scar-faced man.

The clinking coins make me feel a surge of anger as I watch the man pocket his money. 'What happened to Samuel Cleaver?'

The man scratches his head. 'I've no loyalty to Cleaver. You'll find him working as a cook at *The Swan* in St Albans. He uses a different name—but I'd stay away from him if I were you.' The threat in the man's voice brings back long-forgotten memories as he disappears into the morning mist.

I turn to Nathaniel. 'How did he manage to get us out?'

'The gaol was designed to keep people in, not out. It seems it is quite easy to break in, although we still needed the key to your cell.'

'How did he manage that?' I can't imagine either of my keepers handing over the key without a fight or a significant bribe.

'I have no idea.' Nathaniel looks relieved our rescuer is now gone.

The boatman helps us aboard and I see the tide is against us as we head to the opposite bank. We make slow progress and the murky brown water, littered with floating debris, seems sinister. The grey mist seems like the ghosts of the dead who drowned there, and the dark outlines of buildings are full of shadows, any one of which could hide witnesses to our escape.

'Take an oar, if you will, sir?' The boatman struggles against the flow of the river and nods towards a second set of oars stowed in the bows. I unfasten the spare oars and fit them into iron rowlocks. Pulling with all my strength, I feel a satisfying improvement in our passage up the dark, swirling Thames.

We round the bend in the river and I recognise the silhouetted tower of Westminster Abbey rising out of the mist, a useful landmark to show our steady progress. Rowing against the stream is hard, physical work, but it is good to feel the fresh air in my face after so long in the dismal prison. With each stroke we move further from the horrors of Newgate and closer to my new future. I grit my teeth, pulling hard on the oars, keeping pace with the boatman and tasting brackish spray.

I row facing Nathaniel, who cowers in the stern of the boat, making himself useful as a lookout. I can see the strain our time in Newgate has taken on him, as his pale face is thin and his eyes dart from bank to bank, scanning ramshackle buildings. I have already asked too much of Nathaniel and decide we will soon have to part, at least until I secure a royal pardon.

At last the river narrows and the buildings begin to give way to open ground. A rickety wooden jetty reaches out into the river from the southern bank, with several old boats tied up, waiting for the morning trade. There are no signs of movement, so although the area is unfamiliar to me it will have to do.

I call to the boatman. 'Drop us off here, if you please.'

We reach the old wooden supports and I grab hold of one to pull our boat in before climbing out onto the jetty. I help my friends out of the boat and raise a hand in thanks to the boatman, then we head into the mist. The path leading to the jetty widens to become a road and I hope it will soon lead us to a town or village.

The cold morning air freezes in my lungs but we keep a good pace until we cross what I suppose is Wandsworth Common before slowing to walk again. The pinkish tint of dawn begins to brighten the sky and it will soon be light, so the risk of being spotted is increasing with every passing minute.

Nathaniel glances back towards the river as if expecting to see soldiers chasing after us. 'Where are we heading now?' He sounds out of condition.

I must keep an eye on him but continue at a brisk pace. 'I thought to head due west, towards Windsor, about twenty miles.'

'Are you going to give yourself in at Windsor?'

I shake my head at the thought. 'They would send us back to Newgate. We could make it to Kingston by noon, then buy horses and press on to Wallingford.'

Thomas is uncertain. 'Why Wallingford?'

'Windsor is too close to London. We know the Wallingford area well and should be able to find a bed for the night.'

Nathaniel stares up at the wintry sky. 'We are lucky it's dry now but I fear the weather is going to change soon and we're not dressed for a long journey.'

We continue on foot until we reach the busy town of Kingston, where I stay out of sight while Thomas and Nathaniel use some of my remaining money to buy horses and cloaks to keep out the winter chill. Keen to put a good distance from any pursuers, we make good time on the back roads towards Wallingford, riding until a bright moon appears in the sky. I am tired by the time we reach a popular stopping place at a busy crossroads on the outskirts of the town.

Nathaniel finds an inn with a room and after stabling our horses we look for something to eat. Dimly lit and low-ceilinged, the inn is warmed by a roaring log fire and full of travellers drinking and sharing stories. Several men are gambling while others sing with drunken enthusiasm.

A woman with a low-cut bodice and rouged cheeks catches my eye and gives me a welcoming smile. I see Thomas scowl and laugh as I realise she makes a good living from passing travellers. We manage to find an empty table in the corner and the portly innkeeper, wearing a grubby apron, serves us with steaming bowls of meaty stew and tankards of strong ale.

I allow myself to relax a little for the first time since leaving Newgate. Although we are still some way from the relative safety of Wales, it is good to be on the road after the misery of the gaol. The landlord returns when we finish our meal and replaces our empty bowls with an earthenware jug of ale. I nod thanks and hand him a silver half-groat in payment, then take the heavy jug and pour us all another drink, as the salty stew has made me thirsty.

Nathaniel raises his tankard in a toast. 'Here's to a safe journey!'

Thomas touches his tankard to Nathaniel's. 'And to seeing Wales again, God willing.'

'Fortune's Wheel turns again.' I look at my friends. 'To new adventures!' Our tankards clunk together, splashing ale on the battered oak table.

Nathaniel is curious. 'What is our plan when we reach Wales?'

'I thought to head for the island of Ynys Môn off the northern coast.' I take another mouthful of ale. 'I'm hoping that's too far for the duke's men to travel. With luck they will soon forget about me.' In truth I doubt it but feel it is time for our luck to change.

'It should be easy enough to buy a passage on a ship to Ireland if they come after you.' Thomas sounds thoughtful. 'If they don't, I'm sure we will find plenty to keep us busy. 'I'm looking forward to seeing the place after all these years. I may even be able to track down some relatives.'

'We can earn our keep.' Nathaniel looks reassured. 'I would like to visit Ireland—if you do go there I'll be happy to accompany you.'

'I hope it won't be necessary, but I will be glad of your company Nathaniel.'

Thomas drains his tankard and places it on the table. 'We'd better turn in, as there's a long ride ahead.'

I agree. 'We should be able to reach the border tomorrow—then I want to head across the mountains, away from the coast road.'

We check on the horses and retire for the night but I lay awake for a while, trying to remember what I can of my parent's home in Penmynydd. There is nothing for me there now, so I will settle in the nearby town of Beaumaris. I recall the narrow streets and the long seafront with its imposing castle and stony beach. As a boy I sailed to the mainland on one of the many little fishing boats that ply their trade in the often treacherous Menai Strait. I drift off to sleep dreaming of my parents and wishing they were there to greet me on my return.

A bright lantern shines in my face and I wake to the sound of men shouting and heavy boots clattering on wooden floors. I rub my eyes and find the room full of armed men. One is tying Nathaniel's hands with a length of rope and another is arguing loudly with Thomas.

'Owen Tudor?' A bearded man stares at me with questioning, blood-shot eyes.

I nod and am rewarded by being roughly pulled from the straw mattress that serves as my bed and pushed against the wall next to Thomas. I see right away these are not the king's men. They look like farm workers. One is armed with a cudgel and another carries an old sword with a broken blade.

I dimly recognise the man and struggle to recall his name.

Nathaniel beats me to it. 'Thomas Darwent. You worked at Wallingford Castle.'

The man nods and studies me again. 'Wasn't certain it was you, Tudor, until I recognised your accomplice.'

'What do you want with us?'

He shows blackened teeth. 'I hope to be well rewarded for capturing you.'

'I can reward you, if you let us go.'

'How much?'

I sense I can't trust Thomas Darwent but dread the prospect of returning to Newgate Gaol. I take my purse from its hiding place and hold it in front of him. 'Let us go and this is yours.'

Darwent lunges forward, snatching the purse from my grip. 'You probably stole this.' He turns to his men. 'Take them to the castle. I'll be happier once they're safely locked up.'

My hands are tied behind my back and I am dragged bodily out into the cold dawn by two men and lifted into a cart, soon to be joined by Thomas and Nathaniel. The men may not be professional soldiers but they planned their attack well. I stare at my friends and feel a surge of remorse. I should have separated from them when I could, as once again I have led them into danger.

☆ ☆ ☆

I find it strange to be confined in the familiar surroundings of Wallingford Castle, a place with so many happy memories. The castle was once the county gaol and still functions as a prison, with a row of securely locked iron-barred cells. Although we are the only inmates, we know Wallingford is a temporary home. Nathaniel has already discovered from the men guarding them that it will not be long before Lord Beaumont arrives from London to escort us back to Newgate. We also learn the castle has a new constable, Sir William de la Pole, Earl of Suffolk, an ambitious man who commanded the English army at the siege of Orleans.

I brighten a little at the news. 'Suffolk is a supporter of Cardinal Beaufort. There is hope he might listen to our case.'

'If only to spite Duke Humphrey,' Nathaniel agrees. 'We have nothing to lose by trying.'

Thomas has been listening to our exchange. 'What do you have in mind?'

'We have to ask for something which is in his power. Sir Walter Hungerford is still constable at Windsor, so I will ask if you can both be released on surety and for me to be transferred to Windsor. It will be a lot easier to bring your case to the attention of the king once I am there,' I grin to my friends. 'I could be a free man in a month.'

Chapter Fifteen

The Duke of Suffolk refuses to see me and once more we find ourselves in Newgate Gaol. Through some oversight I am now with the others in the communal cells known of as the wards. I am relieved to be spared the loneliness of my solitary cell, although I fear what will happen if my former keepers find I have returned, especially Master Griffin, who once threatened me with his iron-studded truncheon.

The problem we now face is the lack of any money to bribe the keepers to remove the shackles and chains fitted to prisoners who might otherwise escape. We also have no way to pay for a mattress or extra food. At first this means trying to sleep on the hard ground, although it is not long before the need for survival drives us to take unguarded bedding from other prisoners. I curse our luck when I discover the stolen mattresses are infested with tiny fleas and biting lice, which keep us all awake at night.

Nathaniel tries to see the positive side of it. 'At least our poverty means we won't be beaten up and robbed.'

I know the truth of Nathaniel's words. We are fortunate to be of no interest to the dangerous gangs that roam the wards, as I see one man being beaten half to death before being robbed. The keepers turn a blind eye to such acts of violence and although my instinct is to help, there is nothing we can do. At best, it would earn me a beating and make me a target for the bored thugs.

My teeth feel loose due to the poor diet of pottage and stale crusts, and I find a small white bone in my stew but know any complaint will only bring a beating. Fortunately

Thomas helps to improve our rations by hearing confessions and praying for those facing death sentences. Despite my friend's efforts I am becoming concerned at how all three of us are losing weight.

For four long months we simply survive from one day to the next. A virulent illness sweeps through the wards and the stench of vomit and worse becomes overpowering. Nathaniel is the first to succumb. Thomas tries to nurture him through his sickness but Nathaniel's strength is waning as surely as a candle burns to the end of its wick.

I can see the sweat glistening on my sleeping friend's brow as the fever takes its deadly hold. 'What can we do, Thomas?'

'Pray—and trust that God still has some use for him.'

'He needs to get out of here. Can you persuade the keepers to have him moved?'

Thomas shakes his head. 'It's no use. Before we escaped, perhaps, but now we are marked men.'

'I'll give him half my ration until he's better, it's the least I can do.'

I wait for Thomas to reply but he sits in silence and stares into space, his sense of humour gone. I feel my protruding ribs and wonder how long we have to wait for the council to make their deliberations. I curse Duke Humphrey, as I suspect he is content to leave me to rot in Newgate, if he thinks of me at all.

There is a shout as someone raises his voice over the constant murmuring and groaning. I realise they are calling out my name. I shout back and a belligerent keeper produces a key and unlocks my iron shackle. I massage my dirty, swollen ankle, which has grown calloused where the shackle rubs against my skin.

'You Owen Tudor?' The keeper looks at me doubtfully.

'I am.'

I fear my former keepers are going to take their revenge on me for escaping. I am in no condition to take a beating and remember how Master Griffin threatened that no one would know or care if they killed me.

'You're transferred to Windsor.' The keeper gestures for me to follow.

I can't believe my luck. 'What about my companions?'

The keeper shakes his head. 'The order is only for you.'

I turn to my friends. Nathaniel is sleeping but Thomas has been listening to every word. 'It seems the Duke of Suffolk finally got my message.' I manage a smile. 'Take care of Nathaniel. I'll be back for you as soon as I can.'

'God bless you, Owen.' Thomas seems close to tears. 'We'll be here waiting.'

☆ ☆ ☆

Even though returning as a prisoner under escort, I feel an increasing thrill of anticipation as I enter the gates at Windsor after so many years. It is now the middle of July and the sun dazzles my eyes, the long, cold winter already a distant memory. The castle looks magnificent, with exotic blue-green peacocks strutting in the perfectly tended gardens. If I must be imprisoned, I can't think of a better place.

The last time I had been there was when Catherine went missing and I'd gone in search of her. A sad day when I thought our son Owen was dead. Now I know the boy lived after all I draw strength from the thought of returning to Westminster Abbey to see him. It is another reason to keep going, another reason to secure my freedom.

My new cell would be considered palatial by the inmates at Newgate. In the Curfew Tower at the north-western corner of the castle, an iron-barred window looks out into the street and I pass the time watching the comings and goings of the people of Windsor. Built over two hundred years before, following the siege during the reign of King John, the tower has stone walls thirteen feet thick at the base and stands over a hundred feet high.

A guardroom is located above my cell, and as I am their only prisoner my guards treat me well. I feel a pang of guilt as I tuck into a bowl of steaming stew, with chunks of beef and seasoning of herbs, washed down with a goblet of red wine. I have never tasted anything so good in my life and promise myself I will never complain about my food again.

I ask to be visited by the constable, Sir Walter Hungerford, as soon as I arrive but several days pass without my request being granted. It crosses my mind that this is not a good omen but there could be many reasons for the delay. Sir Walter is close to sixty now and still a busy man.

When at last Sir Walter appears his old face looks grim and lined with worry. 'I wish it was under better circumstances that we meet again, Tudor.' His voice, once so commanding, sounds frail.

I am relieved to see the man who can free me. 'Sir Walter... thank God you've come.' I cross to the bars of my cell so my words cannot be overheard. 'I need your help, my lord.'

Sir Walter gestures for the guard to bring him a chair, which he pulls closer to the bars before sitting. I notice how Sir Walter groans like an old man as he sits and realise the years are catching up with him. I also see the guards discreetly return to the guardroom and guess it is on the constable's orders.

'What would you have me do, Tudor?' There is a hint of annoyance in his voice.

'I need an audience with the king, to present my case.'

'Your case?'

'The king granted me permission...'

'This is a council matter,' Sir Walter interrupts. 'You are to be detained until the council has made a decision.'

I study Sir Walter's face for a clue as to what is going on. 'All I ask is that you arrange for me to see the king, my lord.'

'I regret... I cannot do that, Tudor.'

'Why not, my lord?'

Sir Walter regards me for a moment before answering. 'Because... I am Duke Humphrey's man. How did you imagine an old soldier like me became Treasurer of England when Bishop Beaufort resigned the great seal?'

I understand. 'Was it because of you the duke chose me as his man in the queen's household?'

'It was.' He frowns. 'We thought you were going to marry the queen's maid, yet you chose to marry the queen instead. Surely you knew what that would mean?'

'I did—and I would do it all again.'

'Well, you are a fool, Tudor.' Sir Walter stands, his chair scraping on the hard stone floor. 'And now you are learning the consequences.'

I have to think quickly before the constable leaves. 'I was arrested with two travelling companions, my lord. Their names are Nathaniel Kemp and Thomas Lewis.' I look him in the eye. 'They are innocent but still held in Newgate Gaol.'

Sir Walter sits down again and thinks for a moment. 'I'll tell you something, Tudor. I see something of myself as a younger man in you.' He smiles for the first time. 'I was amused when I heard you married Queen Catherine, if only to see Duke Humphrey so completely unable to do anything about it.'

'Will you help to free my companions, my lord?'

'I will do what I can—although I make no promises, as I doubt the duke will take kindly to it.'

'Thank you, my lord. I am indebted to you.'

Sir Walter stands again and turns as he is about to leave. 'Trust in God, Tudor, and include me in your prayers.'

After Sir Walter has gone I sit in the corner of my cell, thinking over what I have learned. Sir Walter is right. I have been a fool, not because I married Catherine but because I should have known I could not ask the old constable to help me. At least there is hope for my friends, if they are still alive. I recall how Nathaniel shivered with the fever and thank God I might have found a way to end his suffering.

Another week passes without any word from the constable, so when my guard tells me I have a visitor I am relieved to be seeing my former master again.

'Owen Tudor...'

I recognise the voice from my past immediately, although it is not Sir Walter. The trace of a French accent reminds me of Catherine, yet it is no ghost. The speaker steps from the shadows into a shaft of summer sunlight and I stand transfixed, my fingers tightening their grip on the iron bars of my cell.

'Juliette.' I say her name almost reverently. She wears an ornate coif over her braided hair, covered with a delicate mesh net. Her dress is made of dark blue damask and around her neck is a silver necklace with a jewelled pendant that sparkles as it catches the light.

'Sir Walter told me you were here. I didn't know what had... become of you.' Her voice falters. She clasps her hands together. 'There is something I have to tell you. Sir Walter has been relieved of his post.'

I know it is my fault. Duke Humphrey has found another way to exact his revenge by punishing the elderly constable. It is an unexpected blow, as I had allowed myself to believe my friends were as good as free. I even started to hope Sir Walter Hungerford could arrange for me to be brought before the king, even if it meant risking the anger of the duke.

'Do you know who is to replace him?'

Juliette hesitates before answering. 'The new constable is someone known to you, Owen. It is the Duke of Somerset, Sir Edmund Beaufort.'

I lean against the cold metal bars of my cell and regard Juliette while I try to think through the implications. I remember my jealousy at how Edmund Beaufort planned to marry Catherine all those years ago. The appointment of a Beaufort meant Duke Humphrey's influence at the council could be waning, but I have not forgotten how Cardinal Beaufort publicly mocked me when we last met. I see Juliette is waiting for me to say something.

'You look... beautiful, Juliette.' I say it without thinking.

She smiles at the compliment. 'You look like a vagrant, Owen.'

I look down at my clothes. They are the same I wore when I last appeared before the council but are now ragged and soiled. I have no way to trim my beard and my hair, which is starting to turn grey, has grown long and is matted with dirt.

'You are right. I have nothing now. My money has been confiscated. Even my sword was taken by Duke Humphrey's men.'

'I was sorry to hear what happened to Queen Catherine...' Her voice is softer now and she glances over her shoulder to see if the guards are listening. She takes a step closer to the bars. 'The first we knew was when her funeral was announced.'

'You heard we were married?'

'You kept your secret well, although... I guessed the truth long before the rumours began.'

'When we last met you asked if I would come back to you.'

'You remember—and do you remember what you said?'

'You should find someone... more worthy.'

'It seems you've done your best to make that easy for me, Owen.' Her hand moves to the bars and rests on mine. 'You know... I never found anyone?'

I like the caress of her hand. 'I lay in my cell in Newgate Gaol and I wondered about you, Juliette.'

She backs away. 'I must go before I am missed.'

'You will come and see me again soon?'

'I will.' She smiles again. 'And I shall have to find you some clean clothes!'

She is gone before I can reply, leaving me with a strange sense of loss, mixed with new hope. I sit in the corner of my cell and try to make sense of it all. Sir Walter's choice of Juliette as his messenger is not a coincidence. He could have sent anyone, yet I wonder if he has chosen her for a reason.

Juliette must have an important position in the king's household, as she no longer dresses as a maid and has the confidence that comes with authority. I remember how surprised I'd been when she was chosen to remain in the young king's household. Now I realise Juliette would be the perfect spy for Duke Humphrey. With her privileged access she can tell him all he needs to know about the king and his visitors.

I sleep fitfully that night, dreaming about how Juliette reached out and touched my hand with the easy familiarity of a lover. Something was rekindled in me at that moment. I dream how different my life would be if Juliette stayed with Catherine. I might have expected awkwardness between us, even bitterness after everything that happened, yet it is as if we have never been parted.

On her second visit she brings the promised parcel of clothes. 'You must forgive people for treating you as a criminal while you have the appearance of one.'

'All my other clothes were lost when I was arrested—as well as everything I owned.' I shrug. 'All I have is the shirt on my back.'

'As you did when you first came to the royal household.'

'You are right—except for something which is very precious to me.' I reach inside my doublet and unfold the square of yellowing cloth to show her the embroidered red dragon.

'My God... you kept it, all these years!'

'I consider it my good luck charm.' I grin at my own joke.

Juliette wipes a tear from her eye. 'I worried the other maids would see me sewing and guess who it was for.'

'Well, now it is all I have.' I see she still has tears in her eyes. 'It may not have brought much luck but you should know it has been a comfort to me.'

She doesn't answer but hands the folded clothes through the bars. A clean linen shirt, a dark wool doublet, a pair of breeches and a good leather belt with a brass buckle. I thank her and turn my back while I strip off the old clothing I have worn for so long. The new clothes fit surprisingly well and make me feel human again.

Juliette has regained her professional composure while she waits for me to change my clothes, and I realise I must do the same. 'How can I arrange an audience with the king?'

She seems uncertain. 'The king is surrounded by his advisors at all times. After what happened to Sir Walter...'

'I wouldn't ask you to speak on my behalf—but I worry about the health of my companions in Newgate.' I look into her eyes. 'You remember Nathaniel?'

'Of course. I liked Nathaniel.' Her voice sounds sad. 'I hate to think of him wrongly imprisoned.'

'He is being cared for by a friend, a Welsh clergyman named Thomas Lewis, although I fear they will both die if they remain there any longer, Juliette.'

'Do you think the king would order their release?'

'If I can see the king he will pardon us all, God willing.'

Juliette understands. 'You will need the support of Edmund Beaufort before you see the king.'

'What is he like these days?'

'Well, he is married—to Lady Eleanor Beauchamp, a rich widow. They say her late husband, Baron de Ros, was thrown into the Seine and drowned. Lady Eleanor has his fortune, until his son comes of age. She seems to have failed to tame Edmund Beaufort though.'

'He still has an eye for the ladies?'

'Several of the maids have already complained to me, although I fail to see what I can do other than caution them to take care.' She brightens as an idea occurs to her. 'I could find an opportunity to ask Sir Edmund to come and see you?'

'I should ask the guard commander first, Juliette. You have done enough for me already.' I don't like to think of the consequences of her asking favours of Sir Edmund Beaufort.

'At least you look a little more presentable now.' She raises a hand in a wave as she leaves.

I feel a tingle of pleasure at her parting compliment and suspect that the barber who visited to trim my hair and beard had also been sent at Juliette's instigation. Pride prevents me from asking her, although she said it is a good improvement.

Edmund Beaufort is quite different from the young noble I knew all those years ago. Now he is wealthy and wears the sword and gold-braided uniform of a commander of the king's army. His successes in France have given him a soldier's swagger and he sounds a little arrogant.

'I didn't like what you did, Tudor.' Sir Edmund looks at me as if I am a strange creature washed up on the foreshore. 'Queen Catherine deserved better.'

I know what I must do. 'She always held you in great esteem, my lord. She named our first son Edmund in your memory.'

He seems surprised and his attitude changes. 'I was sorry to hear of her passing. Did she suffer?'

'It was mercifully swift, thank God.' I force the truth from my mind as there is no need for Edmund Beaufort to be told.

'It may comfort you to know your sons are both well.'

'Have you seen them?'

'No—but the king has regular reports from the Abbess of Barking.'

'Thank you, my lord. Do you know if the king recognises them as his half-brothers?'

'He does. I expect he will find a title for them when they are of age.'

'I should like to see them—but not before my situation is... improved.'

'I know you want to see the king, Tudor, to plead for your freedom.' He shakes his head. 'And I know you are concerned about your friends in Newgate. You could be useful to me. A loyal servant is hard to find. I am prepared to order your companions to be released—but I must ask something of you in return.'

I am relieved and concerned in equal measure. 'What can I do for you, my lord?'

'My uncle,' Edmund glances behind to see the guards are not listening. 'Cardinal Beaufort has taken some satisfaction from the way you outsmarted Duke Humphrey—but he warned me not to let you out of here too soon.'

'Why?'

'It's all a matter of timing, Tudor. You are here as a punishment. If I had ended the siege of Calais earlier, they would all have thought it an easy victory.'

I recall hearing how Edmund Beaufort relieved the Burgundian siege of Calais before Duke Humphrey arrived with his army. The victory marked the start of the duke's declining reputation and boosted the Beaufort cause. 'How long must I wait, my lord?' It is becoming harder to show respect, but I know I must.

'I need you to promise not to try to see the king until I say you can,' he looks around the cell with distaste, 'and also not to escape from this place.'

★ ★ ★

I turn over the letter in my hand and read it a second time, feeling elated and saddened. It has been delivered to me unsealed and the hand is neat but unfamiliar to me. More a note than a letter, it seems to have been written with the expectation it would be read by my gaolers. Thomas and Nathaniel have been released from Newgate and are now in the infirmary at Bermondsey Abbey. Then I notice the letter is signed, so discreetly I had overlooked it at my first reading. There at the bottom, after the words *God be with you*, is a letter B, written in a less skilled hand.

Briony is taking care of my friends and I smile with relief that Edmund Beaufort has kept his promise.

The sparse words of the note bring painful memories. I remember the despair on Briony's face and how helpless I felt when Catherine lay dying in the same infirmary, begging me to bring her sons to her. I picture Nathaniel in Newgate Gaol, his body shaking with the fever and am glad I was able to help him. My mind is full of questions. I have been spared—but for what purpose? How could a merciful God punish good men so cruelly?

Chapter Sixteen

Summer 1439

If I had known I would remain imprisoned for so long I doubt I would have so easily agreed to Edmund Beaufort's deal. Juliette visits as often as she can, bringing news of the world outside and helping keep my spirits up. The release of Nathaniel and Thomas gives me hope and within two months Nathaniel is sufficiently recovered from the sickness to visit me in Windsor.

Nathaniel seems like his old self again, having trimmed his untidy beard and put on weight from eating decent food. Although dressed in a cheap woollen smock and a floppy hat that makes him look like a farmer, he has a new dagger at his belt, a sparkle back in his eyes and a broad grin.

I clasp his hand through the bars. 'I feared Newgate would be the end of you, Nathaniel.'

'I know what you did for us... and will always be in your debt.'

'You owe me nothing. I am glad to see you again after so long. How is Thomas?'

'He wanted to travel with me to see you, but is still weak from his illness. He busies himself helping Briony in the infirmary and plans to return to Wales when he is well enough.' He smiles. 'I think he might even take Briony with him.'

'And what are your plans, Nathaniel?'

'To find a way to have you released from here, for a start. You know no proper charges were ever brought against you?'

'They have forgotten about me.'

'You are not forgotten, Owen.'

'Then why don't they charge me—or let me go?'

'I suspect that Cardinal Beaufort is deliberately preventing the council from discussing your case.'

'Why would he do that?'

'He opposes anything the Duke of Gloucester wants. I fear you are simply caught up in their squabbles.' Nathaniel shrugs his shoulders. 'All I can do is make enquiries with the clerks who understand the legal process. There must be a way—there always is.'

'I appreciate your help, Nathaniel. I was starting to wonder if I will be imprisoned in this place forever.'

Nathaniel turns as he is about to leave. 'Is there anything I can get you, Owen?'

'There is. I don't expect I'll ever see any of my property again but I would like my papers returned, if they haven't been burned. I may need to prove I have the rights of an Englishman!'

After Nathaniel leaves I feel new hope. I begin exercising in my cell for long hours and am relieved to see how soon my muscles regain their firmness. I also secure permission from Sir Edmund to walk within the courtyard in front of the chapel. My bored guards become complacent as they watch but I honour my promise to Edmund Beaufort. I fear that even if I could escape, the duke's men would hunt me down. I will never again do anything that could see me returned to the horrors of Newgate Gaol.

King Henry often visits the chapel, spending long hours in prayer when he stays at Windsor, so it is not long before I see the king's retinue emerging from the entrance. It would have been easy for me to create a disturbance and bring my plight to the king's attention but instead I allow my guards to escort me from royal view.

Sir Edmund seems to appreciate this and a simple bond begins to develop between us. He becomes more talkative on his occasional visits, sometimes sharing news of the king and parliament. Sir Edmund is scathing about the claims of Richard, Duke of York, and open about his distrust of Duke Humphrey. At the same time, he speaks frankly about my future.

'The king will see your sons are looked after, but you must understand, Tudor, you are an embarrassment at court.'

I have heard it before. 'I tried to go to the furthest coast of Wales—twice.' I shake my head as I remember. 'Both times I was dragged back to London by Duke Humphrey's men.'

'What do you intend to do in Wales?'

'There is a castle in Beaumaris, close to the village where I was born. I hope to find a position under the constable there, Sir William Bulkeley.'

'I may be able to put a word in for you, Tudor—but perhaps you would do better with the Merchants of the Staple?'

'In Calais?'

'Why not? There is always need there for men with your... resourcefulness.'

'I will think on it, my lord.'

After Edmund Beaufort leaves I reflect on my future. If they want me out of the way I might be able to turn that to my advantage. It could take a long time before I can save enough to buy a house fit for my sons to return to, so I need money. Catherine's estates and fortune all reverted to the Crown on her death and any money I accumulated over the years has now been spent or confiscated.

I don't share Nathaniel's hope it will ever be returned, so I will have to find any work I can and buy a passage to Calais to seek my fortune there. Sir Edmund told me there are always ships in the busy harbour, laden with bales of wool and returning with goods from all over the continent. On Juliette's next visit I explain my plan. If I can persuade Nathaniel to accompany me, we could perhaps find work with the men of the Staple, who have a monopoly on the trade and act as agents for the wealthy wool merchants in London.

Juliette contemplates my idea for a moment. 'Calais is a long way from here.'

I hear a hint of sadness in her voice. I have had plenty of time to think about what I want from the future. I am close to forty years old now and have learned not to regret mistakes made in the past. I must take my chances while I can or live with the consequences.

'Would you consider coming with me?'

She hesitates before answering. 'I used to dream about one day returning to France. I will consider it.'

'That is all I can ask.'

'And that is all I can promise.' She glances back to where the guard could be listening and lowers her voice almost to a whisper. 'You hurt me once, Owen. I don't know if I could go through that again.'

I am so preoccupied with my own situation it comes as something of a shock to realise how difficult it must have been for her when I vanished with Catherine. I never wrote to her after we arrived at Wallingford Castle. Even when I visited Windsor I only met her by chance.

'I'm... sorry, Juliette.' I struggle to find the right words. 'I hope whatever the future holds for me, it can include you.'

She studies me without speaking for a moment. 'I have always loved you, Owen.' She leaves without looking back, her words hanging in the air like a whispered prayer.

⋆ ⋆ ⋆

When Nathaniel eventually returns he seems pleased with himself and is wearing a smart velvet doublet and breeches and a hat with a colourful jay feather. The guards allow him to bring a letter, quill and ink.

'Did you know Juliette is the king's housekeeper? She has helped me secure a position, much like that I held years ago, keeping tallies of the king's supplies.' He smiles. 'I have a little money again and will be able to visit you more easily.'

'That's good news.' I glance at the letter. 'What have you brought me?'

Nathaniel hands the letter through the bars. 'I drafted this authority for me to act on your behalf, as your agent. It needs your signature.'

I take the quill and uncork the flask of ink, then sign my name. It is the first time I've needed to do so for a long time. 'I doubt you will be able to recover any of my property, as it will be long gone now, but we have nothing to lose by trying.'

'I consulted with a lawyer friend. I was correct in thinking there have never been formal charges against you, so you are only on a holding order from the council. That means you can't apply for bail—but you could be released on a mainprise, an agreed sum of surety.'

'I have no money, Nathaniel. Not a single groat.'

'I've thought of that. The application would be considered by the Sheriff of Berkshire, Sir Walter Sculle.

The granting of a mainprise is at his discretion—and he can require whatever conditions he pleases.'

'I wish I felt able to share your optimism.'

'The sheriff is a fellow countryman of yours, from the town of Brecon—and also the King's Attorney in the Welsh courts. I am hopeful he will be sympathetic to your case.'

'You've been busy on my behalf. I promised Edmund Beaufort I would not try to escape or ask to see the king. I will ask Beaufort to agree your plan, Nathaniel. It could offer him a face-saving way forward and remind him that he has yet to honour his promise to me.'

Edmund Beaufort seems relieved to have a solution and agrees to release me in the middle of July. Juliette is nowhere to be seen but Nathaniel is waiting for me as I emerge into the bright summer sunshine a free man, almost one year after I arrived at Windsor Castle. I feel as if a huge weight has been lifted from me and embrace him warmly.

'I don't know how you did it, Nathaniel.'

'I told you there must be a way. I arranged a surety of two thousand pounds with the sheriff and I was right—he is appalled at the way you have been treated.'

'Two thousand pounds is a fortune. I will never be able to pay it!'

'That is the point, Owen, you should never have to. I conveyed your promise to the sheriff that you will appear before the king as commanded. A date has been set for the eleventh of November.'

'Why so long?'

'It is the best I could do.'

'Thank you, Nathaniel. I don't know how I can repay you.'

'I have thought of a way. You will work for me while you wait. I need to keep an eye on you—and you can help me with keeping records of the household accounts.'

I laugh at how our roles are now reversed. 'A fair price.' A thought occurs to me. 'Will I be allowed to visit my sons at Barking?'

'You can. You are a free man, Owen.'

Barking Abbey is some sixty miles east of Windsor on the other side of London. I arrive in late summer sunshine on a borrowed horse, wearing new riding clothes paid for from the first wages I have earned since my days at Wallingford Castle. I know little of the abbey, other than it had once been the wealthiest nunnery in England before its lands were inundated by flooding from the Thames.

I am greeted by impassive nuns, who direct me to the abbey stables then lead me to the office of the abbess, Katherine de la Pole. The abbess is the sister of the Earl of Suffolk, William de la Pole, and a favourite of the king. She dresses simply, with black robes and white linen headdress of the Benedictine order, making it hard to judge her age.

Her room is sparsely furnished, with clean rushes on the floor and a scrubbed oak table, in front of which are two wooden chairs. The walls are recently whitewashed and the sun streams through the leaded-glass window onto a painting of a serene Madonna, dressed in faded azure robes.

'Welcome, Master Tudor.' Her sharp eyes study my face as if trying to read my thoughts. 'Have you come to take your sons from the abbey?'

I hear a trace of concern in her voice. 'No, I simply wish to see them.' I chose my words with care. 'I have been... unable to for two years, Your Grace.'

'You will see them soon—but first we need to talk.'

'Something is wrong?'

'Your sons are doing well.' She smiles. 'They make good progress with their studies.'

'They were told about their mother?'

'Yes, may God be with her. We were sorry to hear of her passing. It was decided they were too young to attend her funeral.'

'What have they been told about me?'

'They often ask after you, Master Tudor. The sisters tell them you are in the service of the king.'

'Thank you, Your Grace. I am grateful for that kindness. What is it you wish to discuss before I see my sons?'

The abbess clasps her hands together and hesitates before answering. 'I regret to say... the costs of keeping your sons here have not been met for almost a year now.'

I am relieved it is not something more serious. 'I was not aware of this—how much is due to the abbey?'

'The amount is over fifty pounds.' The abbess leans forward in her chair. 'Since the floods the income from the abbey lands has fallen to almost nothing. As well as the costs of food and clothing, we were told to provide your sons with servants.'

'I will do what I can to see that you are paid in full.'

'We would be most grateful.'

I expect it will be a simple matter for Nathaniel to track down the requests for payment and, if necessary, I am prepared to raise it with the king. I hope the failure to pay for the education of my sons is not a sign of how King Henry views Edmund and Jasper.

'I would like to see the boys now, if I may. I have travelled a long way.'

'Of course. Please follow me, Master Tudor.'

She leads me out into the cloisters and through an arched doorway to an oak panelled room, decorated with colourful pictures of saints and an overly realistic figure of Christ on the cross. Edmund and Jasper are waiting on a wooden pew and stand as they see me with the abbess.

They are both simply dressed in plain tunics. Now aged nine, Edmund is the tallest, with his mother's bright blue eyes and golden-blond hair. The nuns have cut their hair short, making them look more like page boys than step-brother's to the king. I am struck by how my youngest son has changed since I last saw him. Jasper is eight years old now and has my dark eyes and black hair.

I walk up to them and embrace them both, surprised at the unexpected awkwardness I feel. I also hadn't expected such a painful reminder of Catherine and feel a stab of regret that I didn't try harder when she pleaded with me to bring them to her at Bermondsey Abbey.

'Have you come for us, Father?' Jasper stares up at me with enquiring eyes.

'I must buy a new house before you can come home with me.'

'Will it be in Wales?' Once again it is Jasper who speaks.

'Would you like that?'

'Yes, Father.'

'And how are you, Edmund?' I turn to my eldest son.

'You told us this would be... an adventure, Father.' He glances at the abbess, who is listening to every word. 'All we do is study—and pray you will come for us.'

'I'm sorry it has been so long. I came here as soon as I could.'

'We are not permitted to practise archery.' Edmund glances again at the abbess. 'The sisters say it is a distraction from our learning.'

The abbess turns to me. 'They can read and write in French and Latin, as well as English.' Her voice softens a little. 'We are impressed with the progress your sons have made. They are excellent students.'

I look at their serious, pale faces and resolve to take them from here as soon as I am able to. 'I am proud of you both—and I know your mother would be.' I fight to control my emotions. 'You know why your studies are so important?'

'Because we are half-brothers to the king?'

'That's right, Edmund. If you do well, one day the king will make you both lords.'

'Will we live in a castle?'

'I am sure you will.'

Jasper smiles. 'What is he like, our brother the king?'

'He is more like your mother than his father.' I did a quick calculation. 'He must be seventeen now. He has no other family than you—and he was taken from his mother when he was about your age.'

'If he is the king he should be allowed to do as he wishes?'

'I agree, Jasper. The thing is... after his father died in France, he was put under the care of his uncle, until he came of age.'

The abbess steps forward and addresses the boys. 'Your father must rest now. He has ridden a long way to see you.'

I take her cue. 'The abbess is right. I will see you both again in the morning before I leave.'

As I make the long journey back to Windsor I look up at the warm sun and thank God for keeping my sons safe and well. I have much to be grateful for and my time in Newgate has made me more appreciative of even the most basic things in life, the freedom to walk in the sunshine, a clean bed and a jug of strong ale.

I am sure my sons are receiving an education that will stand them in good stead in the future. I recall how they stood straight and proud as I left the abbey, Edmund still a little reserved, like his mother, Jasper raising a hand and shouting I must return soon. I am fortunate they are in the care of Abbess Katherine, as I don't like to think what could have become of my sons if they had remained with me.

As I see the huge round tower of Windsor Castle my thoughts turn to Juliette. It is as if she felt safer when there were iron bars between us, for now I am free it seems she ensures we are never alone together. Her manner towards me is a professional barrier as real as any prison bars. I had been disappointed when she wasn't there to witness my release and was right to wonder if that meant she would not travel with me to Calais.

Now, as the date of my official audience with the king draws nearer, I decide there is much to be said for staying at court in Windsor after all. King Henry has no other family still living, so there is a chance he will look favourably on his half-brothers. He has known me since he was a boy, so even if his advisors tell him differently, there is hope those memories can enable Edmund and Jasper to have the future they deserve.

I wait in the royal apartments recalling the first time, seventeen years before, when I waited in these same rooms to meet Catherine. Now her eldest son is King of England and France. The fair-haired little boy who once played with wooden toy soldiers in this room now holds the future of my sons in his hands.

King Henry arrives, flanked as ever by his lords who act as court advisors. One will be Duke Humphrey's man and another there to represent the interests of Cardinal Beaufort, although I recognise neither of them. I feel their judging eyes upon me but focus on the king. Henry has the pale, white skin of his mother and the only sign of his authority is a heavy gold chain around his neck with a gold cross ornamented with bright diamonds. He wears a simple velvet cap over his curly hair, now turned darker than I remember.

Looking again at Catherine's eldest son is like seeing her shadow. He has her long, fair eyelashes but not her bright blue eyes. Instead, I find myself looking into the light hazel eyes of the late King Henry. He has Catherine's delicate mouth but it seems too small in his Plantagenet face. I notice a gold ring, set with a large ruby, on the king's left hand and recognise it as the one she sent him on the eve of his coronation in France. She said her late husband told her a ruby could safeguard against poison. I must remember one day to pass this knowledge on to the king, if the opportunity ever arises.

Henry takes his place on the raised, gilded chair that serves as a throne and watches as I walk forward to stand before him. I remove my cap and bow, before placing it back on my head.

'It is good to see you again, Master Tudor.'

'At your service, Your Highness.'

Henry glances to the advisors on either side. 'I understand life has not been easy for you since my mother's passing.' His hand goes to the gold cross he wears, as if it offers him some comfort. 'I remember your kindness, Master Tudor, and pardon you of any charges.'

At last I feel able to relax a little, for the first time since the arrival of the king. 'Thank you, Your Highness.'

Henry gives an almost imperceptible nod of acknowledgement. 'I welcome you to my household and have decided to grant you a pension from my privy purse.'

'I am most grateful, Your Highness.' I see the lack of surprise on the faces of the king's advisors and realise why it has taken so long. This is not a spontaneous decision.

Someone has encouraged the king's generosity. I wonder who it could be and what their motive is, certain I will learn in due course.

'You are welcome to remain here or travel to your homeland in Wales if you wish, Master Tudor.'

'I would like to remain, at least until my sons are introduced at court, if it pleases Your Highness.'

'I look forward to the return of my brothers.' Henry smiles and I catch a glimpse of the boy I had known, Catherine's son.

Chapter Seventeen

The fresh warmth of spring is a blessing after a hard winter. Everything has changed for me over the past two years. It has not been easy, yet I am back where I started, in my comfortable, low-ceilinged room at Windsor. Bright yellow daffodils from the castle gardens stand in a battered pewter jug on my table and a blackbird sings outside my open window, tunefully claiming its territory.

I wake early with a sense of anticipation, reach out and caress the sleeping figure at my side. She is the reason why I never travelled to Calais to seek my fortune. I have no regrets. The horrors of Newgate and my long imprisonment are now a fading memory but the experience taught me to appreciate the simple things in life. I am thankful and truly grateful for what I have.

Juliette wakes and takes my hand in hers. 'I was dreaming about when we were here together for the first time... all those years ago.'

I trace the curve of her breast with my fingertip. 'You seduced me.'

'You led me on!'

'Ah—but now I have the king's pardon.'

'That was for running off with his mother.'

I pull her closer and whisper. 'You forgive me?'

She answers with a passionate kiss.

I brush her long auburn hair from her face, as I used to long ago. My own hair, once jet-black, is now peppered with grey. Hers is still a luminous reddish-brown in the morning sunlight and feels like silk to my touch. I thank God she has returned to me, after I treated her so badly. Sometimes it feels as if we have never been apart, yet the ghost of Catherine will always be there, even more so now my sons are coming to Windsor.

Juliette strokes the curls of greying hair on my chest. 'It will be different when your sons are here.'

Not for the first time she seems to read my thoughts. 'I will have to learn to be a father to them again.'

'You never stopped being their father, Owen.'

I smile at the plain truth of her words. 'You are right.'

'You have to give them time... but they are young—and they are Tudors.'

I lie back on the bed and watch as Juliette sits and begins to plait her hair, combing out tangles with her fingers. I never tire of seeing how she tames the long strands into a perfect French braid, gathering handfuls from each side with practised ease as she works.

She coils her finished plait and tucks it into place. 'What are you going to tell your sons about me—about us?'

'The truth.'

'Are they ready for the truth?'

'Edmund is eleven now, so Jasper must be ten, old enough to understand.'

'I hope they do.' She finishes her hair and smoothes the creases from her dress, frowning as she sees the hem is fraying where it touches the ground. 'The king has plans for them?' It is not so much a question as a statement, with the faintest hint of jealousy.

I forgive Juliette's unspoken resentment of the life I had with Catherine and understand why she must envy the apparent ease with which she gave me such fine sons. If Juliette chose to never speak to me again it would only be what I deserve.

'As you know, they will have titles.' I smile. 'Then you can help me find good wives for them both.'

'You must make sure they have a proper education. I met the priest who is to be their new tutor.' Juliette grimaces. 'He seems a little... dour.'

'He is the king's choice—I want them to learn about the real world. They have spent too long in a nunnery.'

'The king has become very devout. He is one of the richest men in the world, yet he spends so much time in that cold chapel. The other day he knelt in prayer for so long he needed help to stand.'

'It suits Duke Humphrey and Cardinal Beaufort if the king takes more interest in his faith than matters of council. They became too well used to the taste of power when he was in his minority to wish to surrender it now.'

'You must teach your sons to be wary of men like the cardinal and Duke Humphrey.'

'I would be living in Wales now if not for them.'

'Do you regret that, Owen?'

'I did once, when I was locked up. Now I have no regrets.'

'If Duke Humphrey hadn't brought you back, I don't know if I would have ever been able to find you in Wales.' She pulls her dress over her cotton shift and turns so I can help her fasten the bodice. 'Now the duke has no power at court. After what happened to his wife, Duchess Eleanor, I doubt he will trouble you again.'

'Whatever became of the duchess?'

I recall the first time I saw her, at the royal summer banquet at Wallingford Castle. Beautiful and mysterious, she seemed an odd match for the ambitious duke, more like his mistress than his wife. Lady Eleanor had been the centre of attention, but she smiled when she noticed me staring at her.

'She's plain Eleanor Cobham now. You know the duke agreed to dissolve their marriage in the hope of saving his reputation?' Juliette puts her hand into one of the long sleeves of her dress and pulls it up her arm. 'Well, Eleanor is imprisoned for life at Leeds Castle.'

'And the duke is now a shadow of the man he once was. His wife is lucky to be a favourite of the king. Henry Beaufort would have burned her as a witch if he could.' I help tie Juliette's sleeve in place and tuck the loose ends of thin silk ribbon from view. I like the simple intimacy of helping her to dress and she can't do it on her own.

'There are worse places to be imprisoned than Leeds Castle. I stayed there once, with Catherine.' She pulls on the second sleeve. 'King Henry V granted it to her as a present. It is a beautiful palace.'

Once again Catherine's ghost comes between us, as surely as if she lives and breathes, and I can see in Juliette's eyes that she knows I am thinking of her now. Juliette is right, as it will be difficult for us to live like this when my sons come to Windsor. I lace the second sleeve to Juliette's bodice and tie the loose ends.

Last of all is the high hennin headdress, wire mesh covered with white fabric, and a cloth lappet which covers her brow. Juliette fixes the fabric to her coiled braid with silver pins and the transformation of my lover to the king's prim housekeeper is complete.

☆ ☆ ☆

The abbess and sisters look saddened to see Edmund and Jasper leave Barking Abbey. At least the money owed for the care of my sons, now totalling over a hundred pounds, will be paid to the abbey from the Exchequer. It was necessary for me to carry out my threat to bring the debt to the attention of the king before the officials agreed to settle the account. Their deliberate oversight is a timely reminder that, despite my royal pardon, I still have enemies and I worry my insistence serves to provoke them further.

It takes little time to pack the boy's few belongings and I am keen to be back on the road as soon as we can. Edmund and Jasper are unused to riding any distance and soon grow tired, so it is necessary to make several stops to allow them to rest along the way. I share my leather flask of ale when they grow thirsty and begin to know them both again.

Edmund is full of questions when we arrive at Windsor Castle. 'Where will we live, Father?'

'In the Upper Ward lodgings, which were built by King Edward III.' I point ahead. 'You have better rooms than at the abbey. Better even than me—the king has ordered it.'

'When will we see the king?'

'He is still in Westminster Palace, which is why he isn't able to welcome you today. I thought it best for you to have a chance to settle in to your new lodgings before he returns to Windsor.'

I personally arranged the preparation of their rooms, even securing consent of the king to have some of his collection of priceless tapestries to decorate the walls. The king would have wished them to have religious themes but I selected scenes of mounted knights hunting stags in exotic forests. Good oak-framed beds with new feather mattresses and wool blankets are now installed in what was once a dining-room and tall windows flood the place with light. I watch as my sons stand wide-eyed, taking it all in.

Edmund is a head taller than Jasper and his blue eyes miss nothing, his quick mind storing every detail for future use. Jasper is more like I remember being at the same age. Dark eyes peer out from unruly black hair. Where Edmund has the natural bearing of a young noble, Jasper could pass as a street urchin, if it were not for his smart new clothes, provided from the king's own purse.

I have been looking forward to their arrival in Windsor for many months and saved my pension to buy them each a present. I open a wooden chest and take out their gifts. Wrapped in dark velvet, each has cost me a small fortune. I hand one to Edmund and the other to Jasper, then stand back as they unwrap the covering to reveal finely crafted daggers on tooled black leather belts with silver buckles.

Edmund straps the belt round his waist and draws the dagger, which slides cleanly from its scabbard. Sunlight from the window flashes from the polished blade as he holds it up to inspect the sharpness of the edge. 'Thank you, Father. This is the finest knife I've ever seen.'

'Your mother gave me one like it once. The blade is German steel and holds its sharpness well.'

Jasper tries on his belt and finds it hangs a little low on his slim waist. 'I think I need you to make another hole for the buckle, Father?'

'It's supposed to be low, as that's how men wear them now.' I laugh as Jasper tries walking with the belt hanging around his middle. 'You'll soon grow once you start eating the food from the kitchens here.'

Jasper takes his own dagger from its scabbard. 'It has a bird on the handle.' He sounds disappointed.

'That's a martlet. It's my badge.'

Jasper studies it more closely. 'What does it mean, Father?'

'You see—the martlet has no legs, so never rests. It's the symbol of our quest for knowledge and adventure.' I ruffle Jasper's dark hair. 'We Tudors have to make our own way in the world, as we inherit nothing—and you, Jasper, as the second son, have to work extra hard.'

Jasper looks serious. 'I work hard. The sisters said I was one of the best students they ever had.'

I hear an echo of my own youthful boasting in his young voice. 'Good. I am proud of you.' I glance at Edmund. 'I am truly proud of you both. You have a lot more learning to do here—and I don't just mean from your tutors. I doubt the sisters taught you how to conduct yourself at court?'

'No, Father—and can we practice with the longbow again, like we did at Hatfield House?'

'You remember?' I am pleased, as I'd thought them both too young to remember much of their happier times together. 'I will buy you both new bows—and if you do well, a sword.'

Edmund is pleased. 'I wish to learn to joust as well. I must learn to fight like a knight.'

'All in good time, Edmund. First we must discuss how you will behave in the presence of the king.'

'How should we address the king, Father?'

'Your Highness.' I demonstrate how to bow, flamboyantly removing my hat. 'Although that is for when his advisors are around. You are his half-brothers, after all.'

'Why does he need so many advisors?'

'King Henry is young and there are so many decisions to be made.'

Jasper has practical concerns. 'What if he doesn't like us?'

'He will. You are the only family he has now—and you share many of the qualities of your mother. I have known the king since he was a baby. He is a good man and will treat you well.'

'Does he ride—and fight with a sword?'

'He had the finest teacher in the country.' I recall Sir Richard's patient tutoring. 'He likes to pray and read the scriptures, so remember to show the king your faith is important to you. I will arrange a service of thanksgiving in the chapel, to mark your safe arrival. He will like that. Then we will have a royal banquet in your honour.'

Several days pass before the king returns to Windsor, escorted by the royal guards and followed by his retinue of over a hundred riders and wagons. The king needs to rest after the journey from London, so it is not until mid-morning on the following day that he is ready to meet his half-brothers and orders them to be brought to him. I introduce Edmund and Jasper, who take off their caps and bow to their older brother as rehearsed.

Henry studies them. 'The abbess reported that you are most diligent students. You are a credit to our mother, may God rest her soul.'

Edmund steps forward. 'Thank you, Your Highness, for taking us into your household.'

'With God's help, I will keep you from mortal sin and ensure you complete your education. You will have the best tutors and your studies will continue under the guidance of Master John Blackman, a great scholar.'

Jasper glances at me to see if he is allowed to reply. I nod, relieved my sons have so easily adjusted to the formality of the royal court. This first meeting has gone better than I dared to hope, yet I wonder what Jasper is going to say.

'Will we be allowed to practice with a bow, Your Highness?' Jasper casts a quick glance at Edmund. 'I would like to learn to use a sword as well.'

'You will have proper military training, as I did.' Henry looks at him. 'I trust you are also diligent in your worship of God, and know prayer is more important than practising vain sports and trifling pursuits?'

Edmund replies. 'The sisters at the abbey taught us the scriptures, Your Highness, and we pray every day for the soul of our mother, our father and our king.'

'I am pleased to hear that.' Henry beckons to a servant. 'I have something for you both.' He takes the gift from the servant and hands it to Edmund. 'This is very precious to me, as it belonged to our mother. I give it to you as my brother.'

I recognise the distinctive gold crucifix in my son's hand. It has a thick gold chain and is one Catherine often wore.

Next Henry hands a gold ring to Jasper. 'This also belonged to our mother.'

Jasper tries the ring on his finger. 'Thank you, Your Highness.' His mother's fingers had been so slim it fits perfectly.

Finally Henry turns to me. 'I have not forgotten you, Master Tudor.' He beckons again to his servant, who this time steps forward with my sword. 'This was taken from you by the officers of my council. It is only right it is now returned.'

I take my sword and for once am lost for words, as I believed I would never see it again. The sword had been a symbol of my place in the world, a precious memory of my wife. I could have replaced it with another but it would never have held the same meaning.

'I thank you for your kindness.' My voice is filled with unexpected emotion.

Henry nods in acknowledgement and then stands. 'Accompany me, Master Tudor. There is a private matter I wish to discuss.'

I follow Henry to the inner chamber, a private room which once served as Catherine's dressing-room. Now simply furnished to Henry's austere taste, her tapestries are replaced with bare, whitewashed walls. Whatever the young king has to say, he doesn't want it overheard.

Henry turns to me. 'I have decided one of your sons will be granted an earldom when he comes of age, together with the lands and property to enable him to take his place at court.' He continues, without waiting for my reply. 'The other will enter the church. I will see he has a rewarding career and is prepared for high office.'

I take a deep breath. 'My wish is that Edmund and Jasper will both take up their role at your court, when they are of age, Your Highness.'

'You must know, Master Tudor, that a life in the church is a worthy career. If I were able to, it is a path I would have chosen for myself.' The king seems ready to return to the royal apartments.

Another approach occurs to me. 'Neither of my sons has the calling to devote their lives to the church. With respect, Your Highness, I ask you to reconsider?'

'One of them must.' Henry stares at me, unblinking. 'They are too young to decide for themselves, so I ask you to choose which of them it will be.'

Later I discuss the king's proposal with Nathaniel. It casts a cloud over an otherwise perfect day and I can't contemplate the thought of having to tell either of my sons the news. I rashly promised they would both have titles and now one will have to be disappointed.

Nathaniel ponders the problem. 'Do you think all it needs is a little time, until the king has the chance to know Edmund and Jasper? He has only met them once.'

'I'm not so sure. King Henry seems to have made his mind up.'

'At least he has said that one of your sons will be made an earl.'

'Yes—but neither of my boys would wish to enter the church.' I look at Nathaniel as a thought occurs to me and curse my oversight. 'I've been so preoccupied with Edmund and Jasper coming here that I never mentioned their brother Owen, even to them, let alone to the king.'

'Is it possible there might be a way to turn this to your advantage?'

'I have never seen my other son—and it is high time that I did.'

'What are you thinking?'

'I will see if I can bring my youngest son to meet his brothers—and his half-brother. The king agreed to a service of thanksgiving for the safe return of my sons. It is only right that we all attend.'

Edmund Kirton has been a monk at Westminster Abbey for some thirty-seven years before being elected abbot. Sympathetic to my dilemma, he approves the visit of young Owen, now aged nine, to attend the service of thanksgiving in Windsor.

'I remember how hard you worked here as a postulant, Master Tudor.' The abbot smiles. 'I knew you would never join the order.'

'I will always be grateful to the Benedictine order—for granting me sanctuary and helping me rediscover my faith, Your Grace. I learned a great deal during my time here but you are right, I did not have the calling and it is the same for my other sons.'

'Some are called to serve the world by devoting all their energies to preaching the Gospel and tending the poor.' The abbot looks directly at me. 'Others are called to bring new life into the world through the sanctity of marriage. A few are called to give themselves over to God in prayer and willing penance.' He nods to a waiting monk, who leaves the room and returns with my youngest son.

Dressed in a novice's dark woollen hooded tunic with a scapular apron, he wears the black leather cincture belt around his slim waist. Young Owen looks more like his brother Edmund than Jasper. He pulls back his hood to reveal cropped, gold-blond hair and studies me with Catherine's blue eyes but doesn't smile or speak.

I try to control my emotion. 'You know I am your father?'

Young Owen glances at Abbot Kirton for reassurance. 'I have been told about you, sir.' His voice sounds confident for his age.

'The abbot has agreed you can visit the king, your half-brother—and your other brothers, Edmund and Jasper.'

'I should like to see my brothers.'

I have to remind myself of the disciplined upbringing my son has been given. The novice master, one of the most experienced brothers, will have tutored him every day. Unlike my other sons, who had servants even during their care with the Abbess of Barking, young Owen will only have known the life of the monks.

'They will be pleased to see you. For many years we thought you had... died, here in Westminster Abbey, so it is something of a miracle to us that you are here now.'

The abbot replies. 'It is God's will.' He looks at young Owen. 'We are all born with a purpose.'

On the journey back to Windsor I learn a little more about the life my youngest son has led as an oblate. He has been given the name of Edward Bridgwater, for reasons he is unable to explain, as he has no recollection of ever visiting the town of Bridgwater, although he has once been on a pilgrimage to the Benedictine Abbey of St Mary at nearby Glastonbury.

'What do you know of me, your mother or your brothers?'

Young Owen thinks for a moment before replying. 'Until yesterday all I knew was that I had been given into the order when I was born.'

'They told you who your mother was?'

'The abbot said she was the Queen of England.'

'She was...' I look at my youngest son and know how happy Catherine would have been to see him now. 'Her eldest son, your brother Henry, is King of England and France.'

Young Owen looks back at me. 'Why are you taking me to see him?'

'He has no other family, so it is only right he should meet you and know who you are.'

'My family is God's holy church.'

'Do you remember what the abbot said?'

He tries to recall Abbot Kirton's exact words. 'We are born... with a purpose?'

'Yes.' I regard my son, wondering how much to tell him. 'You were given to God so that your brothers can take their place at the side of the king.'

The service in the old chapel at Windsor is a simple one, witnessed only by members of the king's household. I had wondered if the king's uncles, Cardinal Beaufort or Duke Humphrey, would make an appearance, if only out of curiosity. They must have more important matters to attend to than the king's half-brothers.

I introduce my youngest son as the one I have chosen for a life in the church. Henry is pleased to learn of another half-brother and hear of his devotion to a pious life as a monk. Young Owen takes everything in his stride, seemingly unimpressed by the splendour of Windsor Castle or the bravado of Edmund and Jasper, who seem unsure how to deal with him. After the service they are full of questions for their new-found brother, who answers them calmly, although he has few of his own.

Jasper is intrigued. 'Did you take a vow of poverty?'

'Vows of poverty, chastity and obedience.'

'I would not want to take any of those!'

Young Owen is undaunted. 'It is the life God has chosen for me. I don't wish for anything else.'

Edmund has been listening. 'I would never take a vow of chastity. I must have a son, to inherit my fortune!'

'I must serve the Lord without distraction.'

'You can never marry?' Edmund's brow furrows at the thought.

'We give up marriage for the sake of the kingdom of heaven.'

'Well I plan to marry as soon as I can—and have plenty of good strong sons!'

Chapter Eighteen

Spring of 1445

The old stone wharf at Portchester echoes with shouts and the blaspheming curses of sailors as they make our ship ready for the journey to France. A year has passed since a young French wife has been found for the king, who is now twenty-two. Margaret, daughter of Duke Rene of Anjou, is barely fifteen and speaks almost no English but is rumoured to be beautiful, proud and strong-willed.

King Henry sent Sir William de la Pole to France to represent him at the betrothal. Since then Sir William and his wife Lady Alice have remained with Margaret, making arrangements to bring the new queen back to England. Sir William's reward is to be made Marquess of Suffolk. Lady Alice, daughter of the late Thomas Chaucer, once constable of Wallingford, is now Margaret's English lady-in-waiting.

Juliette is pleased when Lady Alice chooses her to assist with the new queen's household and in turn secures a place for me as a member of the royal escort. We stay at Portchester Castle, waiting for favourable winds for France. Old and in need of maintenance, I think the castle is a poor choice for the new queen's first sight of England, despite the hasty work which is still in progress as we hear it is time for us to sail to France.

I steady Juliette's hand as she nervously walks up the narrow gangplank to board the ship. We find a space on the taffrail at the stern and watch the final preparations for sailing. Wooden crates, coils of thick rope and barrels of supplies still stand on the quayside and a rowdy group of men noisily persuade a fine black mare to board the ship.

'Perhaps the horse knows better than us.' I watch the mare protest with loud whinnying as the men haul her onto the deck.

'Don't be so superstitious, Owen.' Juliette stares up at the high mast where sailors precariously balance as they prepare the sails for use. 'This seems a small ship for such important cargo?'

'Too small.' I cast a glance across the deck to see if we are being overheard. 'The king refuses to replace his father's flagship. *The Grace Dieu* was struck by lightning and burned at its moorings and the best ships of the old fleet are all sold off, so now he must commission whatever is available.'

'The king has no need of warships. All he wants is peace with France.'

I give her a wry look. 'And he will have it—at a price...'

'Don't even speak of it, Owen.' Her voice is unexpectedly sharp.

Before I can answer the mainsail drops and heavy canvas flaps in the freshening breeze as sailors trim the sheets. The final stores are now carried on board and the captain orders the mooring ropes cast off. Wind fills the sails and the ship lurches away from the quay as we head out into the English Channel.

Taking a deep breath of fresh air I can taste the salty tang of the sea for the first time in many years. It seems a welcome new phase of my life is beginning with this journey to Normandy. I have been content enough with the simple routine at Windsor, yet I know the royal court will not be the same once King Henry has a wife.

Our small but sturdy ship ploughs through the dark waves, despite the choppy swell. Every once in a while the bow plunges more deeply and seawater sluices over the deck, but she is built for the cross-Channel trade. The captain has chosen the timing of our departure well, so I feel reassured that we are in safe hands.

The favourable combination of wind and tide means we make good time on the crossing to the port of Honfleur before beginning the long and challenging sail up the River Seine. I return to the rail with Juliette and we stare at the fast-flowing river, watching as an uprooted tree flows past.

'It seems the spring tides have brought a flood. When I was here last the river was so shallow we ran aground on a mud bank.' I smile at the memory. 'We had to wait until the next morning for the tide to float us off.'

'You were fortunate, as a good many ships have foundered on their way upriver to Rouen.'

'God was on our side that day.' I study the high riverbanks on either side. 'Our ship heeled over so steeply you couldn't walk across the deck—but she righted well enough as the water rose again.'

Juliette takes my arm. 'Let us walk around the deck, Owen, while we can.'

For a moment I wonder if she is referring to the threat of running aground or the need to be discreet when we arrive in Rouen. Our easy relationship is risky enough at Windsor but here there will be many who would disapprove, including Lady Alice. Everyone expects me to marry Juliette and I know I should, but have yet to ask her. She never mentions it, although sometimes I see the unspoken question in her eyes.

Juliette seems oblivious of my silence. 'When we are in Rouen I will look for a new dress—no, I will need at least two new dresses, as there is a royal wedding as well as Margaret's coronation.'

'I heard Duke Humphrey is trying to prevent the Treasury meeting the expenses of the marriage and another coronation.'

Juliette seems surprised. 'Why would he?'

'You must know that Margaret is Cardinal Beaufort's choice?'

'Yes—but the king has more than enough money of his own?'

'He should, but his father bankrupted the crown with his wars in France.'

'I heard the celebrations are to be the grandest ever seen.'

'They are, which is why Margaret has been kept waiting in France for so long.' I lower my voice. 'The king has been obliged to pledge the crown jewels, as well as his gold and silver plate, to raise the money.'

'That's terrible. Who is lending the money?'

'Bankers and merchants—and I expect the good cardinal will all grow even richer at Henry's expense.'

'Can nothing be done about it?'

'Not while he takes so little interest in such matters.'

She points ahead as the spires of Rouen appear on the horizon. 'I wonder what Lady Margaret of Anjou will make of our king—or him of her, for that matter?'

I understand what she means. King Henry has never spoken of marriage or of any woman within my hearing. He spends long hours in prayer and lives a simple, almost monkish life, so it is difficult to imagine him with a fifteen-year-old wife. Particularly one as forceful and outspoken as young Margaret of Anjou is rumoured to be.

'Perhaps she will be good for him.' I smile at Juliette. 'Give him an heir and bring some joy back to the royal court.'

'Let us hope so.' Juliette sounds uncertain. 'She will need time to understand our ways.'

'Are we really so different?'

'The Duke of Anjou has fathered more children with his mistresses than can be counted—and her mother, Isabella, Duchess of Lorraine, led an army to rescue her husband when the Duke of Burgundy held him prisoner.'

'Sir William de la Pole seems to think she is a good match for the king.'

'I worry that Sir William might have been blinded by his... admiration for Lady Margaret.' Juliette frowns. 'Let us hope this choice is the right one.'

Weary after their long sea voyage I find the prospect of the farewell banquet tiring and dread the inevitable long speeches in French. Margaret of Anjou seems older than her fifteen years, with her elaborate headdress and pale make up. Slim and attractive, if not conventionally beautiful, she is the centre of attention in the crowded banqueting hall. When she speaks in French her voice is confident, yet she falters a little when she tries her heavily accented English.

The host is the Governor of Normandy, Duke Richard of York, a serious, abrupt man with a permanent frown, who eyes young Margaret with poorly veiled disdain. Duke Richard is the king's cousin, with a strong claim to the throne through a direct line of descent. The duke would not be expected to welcome the prospect of an heir for King Henry. His wife, Lady Cecily Neville, Duchess of York, does her best to cover for the duke's surly mood, chattering loudly with Lady Alice.

The liveried servant standing behind me leans forward and splashes red wine on my sleeve as he refills my goblet. I curse the man's carelessness and am about to take him to task when Duke Richard calls the crowded hall to silence. An old priest rambles through a grace, which includes the blessing of the forthcoming coronation of Lady Margaret as Queen of England and France. When at last he finishes, the duke gives the signal for more servants to appear, laden with platters of food.

I am interested to note how the duke's tastes have been influenced by Normandy tradition, for the centrepiece is a roasted boar with one half coloured green and the other golden yellow. The music is also very French. Playing their high-pitched, reedy instruments, the musicians repeat the same phrase over and again until I wonder if I will ever be able to get it from my head.

My appetite waning, I am feeling a little drunk and am annoyed at Juliette, who has abandoned me to talk to a group of French ladies. I am planning to slip away and catch up on much-needed sleep when I hear Sir William, now Marquess de la Pole, call my name.

'Tudor!' He beckons to me. 'Come and be introduced.'

I feel eyes on me as I approach the top table. I have not forgotten that Sir William was constable at Wallingford and knows far more about my past than I would wish. The Duke of York is paying no attention, deep in conversation with a French nobleman, although Duchess Cecily and Lady Alice are watching me approach with undisguised interest.

'This is the man who married Queen Catherine of Valois—in secret?' Lady Margaret speaks in French but I hear the seductive note of admiration in her voice.

At once I understand how Sir William might have fallen for her. I miss Catherine so deeply that hearing her name spoken in French is more than I can bear. In a flash of insight I realise that I will never stop loving her. I will never be able to commit to marrying Juliette and I can never be truly happy with any other woman.

The noisy banqueting hall has fallen silent as Margaret's loudly voiced question coincides with a break in the raucous French music. Realising they are all waiting for me to reply, I take off my hat and bow.

'Owen Tudor, at your service, my lady.' I speak in my best French.

'We thank you for coming to escort us to England.' I see her eyes go to the red stain on my sleeve.

'It is an honour, my lady.' I replace my hat and take a step backwards, trying to hide the wine stain and cursing the careless servant.

Margaret glances in the direction of the Duke of York, who is still paying us no attention. 'We will need loyal men once we arrive in England.'

I feel flattered and wonder if the wine is affecting my judgement. Margaret is right, she will find more than enough enemies waiting for her in England. Sir William is Cardinal Beaufort's man, so there is no mystery about who will plot against her. I had not expected to like her, but now feel protective towards this young girl, barely a woman, her life changed forever by the cardinal's intrigue.

'You can rely on my loyalty, my lady.'

'You have known the king since he was... a baby?' She speaks in her faltering English now, hesitating as she finds the right words.

'I joined his household when he was less than a year old.' I see Sir William give me a cautionary glance. 'The king has been kind and generous to me—and to my sons.'

She leans forward and lowers her voice almost to a whisper. 'Do you think the king will like me?'

I am surprised at the intimacy of her question and realise how young and vulnerable she is. 'I am certain he will, my lady.'

The musicians begin another raucous tune before she can ask more questions and I see my chance to leave, yet as I go in search of Juliette I recall her doubts. They are so different in character it is difficult to predict what the king will think of Lady Margaret—or what she will make of him.

I wake with a headache and lie in my bed alone, recalling the events of the previous night. Juliette thought it best she should not risk coming to my room, as she said there were too many people who could notice. I disagreed and we argued for the first time in years. She accused me of drinking too much wine, so I shouted at her and stormed off to my lodgings.

My outburst was unwarranted. I can see that now in the cold light of day and know Juliette deserves better. I should have married her years ago or told her why I could not, but now it is too late. I have finally faced the real reason why I will never marry again. The pain of losing Catherine is still too real. I have tried my best to start a new life but there are too many memories time will not erase.

I dress and make my way through dimly familiar narrow streets, remembering the first time I was there, as squire to Sir Walter, after one of the longest sieges anyone had known. The streets had been strewn with corpses. Although I had not been responsible, the staring, accusing eyes of the starving people of Rouen haunted my dreams for months afterwards.

Now the people seem relatively prosperous. The lords and merchants have supported the building of many fine houses and great religious buildings. I walk past a row of impressive churches going from east to west through the centre of the city and stop at the cemetery of Aître Saint-Maclou, used for burials since Roman times. During the pestilence three-quarters of the inhabitants were buried here and this was where, after the siege, I helped bury so many innocent men, women and children.

The city has recovered but is still scarred by the past. I find myself in the market square where young Joan of Arc had been so cruelly burned just fourteen years before. There is no sign it had ever happened now but the people will never forget the terrible cost of their war with the English.

I make my way into the towering cathedral that dominates the city of Rouen and my troubled mind is calmed by the atmosphere of silent reverence. Finding a deserted side chapel, I light a candle in Catherine's memory. I say a prayer of gratitude that she blessed my life with her love, and know what I must do.

☆ ☆ ☆

The captain of our ship makes us wait in Rouen for a week before he is satisfied the winds and tides are good enough for the return voyage. Even then, the skies are darkening as we cast off from the quay. An unseasonably chill wind tugs at the flapping sails as we make our way back down the River Seine towards Honfleur and the English Channel.

With a final wave to the crowds who have come to see her off, Margaret retires to her cabin, followed by Lady Alice and her French servants. I prefer to remain on deck, watching as the historic city of Rouen, dominated by the cathedral of Notre Dame, recedes into the distance. Juliette stands at my side, unusually silent, as if she senses something has changed between us.

I must be direct with her. 'I am sorry, Juliette. You know I still think of Catherine, every day?'

'Has enough time not passed now, Owen?' She puts her hand on my arm, no longer concerned about what anyone might think. 'How long are you going to mourn Catherine?'

'She is not gone, Juliette, she lives... in my thoughts and prayers.'

'I understand—young Margaret reminds you of her?' There is bitterness in her voice now.

'Margaret is nothing like Catherine, but meeting her has made me think... you deserve better.'

'I made my choice years ago, Owen, and knew the consequences.'

Not for the first time I wonder if she would have left me for another if she had been capable of having children. Juliette is still beautiful and I've seen how other men look at her. When I think of all the years we were apart I find it hard to believe she was patiently waiting for me to one day return. I could marry her easily enough, but would be living a lie. It will hurt us both to part when we reach England, yet it is the only way I can set her free.

As we leave the shelter of the estuary at Honfleur and head out into the English Channel I hear a shout from a sailor who has climbed high up the mast. At first I can't understand what the man is saying and then see him shout again and point to the far horizon.

Juliette looks concerned. 'Is he saying there is a storm ahead?'

I glance up at the darkening sky and recall a sailor's saying: Mare's tails and mackerel scales make lofty ships take in their sails. The rhyme may be no use to me, as there are no oddly shaped clouds, but I sense the approaching storm in my bones and see the waves are already crested with white spray. 'This weather could mean we have to return to Honfleur.'

'There are worse places to be stranded than Honfleur.'

'It is always better to be in a safe harbour wishing you were at sea than at sea wishing you were safely in a harbour.'

Juliette holds out her hand, palm upwards. 'I knew it. Rain is coming.'

A stiff breeze nearly takes my hat as I lead her towards the cabins. We barely make it to shelter before the rain starts hammering on the deck, soaking the sailors who are unable to join us in the lee of the cabin. We watch as the visibility reduces to almost nothing and the captain shouts for his crew to reef the mainsail.

A flash of lightning illuminates the deck, followed by a crash of thunder, close enough to startle Juliette. She takes my hand and I am comforted by the feel of her warmth, although this is only going to make it more difficult when we arrive back at Windsor Castle.

'Don't worry, Juliette. It will soon pass.' My lie sounds hollow.

As if to prove me wrong a second crash of thunder makes us both flinch as it booms overhead. A heavy wave swamps the deck, washing away several heavy barrels. A sailor saves himself by clinging to the wet ropes as the ship lurches to starboard in the increasing swell. The barrels float off to sea and are soon out of sight. If any of the crew fall overboard they won't stand a chance in these conditions.

Sir William emerges, holding a handkerchief over his face. He sees us huddled together in the shelter of the cabin entrance. A flicker of understanding shows in his eyes before he dashes past them to the rail and leans over the side, his body heaving. The rain continues in torrents and

Sir William's clothes are soaked before he returns. He runs a wet hand over his face and turns to Juliette.

'Go below, if you will, and see what you can do to help my wife.'

Juliette is used to men like Sir William and hurries down the narrow passage leading to the cabins. I am surprised a veteran of so many Channel crossings is such a poor sailor. Sir William has lost his hat and his hair is plastered to his face like wet seaweed. He clutches at the door-frame to steady himself as the ship heels again, its timbers creaking with the strain. He has to shout to be heard over the noise.

'Find the captain, Tudor. Tell him we must turn back before this storm grows worse.'

I peer out and see how the waves are crashing over the bows and seem to be growing larger as we head further out to sea. The decision to turn back or continue is entirely one for the captain and I know he will not thank me for offering Sir William's advice.

'The wind is behind us, my lord, I think the captain is a capable man.'

'The storm is worsening. I've crossed the English Channel many times and never seen it as bad as this.'

Another wave swamps the deck as we watch and this time cold seawater puddles at our feet. I taste the salty spray on my lips and see the grimace of concern on Sir William's face. I pull my hat tighter onto my head and rush out into the storm. The wooden steps to the upper deck are wet and slippery and hold tight to the handrail as the wind buffets my body.

The captain shouts commands at the top of his voice as the crew battles against the squall and I must tug at his arm to catch his attention. 'Sir Walter wishes to know if we can turn back, Captain.' I shout over the storm.

'By God! Tell him we are in the middle of the Channel!' The captain curses then turns his attention to the helmsmen, who are battling to keep our little ship on course.

Another flash of lightning is followed by a clap of thunder and I nearly fall down the steep steps, barely able to stagger back into the cabin. Sir William is still waiting there and looks at me for news.

I wipe the water from my face with my sleeve. 'The captain says it is too late to turn back, my lord.'

The ship lurches again as yet another wave batters us broadside and the rain intensifies so I cannot understand his shouted curse of reply. I do hear a crack and the sound of splintering wood as one of the spars breaks, causing the sail to flap wildly as the crewmen fail to bring it under control.

I shout at the top of my voice to be heard over the storm. 'Is Lady Alice seasick?'

'Not my wife. It's Lady Margaret.' Sir William glances back towards the cabin. 'She is hysterical with fear and...' He looks at me as if unwilling to share the truth. 'She is ill, with the pox.'

I am shocked at this news. She seemed well enough when I saw her last but the French pox could finish Margaret if she is in a weakened state. Now I understand why Sir William is so keen to return to Honfleur. It is not the best way for a new queen to arrive for her wedding and coronation.

'What are we to do, my lord?'

'She is being tended by her physician, Master Francis. He is a good man—but cannot work miracles.' Sir William looks stoical. 'Pray to God, Tudor, pray and hope.'

The sea calms a little but the thunderstorm continues even as we reach the shelter of the Solent. Our little ship heads into Portsmouth with rain lashing the deck and sails torn and ragged by the powerful gusts of wind. It seems a long time since we left the coast of France and a lot has happened since I last saw the wharf of Portchester Castle.

The quayside is lined with crowds of people waiting to welcome our arrival, despite the bad weather. I say a silent prayer of thanks as the mooring ropes are secured and realise I haven't seen Juliette for most of the voyage. I watch with growing concern as Sir William appears, carrying Lady Margaret in his arms. She is pale and listless. Lady Alice, followed by Juliette and the other maidservants, all look as if they have suffered on the voyage.

I follow behind their procession through the crowds into the rush-strewn streets of Portchester. The wet air is filled with cheering and cries of goodwill as our little group makes progress through the town. Lady Margaret sees nothing of the welcome. She is unconscious before we reach the convent where she will spend her first night and prepare for continuing her journey to meet the king.

Chapter Nineteen

Lady Margaret is young and strong and recovers from her illness, diagnosed by the king's physician as the small-pox. She is soon married and her coronation in Westminster Abbey, where Catherine became queen twenty-four years earlier, is the grandest ever seen. As she makes her way through the city from Southwark she is greeted by pageants, representing peace and the hope the long conflict with the French will now come to an end.

The bells of every church in London compete with the hooves of over a hundred horses, clattering on cobbled streets, almost drowning the cheers of the waiting crowds. A fanfare of trumpets announces the arrival of King Henry's new wife, riding in a gilded coach drawn by a team of white horses. Her long hair is worn loose as a sign of virtue and she looks like a queen, but I know she is a nervous girl, playing her role as instructed.

As she comes closer I see her face is set in a fixed smile. Margaret steps from her coach and is escorted by royal guards, expensively dressed noblewomen and senior clergymen, and is flanked by a dour Duke Humphrey and a self-satisfied Cardinal Beaufort. She turns her head in my direction as she passes and our eyes meet for the briefest moment. I see a flash of recognition and realise she is missing no detail of her coronation day. Margaret of Anjou holds my gaze for less than a second and is gone.

I follow the long procession through the high arched doorway into the abbey. We watch as she makes her grand procession up the nave, escorted by her father, Rene, Duke of Anjou and self-proclaimed King of Naples. Someone behind me asks why King Henry isn't there and another tells him that, by tradition, the king is not supposed to attend his queen's coronation. I suspect he is watching from a private vantage-point and scan the vaulted galleries of the abbey, realising there are many places for him to hide.

As Margaret reaches the altar she kneels in prayer then prostrates herself to show her humility. The Archbishop of Canterbury, John Stafford, leads her behind red velvet curtains for the anointing and places St Edward's crown on her head, the same crown used since the coronation of William the Conqueror four hundred years earlier. The new queen makes her slow procession back past the watching nobles and I recognise Sir William de la Pole, looking pleased with himself, as well he might.

The coronation is followed by three days of extravagant feasting and tournaments. I watch and wait to see where the new queen will wish to live. I expect Margaret to choose Windsor Castle but she prefers the Palace of Westminster and persuades Henry to have an apartment in the Tower of London refurbished for her personal use, at great expense. When not in London, Queen Margaret's unsurprising choice of residence is Cardinal Beaufort's well-appointed mansion in Waltham Forest.

This means Juliette does not return to Windsor, as she attends the queen while I remain in Windsor to be close to my sons. Their tutors prove well chosen, as Edmund and Jasper continue to do well with their studies and are now quite fluent in Latin and French. They amuse me with their sword fights and impress me with their new-found prowess at the tiltyard, yet I feel restless with my easy, undemanding life.

The voyage to Rouen has reminded me of the world of adventure outside Windsor's high walls and I recall my plan to try my luck across the Channel in Calais. I seek the advice of Sir William de la Pole, who recommends me for an appointment in Normandy as Captain of Regnéville, an outpost on the coast around fifty miles south of the port of Cherbourg and close to the island of Jersey. I am to be the king's representative in the region, responsible for keeping the harbour safe for English merchant ships.

The position is an important one and well paid, with allowances from the Treasury to strengthen the existing garrison. Nathaniel is easily persuaded to accompany me and we sail from Portsmouth to Normandy before winter sets in. The crossing is uneventful but no one greets us when we land and there is no sign of the garrison.

I confront our ship's captain. 'Are you certain this is the right place, Captain?'

'What did you expect, Master Tudor, a civic reception?'

We look across the harbour at the old castle, taken from the French by Duke Humphrey in 1418, which is to become my new home. Black crows fly like ghosts of bad omen from one of the high windows, but apart from that there is no other sign of life. The only other vessel in the harbour is a battered fishing boat, rotting at its moorings as a decaying memory of better times.

'I was told there is a garrison here. Regnéville is supposed to be a busy port?'

'I remember when it was one of the most active harbours on the Cotentin Peninsula.' The captain looks interested. 'Do you think you can make it safe again?'

'Safe?'

'Did they not tell you?' The captain gives a humourless laugh. 'The local French and their neighbouring Bretons are vying with each other to recover land they see as stolen by the English.' He points at the derelict castle. 'Regnéville is one of the most vulnerable of the remaining English outposts.'

I feel a dawning sense of apprehension as we make our way to the castle, built at the head of the river valley, with a high tower overlooking the harbour. I count five horses grazing on the coarse turf. Fat chickens scratch in the dirt and a tethered goat offers us a mournful bleat in welcome. The castle has an air of neglect, with a wooden drawbridge leading over a stagnant green moat to the gatehouse, wide and high enough to take a horse and cart.

Unchallenged, we continue through an open courtyard littered with old barrels and bales of hay. A pile of fresh manure is heaped next to a thatched, lean-to stable, built against the thick stone walls. The iron-studded door leading to the accommodation swings open to reveal several men playing cards and drinking beer. It seems more like a tavern inside than a garrison.

One of the older men stands as he sees us. 'Who might you be?' The man scratches his head as he approaches, his eyes taking in my fine sword.

'I am the new captain, Owen Tudor, and this is my first officer.' I gesture towards Nathaniel. 'What would you have done if we'd been French soldiers?'

The man looks puzzled. 'We weren't told you were coming, sir.'

'That much is evident.' I glance behind him at the mess and clutter. 'What is your name?'

'Hue Spencer, acting commander of the castle and the King's Bailiff of Cotentin.'

'Are there any more men than this?'

The others gather in a curious group and I see they are unshaven and ill-disciplined but look like time-served soldiers. Several have battle scars and some wear well used swords at their belts. I heard the English army in Normandy has struggled to remain organised since the death of Duke John of Bedford and proof of this stands before me.

The bailiff glances back at the soldiers. 'There used to be more, sir. After the last captain left I've had no money to pay them.'

I feel some sympathy for the men. 'I will see you are all paid from now on—and receive any back pay due to you.' I turn to Nathaniel. 'Take all their names, please. We will write to the Marquess of Suffolk and explain what we've found here.'

Three armed soldiers ride behind us as we make our first patrol to assess the challenges ahead. The land is flat and featureless, making the castle stand out starkly on the skyline, an inviting target for anyone who wishes to try their luck. The sandy beach curves away into the far distance, wild and barren. Our arrival startles whirring sandpipers, which sweep into the air with their rapid, shrill cries of weet, weet, weet.

Small fishing boats bob in the shallow, sheltered bay but there are no signs of any people this early in the morning. I feel a refreshing sea breeze in my face as I scan the horizon. In the misty distance I can make out the dark outline of Jersey, where we stopped on our way to Normandy.

'It reminds me a little of when I was a boy in Beaumaris, although the Irish Sea is not so blue—and the wind is colder in Wales!'

Nathaniel looks along the seafront and frowns. 'I don't see how we can keep the French out with so few men.'

'Do you think Sir William de la Pole knew this when he sent me out here?'

'It seems he has not done us a great favour.' Nathaniel points to the fishing boats. The French can land an army by sea—and you can be certain that they know they can take back this castle whenever they choose.'

'Well, it's up to us to make sure they don't, Nathaniel.' I look out across the sea to where England lies somewhere in the far distance. 'There are a lot of men who fought here in Normandy who are now without work. You could return to London and speak to your merchant friends, see if we can make this place into a trading port again.'

'It might be possible to defend a smaller area, around the harbour and the castle?'

'We will make of it what we can,' I look back to the castle. 'And we'll start by making that place fit to live in!'

We continue to ride in a wide circle, arriving back at the castle, which already echoes with the sounds of hammering and the smell of newly sawn wood. Two soldiers have stripped to the waist and are busy with shovels, filling in potholes to improve the road to the harbour. It is evident we will never be able to do the necessary work on our own but the local villagers have long since been driven out. Apart from the furtive fishermen who cast their nets for langoustines in the shallow bay, the French stay away.

'We need a blacksmith, to fire up that forge again, as well as a team of stonemasons.' I look at the pile of stones which still lay where they have fallen from the castle.

The bailiff Hue Spencer explains in his matter-of-fact way. 'We keep the Frenchies out, Captain Tudor. It's the best way—they are not to be trusted.'

'Where are the nearest locals who could help?'

'That would be the town of Coutances, sir. A short enough ride.' He points east, to the distant spires. 'You can see the cathedral.'

'Have you been to the town?'

'For supplies—or if we need a physician.' The bailiff looks as if he is planning to spit on the ground then sees my frown. 'We don't have much to do with the French.'

Nathaniel makes a suggestion. 'I could go and see how the land lies, without drawing attention to myself?'

'I'll ride with you—your French is even worse than mine.'

Travelling light to the outskirts of Coutances we hear the bells of the cathedral chiming to mark the hour. The town is a sprawling confusion of narrow streets and old buildings, reminding me of the back streets of Rouen. There are plenty of people in the busy market, where flies feast on hanging hams and old women in black shawls haggle in high-pitched French over the price of linen from Brittany.

Nathaniel points to a courtyard stacked with bricks and roof tiles. 'We could ask them?'

I engage the owners in conversation. The man is helpful enough but seems fearful of reprisals if he helps us. He warns me there are many in Coutances with long memories of how the castle, which they call the Château de Regnéville, was stolen from them by force. It seems the influence of Duke Humphrey continues to affect me, even here in the wilds of Normandy.

Leaving our horses, we walk to the impressive cathedral in the centre of the town. Instead of the subdued coolness I expect, a cleverly designed lantern tower floods intense light into the centre of the cathedral. My eyes are drawn to the stained-glass windows, showing the last temptation. The figure of Christ is surrounded by trumpeting cherubs while cloven-hoofed devils torment naked people and a handsome French knight holds the scales of justice.

I light a candle for Catherine and kneel to pray in the Chapel of Saint Joseph, under a colourful wall painting of the Holy Trinity. I pray for my sons, for Catherine's soul and that of our little daughter Margaret, and for guidance in how to keep the peace in Regnéville. I am aware now that I was sent on this impossible mission to keep me out of the way, but I have no wish to fight the French and hope to find some way to bring acceptance of our presence here.

✷ ✷ ✷

Nathaniel is working on his ledgers as I enter the room on the second floor of the castle which he has adopted as his study. A collection of seashells gathered from the beach are arranged on the stone sill of the small window, which has a good view of the harbour. Two fine trading ships are moored at the quayside, a common enough sight now, bringing a steady flow of income. Merchant ships often stop to take on fresh water or to shelter from rough weather.

Also moored with them is my newest venture, *La Demoiselle*, an old but seaworthy three-masted carrack we bought from a Portuguese merchant. The ship cost most of the money I have saved but is capable of making the crossing to Portsmouth and now Nathaniel is investigating how she can pay her way on the lucrative trade routes.

Nathaniel looks up from his ledger. 'I've been thinking. We could use some of this money to buy Breton linen and trade it for wool from England?'

'The Merchants of the Staple will never allow it.' I stare out of the window at the visiting ships. One has sailors balanced high on the yardarms, shouting to each other as they make their ship ready to sail. 'I always thought Calais has a monopoly on the trade in wool?'

'I will ask my contacts in London.' Nathaniel smiles. 'I never met a merchant who turned down a profit. There must be a way.'

'Will we buy the linen in Coutances?' I recall the warning from the builder I spoke to on their last visit.

'The best linen comes from Brittany.' Nathaniel grins. 'I have a contact in Rennes who can supply us—for a price.'

'I don't see any harm in trying.'

'We could use more money to strengthen the harbour defences.'

'Can we afford a canon?' I look down into the harbour. 'In Calais they have iron chains they can use to block the harbour—and a row of cannons trained on the entrance. If an enemy ship comes here there is almost nothing we can do.'

The castle has three ancient guns, small cannons called culverins, that can propel four-pound cannon balls a good distance, but without much accuracy. Designed to use on ships, the guns are of uncertain age. The bailiff swears they were brought to the castle by the Duke of Gloucester's men, so it could be thirty years since they were last fired in anger.

'A prominent cannon would be a useful deterrent, show them we mean business.'

'Make some enquiries, Nathaniel. Our defences will be even more important if we can make a success of the trade.'

'Do you think we could still be attacked, Owen?'

'You remember what the man said in Coutances?'

'There are people there with long memories and they still resent our presence here.'

'I wish we could live in peace here.' I examine Nathaniel's collection of seashells and realise they are neatly arranged by type. 'This could be an idyllic place if it wasn't for the threat of being attacked.'

Despite our well-intentioned drills and daily patrols, the first attack takes us completely by surprise. I wake in the night to the sounds of shouts and curses as our men try to find their weapons in near darkness. I pull on my boots and grab my sword, rushing down the steep stone staircase to investigate.

'What's going on?'

One of the soldiers shouts back. 'The French are here—they've set fire to a ship in the harbour!'

I rush to the window. Flames lick high into the sky and billowing smoke fills the harbour. The merchant ship that had been moored there left the previous day. The fire is aboard *La Demoiselle* and grows more intense as I watch, engulfing the painted figurehead at her bow.

In the courtyard Nathaniel glances up as he bandages a wounded soldier. 'We think they were local men. They seem to have run away now.'

I wish they had woken me sooner. 'Are any other men injured?'

'Only this man, as far as I know.'

'Did we wound any of them? Take any prisoners?'

'I don't think so. They were too fast for us.'

I am relieved but the surprise attack has been an important wake-up call, a reminder of why we are here. From now on we will have to keep a lookout at night. Worse still, if it is the work of local men it will be a setback to my plans to find some way of working with them.

I pass through the gatehouse onto the drawbridge and walk down to the harbour. The wind changes direction, bringing the acrid smell of smoke. Glowing embers float high in the night air like dangerous fireflies. The flames are too fierce to even bother trying to put them out. *La Demoiselle* is a wreck. I feel the prickle of heat on my face and hear a sharp hiss of steam as seawater rushes through gaps in the hull to fill the hold.

The old hulk of a fishing vessel which has been there since we first arrived is undamaged by the flames. This is no chance act of destruction. The local people are sending me a clear message: The English will never be welcome in this remote outpost. I turn my back on the scene of destruction and make my way back to the castle, wondering if it would make any difference if they knew I am not English but a Welshman.

Chapter Twenty

Autumn 1449

Standing alone on the high, windswept battlements I look out over the vast expanse of blue-grey sea. A cool, salty breeze tugs at my cape and carries the cry of the gulls as they wheel and soar behind fishing boats. Five years in this tranquil place has changed me, and each year when I return to see my sons I am astounded by the change in them.

Edmund and Jasper have grown into handsome, confident noblemen. King Henry treats them as his favourites, although Jasper secretly warns me of the king's madness. Like his mother Catherine and her father, King Charles, before her, King Henry has increasingly frequent lapses into a dark place. Sometimes he forgets who he is. Other times he is gone for a day or more, yet they have all become skilled at hiding the truth.

From everyone, that is, except the queen. Margaret has grown into a remarkable, beautiful and powerful woman. Her marriage remains childless, sparking ribald speculation, so she must be concerned that she has failed to provide the king with an heir. Despite that, she has won the popular support of the ordinary people of England. Most importantly, Queen Margaret has also proved herself capable of dealing with those who seek to steal the king's power.

Duke Humphrey died in strange circumstances two years before, after being arrested by Sir William de la Pole. With his wife Eleanor Cobham still languishing in her prison at Beaumaris Castle, Queen Margaret promptly took over the duke's mansion, Baynard's Castle in London. She also seized the duke's lavish estate at Greenwich and renamed it the Palace of Placentia, making it her favourite personal residence.

I heard the rumours about the death of Duke Humphrey. Some whispered that his food was poisoned on orders from the queen. Others suggested the shock of his arrest was too much for his weak heart. Even when Cardinal Henry Beaufort died soon afterwards, it seems there was nothing to suggest they did not meet their ends from natural causes.

Sir William, the queen's protector, unquestioned favourite and constant companion, has now become the power behind the throne. His days are numbered though, as he has upset many powerful men who blame him for the loss of Maine and Anjou through his over-generous marriage negotiations.

My little empire has not changed a great deal over the five years. The castle is restored but Hue Spencer was right. My plan to engage with the local people could never have succeeded. The surly bailiff retired the previous year and left for England, much to my relief, as there had always been tension between us. Although I understood the old man's hatred of the French, I had hoped we could find some kind of peace.

After the attack on my ship I recruited more men, expanding the original garrison to some fifty soldiers, including fifteen archers and ten crossbowmen. Well trained and well paid, there is barely enough for them to do, so I keep them busy patrolling the perimeter and working on restoring the castle, which I think of as my home.

My lodgings at the top of the four-storey high rectangular tower are comfortable, if a little basic. I like to walk along the endless, curving beach, deserted other than for the sandpipers and oystercatchers which turn over small stones as they forage for food. On a clear day I see the island of Jersey and hear the bells of the cathedral in Coutances.

Now all this could be coming to an end. Nathaniel prospers through his work as an agent of the London merchants and spends much of his time visiting Cherbourg and Rouen, negotiating on behalf of his many clients. This has led to him learning that the ambitious and influential Breton campaigner, Admiral Prigent de Coëtivy, is planning to challenge our ability to defend the harbour.

My reverie is interrupted by the arrival of Nathaniel, who has been out on patrol checking the chain of lookout posts concealed at intervals along the seashore. Each man has built a beacon from driftwood covered with pitch. Ready to light at the first sign of an approaching fleet, they should be easily seen by the lookouts at the castle.

'Have you sighted anything?' Nathaniel scans the horizon, shading his eyes with his hand against the early morning sun.

'Nothing yet. If they do come, God forbid, they'll want to surprise us, when they think we will least expect it.'

'The lookouts are all in place—but we are exposed on the flank. Do you want me to reinforce the eastern perimeter?'

I scan the flat plains of the peninsula. The few trees and low scrub offer little in the way of cover for any attacking force. 'Not if it means taking men from the harbour.'

'You expect the admiral to attack from the sea?'

'I do. You said it yourself—they can easily land an army on the beach.'

'I remember saying we couldn't do much with so few men. Even the garrison we have now is stretched, so what's our plan if they attack?'

'If there are any ships in the harbour it's our duty to protect them—otherwise we need to bring everyone into the safety of the castle and prepare to stand our ground.'

Nearly two weeks pass and we are wondering if Nathaniel's information is good after all, when I am roughly woken by one of the men at dawn. I rush to the high battlements and see the beacons blazing their bright warning. The thought that I will never see my sons again flashes briefly through my mind, then the training we have rehearsed so often takes over.

I look out towards the horizon in the glimmering early light. An ethereal mist floating over the sea is thinning to reveal the sails of at least four ships. I don't need to watch for long to be sure they are on a steady course, directly for the harbour.

There is a chance they could be merchantmen. Even if they are French or Breton it could be a show of strength rather than an attack. All the same, we must prepare for the worst. We have grown complacent over the five years I've been here, almost forgetting the real danger we face is from the French fleet.

Strapping on my sword and wearing a steel breastplate over my doublet, I run down the narrow road to the harbour where Nathaniel is already busy with a group of soldiers preparing the bronze cannon, mounted on a high platform overlooking the harbour entrance.

Each month the team of men practise their gunnery drill and once fired a heavy cannonball far out to sea, although they have never used the cannon against an enemy. It took a lot of work to manhandle into place and our new cannon is impressive, yet now seems inadequate against the approaching warships.

Nathaniel sees me approaching. 'How long do you think we have?'

I look out to sea where the French ships are now close enough now to see their decks are filled with archers and crossbowmen. 'Not long. Make sure your men hold fire until we are sure they are in range.'

'That will mean we are also in range of the French guns.' Nathaniel frowns as he tries to estimate how soon the ships will arrive. 'We could fire a warning shot? They may turn away once they see we are defending the harbour?'

'God willing. If they don't, we must be ready to withdraw to the castle.'

I look at the French ships and can now see the faces of the men crowding the decks. 'Fire your warning shot, Nathaniel!'

The boom of the cannon sounds so loud my ears ring and I feel the pressure wave as the ground vibrates under my feet. The gun crew aim their shot well, as it is followed by a splash in the water ten yards in front of the leading warship. I watch the ships continue on their steady course while the gun crew follow their well-rehearsed reloading drill.

They are taking too long. Even if they manage to hit the leading ship, the others will soon make landfall before his crew reload the cannon. It is a difficult decision but I know what I must order them to do.

'One more round, Nathaniel. See if you can make it count this time—then you and the men must retreat to the safety of the castle.'

'What are you going to do?'

'I'm going to order the other men back. We need to prepare the castle for a siege.'

Running towards the lookout posts on the beach I arrive in time to see the first longboats landing on the distant beach. Armed Frenchmen are swarming up the sand dunes, yelling and shouting. There is no longer any question of their intention.

My men are hopelessly outnumbered, throwing down their swords and pikes without even trying to fight. I order them to retreat to the castle and realise too late that the ships sailing into the harbour are simply a diversion, to distract us while the main force lands on the unprotected seafront.

I rush back to the castle and look down to the harbour where our cannon fires one last brave, ear-splitting shot before the crew retreats. The ships are now so close I see men preparing to disembark. The air is filled with shouts of alarm as the heavy cannon ball smashes into the hull of the leading ship. A jagged hole appears above the waterline, the heavy cannon ball causing untold damage and injury as it rips through the decks inside.

'Hurry!' I shout as loud as I can. 'We need to raise the drawbridge!'

Men run into the castle and I count twenty-six, including myself and Nathaniel. As many again have either been taken prisoner, are killed or have deserted, but there is nothing I can do about it. The drawbridge rises with agonising slowness as the ships begin to moor at the quayside and I know it won't be long before we are surrounded.

The men are hastily barricading the gatehouse with whatever they can find while I return to the top of the tower to take stock of the enemy strength and positions. As well as the four ships in the harbour, I can now see at least another dozen mooring in the shallow bay, some still lowering boats full of armed men. We are hopelessly outnumbered. Worse still, I can see the French are trying to manhandle the heavy cannon at the harbour entrance to point it at the castle. Too late, I realise Nathaniel's men must have forgotten to render the gun useless.

A repressed memory of the siege of Rouen flits into my mind. The castle, with its three-foot thick walls of stone has become our prison and there is no way to escape. Nathaniel has ensured we have plenty of stores, but we have limited water, although there are enough barrels of ale to last us a month if necessary.

I gather the remaining men in the courtyard. 'I've no idea how long we will need to hold out—but I'm not surrendering until we have to. I want the archers on the parapet, crossbowmen at the windows.' I turn to Nathaniel. 'Can you have some men move all the supplies to the second floor?'

'Most of it is already there.'

'It is a shame we had to abandon the cannon in the harbour—I'm certain they'll turn it against us now.'

'We still have the old culverins and plenty of shot and gunpowder.'

'I worry those things could blow up in our faces.' I can't help feeling superstitious about the ancient guns, ever since I found they were left here by the late Duke Humphrey. It would be a cruel twist of fate if they enabled him to have his revenge on me after all.

Nathaniel is more practical. 'That's a risk we'll have to take.'

'Let's set them up in the second floor windows and see what they can do.'

Before Nathaniel can reply, a deafening boom from the direction of the harbour is followed by a crash of splintering stone and breaking timber which reverberates inside the courtyard. Despite the thick stone walls we know there are parts of the castle that won't take such a hammering for long.

'There's no time to waste.' I follow Nathaniel up to the second floor of the tower, where the culverins are already being lashed in place with ropes. We watch as the men load four-pound iron balls and measure out gunpowder to prime the guns, ready for the order to fire.

I lead our small group of archers up to the battlements and have my own bow ready. Although I thought it would never be used against an enemy again I have always practised, to pass the time as much as anything else. I look at the tense faces of my men. We might have food and water to withstand a siege but our limited supply of arrows and crossbow bolts means we will have to use them well.

From my high vantage-point I can see the French have hauled our cannon into position and it is now pointing straight at us. They don't seem in any hurry to reload it and I realise the gun crew only carried a few of the heavy cannon balls to the harbour, as the rest are still in the castle. All the same I curse our failure to prevent the cannon from being used against us, a mistake which could cost us dearly.

On the other side of the castle the French are forming a line to surround us, keeping well out of range. There are so many it is impossible to count them and I feel a sinking feeling as I realise they are preparing to hold us to siege for as long as it takes. The French fleet are well placed to prevent any attempt to support us by sea. Even if I had the foresight to send a man to Rouen it would be too late before reinforcements could arrive.

We spend the whole of the next two days doing what we can to keep the French at bay, taking turns to keep watch at night and sleep. It seems the admiral would prefer to starve us out, although I know the men don't like the uncertainty of waiting for the attack which will surely come.

I make Nathaniel responsible for rationing our supplies, while I make sure the men remain vigilant and are kept occupied with improving our makeshift barricades. We are starting to wonder if they are ever going to attack when the cannon booms and another heavy ball crashes into the castle with a numbing thud, breaking into fragments with the force of the blow. The cannon will do a lot of damage if they can fire through one of the window openings and I see the French gunners are already raising the barrel a little to improve their aim.

I rush down to the culverin crew facing the harbour and give the order to return fire. They are ready and waiting and I put my hands over my ears as the blast echoes around the inside of the castle. It is so loud I think for a moment that the old gun has exploded, then I see the Frenchmen who were trying to reload the cannon scattering as the four-pound ball crashes into the ground in front of them, leaving a small crater in the earth. The gun crew make an adjustment and their next shot destroys the cannon's sturdy wooden mounting with such force the heavy gun tilts over with the barrel pointing into the sky. There is a cheer inside the castle from the men watching our first small victory.

The siege lasts almost a week, with the French holding their line around the castle, shooting arrows at the windows and over the high walls. I always cursed the stagnant green moat but now I am glad it offers some defence, particularly at night, when we hear muffled French voices coming worryingly close.

At times the French seem in high spirits. Like any soldiers holding a castle to siege, they taunt us with shouted insults and sing bawdy Breton drinking songs. They become more daring and archers risk being in range of our guns to launch flaming arrows high over the wall into the courtyard. One burning arrow finds its mark on the thatched roof of the stable, starting a serious blaze.

The men manage to save most of the horses but one is lost in the smoking inferno, despite our best efforts. The agony of the dying horse is a bad omen, even for the least superstitious of the men. I see the exhaustion in their soot-blackened faces and know we won't be able to hold out for much longer.

I check our dwindling supplies of food with increasing concern. 'We must reduce the men's rations, Nathaniel. This castle has become our prison—and now we have to find a way out.'

'We only have enough supplies for another week, Owen, perhaps two.' Nathaniel glances over his shoulder to make sure we are not being overheard. 'There's no way to fight our way out, so I was thinking... we could make a run for it, under cover of darkness?'

'It's too risky. They have us surrounded and we know they keep watch at night.'

'Perhaps we should see if we can negotiate a withdrawal?'

'Surrender, you mean?'

'I can't imagine they will leave us now.' Nathaniel points to the south. 'They are digging in. That can only mean they plan a long siege.'

'If we surrender they could hold us for ransom—and I don't like the idea of another prison.' I know the reputation of the French for holding prisoners for many years, waiting for ransom. I doubt Sir William would be in any hurry to negotiate our release if we lose the outpost.

'They're coming!' Nathaniel points towards the French line.

From our high viewpoint we see a group of French crossbowmen advancing boldly on the castle, regardless of the lack of cover. They intend using their deadly crossbows at close range. Two thundering booms sound in quick succession in the tower below us. The men waiting at the south facing culverins have opened fire on the French and one man is hit in the face and killed. Several others are wounded and are dragged by their comrades to safety.

'It will be harder to negotiate terms for a withdrawal now.' I bite my lip as I make a difficult decision. 'If we're going to surrender, we may as well do it before any more men die.'

Nathaniel agrees. 'I'll have one of the men make a white flag.'

'Make it a big one, I don't want the French to be in any doubt and start firing at me.'

'It's too risky for you to go, Owen. I will write a letter, setting out our terms. One of the men will have to deliver it. There's no point in you risking your life for nothing.'

'I can't ask any of the men to do this, Nathaniel. I have enough lives on my conscience.' I feel a frisson of fear at the thought of becoming an easy target for the French archers when I step from the protection of the castle. 'It has to be me.'

Placing Nathaniel in charge of the remaining men, I warily emerge from the castle gatehouse, alone and carrying our makeshift white flag, which flutters in the light breeze on a long wooden pole. The only sound is a skylark singing high in the air over the watching French, oblivious to the events below.

'I wish to speak to Admiral de Coëtivy!' I call out in French, praying that my use of the admiral's name and the flag of truce will have the desired effect.

The French soldiers are well trained. Two come forward, one with a crossbow aimed at my chest. I look at the tip of the bolt with its deadly barb and realise I have never been this close to death.

'Come with us.' The second soldier speaks in French with a Breton accent.

Admiral de Coëtivy must be on the French flagship, as I am taken to the beach and urged into a longboat. As I am rowed towards the grandest ship in the whole of the Channel I see what looks like the entire French fleet anchored in the bay. I am reassured that my decision to surrender was our only option, as we would never have stood a chance against this many. I look back towards the high square tower of the castle where my friends wait and know all their lives depend on what happens next.

The admiral is younger than I expect and looks at me with undisguised curiosity. 'You are ready to surrender so soon?' His voice is cultured and it takes me a moment to realise I have been addressed in English.

'I am Owen Tudor, Captain of Regnéville. I respectfully request that you allow my men to leave in peace, Admiral.'

'Or else?' There is an unmistakeable challenge in his voice.

'Or else we will fight—to the last man.'

The admiral considers this for a moment. 'You will surrender your arms, Captain Tudor. Then I must decide what is to be done with you.'

'May I be permitted to keep my sword? It was a gift from my late wife, Queen Catherine.'

'You are the Welshman who married Queen Catherine?'

'I am, my lord.'

'I was intrigued when I heard the story of how a servant married a queen. There are many men in France who would have wished to be in your position...' The admiral's voice softens. 'I was truly saddened to learn of Queen Catherine's death.'

I hold my breath, knowing that my life and those of my men are in the hands of Admiral de Coëtivy. There is kindness in the man's eyes I had not seen at first. I notice the admiral carries a book in his hand, more like a priest about to read a sermon than one of the most powerful military men in France.

'I will allow you until noon.'

I cannot believe that Fortune's Wheel has turned again in my favour. 'Thank you, Admiral.'

'I wish you well, Captain Tudor.' He smiles. 'It is a long march to the port of Cherbourg, although you should be able to find a ship home from there.'

Chapter Twenty-One

The voyage is long and dangerous, as the trading ship on which we secure a passage home across the English Channel makes heavy going in the storms of an early winter. Forked lightning rips through a black sky and the deep boom of thunder reminds me of the cannon blasts, shaking the wooden planks of the deck under my feet. It is not a good omen and I worry about the reprisals I will face for the loss of Regnéville.

I can still hear the ribald taunts of the jeering French as my men surrender the castle after having fought so loyally. It would seem that God was not on our side, as our long march to the port of Cherbourg was made more miserable by heavy rain. The constant downpour turned the tracks leading north into a muddy morass which clung to our boots and slowed our pace, as if even the land of Normandy tries to prevent our safe departure.

At least the admiral granted my request to keep my sword. My hand falls to the hilt as if to reassure myself it is still there. I am comforted by the cold, familiar shape of the engraved, weighted pommel and handle of tooled leather. I am not sorry I never had the need to use it against a Frenchman. It is not what Catherine would have wished, unless my life depended on it.

It is the end of November and the first frosts are on the ground by the time we reach London, where I must report the news of our defeat to Sir William de la Pole. Much has changed in England while I have been away in Normandy.

Sir William has been made Duke of Suffolk and found a good marriage for his only son to a young heiress, Lady Margaret Beaufort, daughter of the late John Beaufort, Duke of Somerset. I pray that this will improve Sir William's mood, but I am mistaken.

'You know I could have you thrown into the Tower for this, Tudor?' His face grows red and he curses me as he considers the implications of my failure for his already blighted reputation.

'I deeply regret the loss of my command, my lord. The men fought bravely, and we withstood the siege for as long as we could, but were heavily outnumbered. I would ask you, sir, how our garrison of fifty men could hope to defeat ten times as many Frenchmen, supported by the French fleet and more warships than we could count?'

'You know the king is to confirm a knighthood on your sons? I will put your case to him and, with God's grace, he might show you leniency. Don't think you've heard the last of this though Tudor. The council will have to hear of it and I expect they will demand a full explanation.'

'I am most grateful, my lord, if you will speak to the king and the council on my behalf.' I dread the prospect of appearing before the council a second time, as the outcome is completely predictable.

The knighting ceremony is held at Westminster, two weeks before Christmas. I meet with my sons on the eve of the ceremony in the king's chapel at Westminster, where by tradition they spend the night in a vigil of prayer and contemplation of their duties as knights. The ancient chapel is cool and peaceful, lit by thick yellow candles.

Their fine new swords and regalia are laid out on the altar for the blessing, and on the walls hang their colourful new shields, paid for from the king's personal treasury. Both bear the arms of the kingdom, Edmund's with a blue border of gold French fleur-de-lis alternating with my martlet badge and Jasper's the same, but with a simpler border of gold martlets.

My sons are now of age and grown as tall as me. 'The first Welshmen ever to become English knights,' I smile at them. 'I am so proud of you both—and your mother would be too.'

'Thank you, Father.' Edmund looks towards the altar. 'We will pray in memory of our mother.'

I turn to Jasper. 'You remember what our martlet badge on your shield is meant to signify?'

'Yes, Father. It reminds me to follow the quest for knowledge and adventure,' Jasper glances at his brother. 'And as the second son I must work harder.' He grins at the thought.

'That's right, Jasper, but never let anyone say you are not of noble lineage. You are half Welsh, descended from the great lords of Wales—and half French, of the House of Valois

'And we are half-brothers to the King of England and France,' says Jasper.

'Yes—and what must you never forget?'

'That we are Tudors,' says Edmund, 'and our grandfather fought at the side of the last true Prince of Wales, Owain Glyndŵr.'

'That is the truth, Edmund, you must always be proud of your heritage. There are plenty of English nobles with far less right to stand at the side of our king than you—and plenty more who would seek to usurp him. They mistake his piety for weakness, so he needs strong and loyal men around him, more now than ever before.'

My mind turns to my own future as I witness the knighting ceremony. Although I do not know the actual day of my birth, I am about to turn fifty, a grand age by any standards and something of a milestone. My once jet-black beard is now silvery grey and my hair is thinning, yet my eyesight is still sharp and the outdoor life and clean sea air of Regnéville has kept me fitter than many men of my age.

I tire of the self-serving politics of London and need to escape recriminations for what happened in Normandy, so now my thoughts are of Wales and the idea of finding somewhere to live out my days in peaceful retirement. Bishop Morgan once advised me that out of sight is out of mind, and I always wished to return to the island of Ynys Môn, particularly now there is little to keep me in England. Edmund and Jasper have their own lives and even Juliette now has a high position in the queen's household and our paths rarely cross.

I consider seeking her out to tell her my plans for the future, but by the time I see her it is the first week of May. I am with my son Edmund on a visit to see the king at the Palace of Placentia, once known as Bella Court, the grand home in Greenwich of Duke Humphrey and Lady Eleanor Cobham.

We have come to discuss titles and marriages for both my sons, but as the eldest, it is Edmund who is at the forefront of my mind. I have not forgotten my promise to them all those years ago at Barking Abbey that they will one day be made lords, with lands and castles of their own. The king is generous to his favourites, yet needs gentle prompting as his lapses make him forgetful of his promises.

Edmund is full of questions. 'Why must it take so long for him to decide my title?'

'Because titles pass from father to son. That's the way of it—and how it should be. There are enough disputes over land and titles. The last thing we need is to make more enemies through yours.'

'Why can't he create a new one for me?'

'He can create a new title, but you need the lands and the income from them, to make it worth a jot.'

We turn a corner and Juliette emerges from a side door. I feel longing and regret at the unexpected sight of her and am concerned to see she is red-eyed and distressed. She looks as if she wants to talk but remains silent when she sees Edmund at my side. I notice how she wrings her hands and realise this is something I need to know about. Telling Edmund to continue without me, I take her arm and lead her into the privacy of one of the side rooms.

She stares at me with wide eyes. 'Something terrible has happened, Owen.'

'Is it the queen?'

'It concerns Sir William de la Pole. He was always very good to me.'

'Was? You mean he is dead?' I knew Sir William was always going to take more than his share of the blame for the loss of Maine and Anjou. He was even imprisoned in the Tower until the king ordered his release. Sir William waived his right to trial by his peers to have the king's judgement, yet I was as surprised as anyone to learn the king banished Sir William from England for five years.

Juliette's voice is almost a whisper. 'The queen told me he has been murdered, trying to make his way to Burgundy. His body was discovered on the beach near Dover. She said they… cut off his head.'

I hold her close, feeling her familiar warmth, and she clasps her hands at the back of my neck, as if she will not let me go. For a moment it is as if we are lovers again, then I realise my sons could be in danger. If this is the first sign of a revolt against the king and queen, those close to them need to take care.

'Does the queen know who is behind this?'

Juliette rests her head against my chest as she had done so often in the past, without any awkwardness or bitterness at my decision for us to part. 'Only rumours. The news was brought to the queen by a servant of the Sheriff of Kent, who knows few of the details.'

'How has she taken it?'

'She is distraught. It has all come as a shock, particularly to Lady Alice.'

I remember how pleased Sir William looked at the queen's coronation and how he risked his own reputation to protect me after the loss of Regnéville. I release Juliette so I can look into her eyes. 'I am truly sorry for them. Fortune's Wheel has turned again—but who benefits most from this, I wonder?'

'He had many enemies—it could have been anyone.'

'I remember how Richard, Duke of York, scowled at him when we were in Rouen. He has never forgiven Sir William for the losses in France.'

Juliette's eyes are full of concern. 'They say an angry crowd pursued him from London, calling him a traitor.'

'These are dangerous times, Juliette. I must leave London while I still can.'

'Are you finally going to Wales?'

'It was always my plan, and now I'm worried about my sons.'

'They are grown men now.' She looks into my eyes. 'Edmund reminds me so much of his mother—and Jasper of you when we first met.'

'He is a true Tudor, that one. Perhaps you will help me find him a suitable wife?'

'Before he takes after his father?'

'Am I really so bad?'

She answers by kissing me, surprising me for the first time in many years.

☆ ☆ ☆

The town of Beaumaris feels tranquil, a different world from the noise and dirt of London's crowded, muddy streets. I have a pension from the king of forty pounds a year, more than enough to live comfortably and buy a fine, stone-built house with a slate roof and three acres of good land. My new house is conveniently close to the church of St Marys and St Nicholas, and a short distance from the seafront and the shallow, drying harbour.

On the evening of my second day in Beaumaris I take a walk to see the towering sandstone walls of Beaumaris Castle, with its wide green moat, which dominates the town. The first King Edward ordered his soldiers to evict the entire population of the village of Llanfaes by force so he could build his castle on their land. I curse the English for their contempt for the people of Wales and am not sorry the arrogant king died painfully of the flux, like King Henry V.

I find a tavern in a side-street near the castle, where the helpful landlord recommends a local widow as my cook and housekeeper. With her daughter Bethan, who cleans and serves, I find I soon have my own household. They speak Welsh as their first language and I struggle to understand them or to make my wishes properly understood, although I am learning the language again.

Bethan is an attractive young woman, with dark hair and enquiring eyes, reminding me of how my daughter could have been if God had allowed her to live. Bright and quick-witted, with a lively sense of humour, she offers to improve my Welsh in return for my help teaching her English. She is a fast learner, if a little forward for her age, and I am grateful for her help.

The people of the town are friendly enough and I guard my anonymity well, as there are dangers for me even here, so far from London. On another visit to the tavern I strike up conversation with a soldier from the castle who tells me the Duke of York recently passed through Beaumaris on his return from his post as Lieutenant of Ireland, and is thought to be raising an army to challenge the king.

'The duke was furious,' the soldier takes a drink from his tankard, enjoying his tale, 'the constable, Sir William Bulkeley, denied him supplies and access to the castle, you see?' He waits for me to respond.

I sip my ale and pretend disinterest, but the talkative soldier does not appear to notice. He is already a little unsteady on his feet, having drunk several tankards of the strong ale.

'Men loyal to the king tried to detain him in Bangor! They say the duke has sworn to seek out and punish those who lost our lands in France.' He looks as if he expects me to agree.

This is not what I wish to hear so close to the sanctuary I chose to escape from such things. The Duke of York is rich enough to raise a sizeable army and is a man who can win popular support for his challenge for the crown. I worry that word of the surrender of Regnéville could make me a target for those who resent my favours from the king. Even in Beaumaris it seems there are men who would prefer to see York on the throne.

I pour the soldier a fresh tankard of ale from my jug and change the subject. 'Am I right in thinking Lady Eleanor Cobham is imprisoned in the castle?'

'She is.' The soldier lowers his voice. 'Lady Eleanor is teaching me to read—and write my name.'

I hear the pride in his voice and remember the strikingly beautiful young wife of Duke Humphrey. She is about the same age as me, so must also be nearing fifty years old now. I barely survived twelve months in prison, so it is hard to imagine what life must be like for Lady Eleanor after ten years, particularly now her husband is dead.

'Is she allowed visitors?' I am not sure I wish to see her but am intrigued all the same.

The soldier shakes his head. 'Our orders are not to allow anyone to see her, other than the priest—and the constable's wife.'

I take a silver groat from my pocket. 'Would you ask her if there is anything she needs?'

The soldier pockets the coin. 'I surely will, sir.'

The next day I ride out on the road to Llangefni to visit the village of Penmynydd, the place of my birth. It is little more than a row of alms-houses and farmsteads, although there is a church at the crossroads. I tie my horse's bridle to the gatepost and enter.

The church of St Credifael is small, with a steeply pitched roof, which makes it feel spacious and welcoming. I find an alabaster tomb and decipher the inscription. It belongs to my uncle, Gronw Fychan ap Tudur and his wife Myfanwy. At last I have found my family and returned home. I kneel alone at the altar and pray, first for the safety of my sons, then for the souls of my wife and daughter, Margaret, named in memory of my mother.

☆ ☆ ☆

My peaceful retirement feels more like a lonely exile, so I am cheered when a sealed letter is delivered by a merchant on his way from London to Ireland. Nathaniel has been busy building his fortune amongst the mercers and haberdashers and has lodgings in Westcheap, near London Bridge.

I walk down to the seafront and look across the River Menai at the brooding mountains of mainland Wales, wondering what is happening in far away London. I still worry for my sons. Edmund spends most of his time in Westminster and I have not heard from Jasper. Sitting on the old stone sea wall I take the letter from my pocket and break open the seal, smiling as I see Nathaniel's neat hand.

He writes of a mob gathering to the south of the city, as many as five thousand, including disaffected soldiers and sailors returned from the wars in France and Burgundy. Royal forces sent to disperse them at Sevenoaks were defeated by the rebels and from Wiltshire there is news of the murder of William Ayscough, Bishop of Salisbury. The king's personal confessor was dragged from his chapel and hacked to death because he advised the king that marital relations are sinful.

As far as Nathaniel is aware the king and queen have left London for their own safety. The rebels soon took over the city and their leader, a man who goes by the name of Jack Cade, carried out mock trials, accusing the king's supporters of corruption. The head of Baron Saye, the Lord High Treasurer, was paraded through the streets on a pike and there were several days of drunken looting before the rebels are driven back over London Bridge and routed.

Nathaniel makes no mention of Edmund or Jasper, which I hope is a good thing. I fold the letter and return it to the pocket in my doublet, then continue walking along the shoreline. I search for a round, flat stone amongst the many on the beach and find one that fits comfortably into the palm of my hand. I pitch it into the sea, spinning it with a flick of my wrist as I used to as a boy. The stone hits the water and skips into the air, still spinning, three times before it disappears into the grey-green waves. I have done what I can for my sons. Now they must live their own lives.

Chapter Twenty-Two

Autumn 1455

I take the arm of my son's new bride and escort her up the aisle of the Saxon church of St Mary the Virgin, which serves Bletsoe Castle in Bedfordshire. I cannot help wondering if she is the perfect choice for Edmund, as everyone seems to believe. Her childlike body seems frail and her skin is ghostly pale. I notice her wrists are as small as Catherine's were when I first met her. That is where the resemblance ends. Margaret is as pious as any nun and already better educated than most men. Her sharp young eyes seem to read my thoughts and judge me in an instant.

Margaret is a Beaufort. She is also one of the wealthiest heiresses in England. Her grandfather, Sir John Beaufort, the first Earl of Somerset, was the eldest son of John of Gaunt, made Constable of England and given the confiscated estates of Owain Glyndŵr by King Henry V. This is Lady Margaret's second marriage, for she was married first to the son of the ill-fated Sir William de la Pole. The annulment of that marriage was approved by the king, who made Margaret the ward of Edmund and Jasper. Now Edmund will inherit her fortune and her royal lineage.

Edmund would be next in line for the throne if the queen had not given birth to a healthy son, Prince Edward, two years before. It saddens me to learn the king's lapses have grown more frequent. His physicians had declared him an imbecile, as for more than a year he didn't acknowledge his son or even recognise the queen. Some say the prince is a gift from God. Others say it is a miracle the king managed to produce an heir at all. King Henry's enemies mischievously ask who the real father is—and the king has a good many enemies now.

At the end of May the Duke of York showed his hand. With Sir Richard Neville, Earl of Warwick, and the earl's father, the Duke of Buckingham, he led an army against the king, who was barricaded into the town of St Albans. King Henry was wounded in the neck by an arrow and Jasper narrowly escaped with his life as he fought to protect him. Sir Edmund Beaufort, Duke of Somerset, Margaret Beaufort's uncle, was slain in the battle and York is now acting as Protector of the Realm. The king is now effectively his prisoner and the queen and Prince Edward dare not leave their sanctuary in Greenwich.

My son turns to watch as we approach. Edmund has changed since the king made him the Earl of Richmond, with generous grants of lands and income. His once gold-blond hair is darker now and his blue eyes shine with ambition. Jasper was made Earl of Pembroke, a good Welsh title previously held by none other than Duke Humphrey. Both my sons are now recognised by parliament as the king's legitimate brothers, a mixed blessing, given his situation.

I leave Lady Margaret at the altar and take my seat on the hard pew next to Jasper, who has travelled to Bletsoe from Wales to witness the ceremony. Jasper is every inch a nobleman now, with a fine doublet of dark green velvet and a heavy gold chain around his neck. I try not to favour one son over the other, but I am particularly proud of Jasper for the way he tries to reconcile the warring factions of Lancaster and York at parliament, with no thanks from either.

We watch as Edmund and Margaret repeat their wedding vows. Edmund's well educated voice echoes in the high-vaulted church, yet sounds slightly rushed, as if he wishes the whole business soon over. Margaret sounds softer, surprisingly mature and confident, and her words carry conviction. She told me Saint Nicholas came to her in a vision as she prayed for guidance, telling her she should take Edmund as her husband. I thought that was just as well, for she had no choice in the matter once the king made his decision.

My mind wanders to my own wedding day, so long ago and in such different circumstances. I remember waiting for someone to stop the ceremony and arrest me, but no one came and now I am witnessing my own son's wedding. This is no love match though. I see a calculating satisfaction in my son's eyes as he estimates the net worth of his new inheritance.

Bletsoe Castle is a fine, fortified manor house, now part of Edmund's new life. The birthplace of Margaret Beaufort, it is protected by a moat some fifty feet wide and has a spacious banqueting hall. The high arched roof is a grand construction of carved oak beams and the gaudy, painted shields of generations of Beaufort ancestors decorate the walls. Long trestle tables are set with white linen for the wedding guests, mostly of the extended Beaufort family, few of whom I recognise.

Edmund and Margaret sit at the top table like a king and queen. On one side is Margaret's stern, uncompromising mother, Baroness Margaret of Bletsoe and her third husband, Baron Lionel de Welles, sits with me, with Jasper to my other side. In our brief introduction I learn the baron has travelled from his post as Deputy Captain of Calais for his step-daughter's wedding. He is easily diverted by talk of piracy in the Channel and sea conditions on the crossing.

A brash fanfare of trumpets announces the serving of the first course. This is civet of hare, which Jasper explains is made from a whole hare, marinated and cooked with red wine and juniper berries, then 'jugged' in a tall jug standing in cold water. I wonder how they manage to find and catch enough hares for so many guests, then remember that such things are easily achieved if you have a vast fortune.

A small army of silent servants in blue and white Beaufort livery clear our platters as soon as they are empty and the second course is served. Sweet gilded sugar plums and shiny red pomegranate seeds from Spain decorate enormous pies, each hiding under its pastry crust the meat of roe deer, gosling, capons and pigeons, all covered with bright yellow saffron and flavoured with spices.

Even now, after more than thirty years, the exotic scent of cloves takes me back to my first night with Juliette at Windsor. I still carry the yellowing square of linen embroidered with a now fading red dragon. My maid, Bethan, discovered it when cleaning my doublet in Beaumaris and I told her I carry it for good luck, although the question in her eyes suggests she is not convinced.

I have had enough rich food by the time the third course is served and decline the offer of roasted piglet, laid out on the table as if it is sleeping. Instead I choose sturgeon cooked in parsley and vinegar and covered with powdered ginger. Jasper has a dish of herons, covered with egg yolks and sprinkled with spices. The wedding couple are presented with a whole wild boar, with gold leaf covering its curving tusks.

Edmund seems to be enjoying the feast and throws morsels to his hunting dogs, which prowl under the tables of the wedding guests like hungry wolves. After a final course of plums stewed in rose-water, it is time for me to stand and make my speech of thanks to the assembled guests and dignitaries. I keep it short, thanking God that I have been spared long enough to see my eldest son married, and propose a toast to the happy couple. I am not used to eating or drinking so much and secretly wish I am back in the restful sanctuary of Beaumaris.

When I sit down again Jasper leans over and speaks in my ear. 'Edmund told me he plans to have her with child tonight—if he can.'

I glance across at my eldest son, who is now drinking from a large silver goblet. 'That is his right, I suppose, Jasper, although she is... a little young.'

'She is twelve years old, half Edmund's age.'

'Well, she couldn't have been more than six or seven when she first married the de la Pole boy.'

'That marriage was never consummated, Father, and you know it.' Jasper frowns. 'I fear Lady Margaret is too feeble to have a child.'

'I share your concern, Jasper—but don't underestimate the new Countess of Richmond. She has Beaufort steel running through her veins.' I smile as I wonder what Cardinal Henry Beaufort would have made of this marriage.

Jasper's concern for the girl is touching, but I sense there is more to his anger. The king made Lady Margaret the ward of both my sons, so there could be a little jealousy that Edmund has secured such a prize. Edmund's haste to risk his new wife in childbirth is no mystery to me. By common law, all Margaret's lands and fortune pass to Edmund once she conceives a child.

'And you, Jasper, what are your plans now?'

'I intend to make Pembroke Castle my home. The building work has already started. You must visit and see for yourself when it is finished.'

I take another sip of red wine, appreciating the quality. 'I will do that, Jasper. It will be good to see more of Wales— and you must come to Beaumaris, to see where your grandparents were born.'

'Of course, although I must remain close to the king until the danger has passed.' Jasper looks thoughtful. 'Perhaps you will accompany me tomorrow to Greenwich?'

'To visit the queen?' I find I am wondering if I will see Juliette one last time.

'Yes.' Jasper glances up the table to where his brother is still drinking heavily. 'I think, Father, it is time we Tudors showed our colours in this tussle between Lancaster and York.'

The long ride south to Greenwich provides an opportunity to catch up on developments in England. In Beaumaris I must rely on the occasional letter and the castle guards gossiping in the tavern for news. Jasper is one of the few people close to both the king and the Duke of York, who now governs the country through a parliament of his own supporters—and by the threat of force.

We leave Bletsoe Castle as a low sunrise turns the sky the colour of a ripe peach. My head throbs from the effects of too much rich food and wine, although the fresh morning air is already improving my mood. I am on my trusty Welsh Cob and Jasper rides at my side on his black stallion. He has an expensive fur cape over his doublet and wears his sword with the easy confidence of a man who knows how to use it.

When I asked Jasper about St Albans there were too many Beaufort servants listening at Bletsoe for us to speak freely. I look back down the road. We are followed by a dozen yeomen and a few servants of Jasper's on a wagon with our baggage and supplies, all loyal, trusted men and far enough behind to be out of earshot.

'So tell me what happened at St Albans, Jasper?'

My son frowns at a memory. 'The Duke of York is an honourable man, Father. We nearly negotiated a truce with him.'

'What went wrong?'

'He demanded that the king surrender his advisors.'

'Henry couldn't allow it?'

'It was the first time I have ever seen him angry. We knew what would happen to anyone we handed over, so we had no choice but to fight.'

'I thought York attacked first?'

'He did. We barricaded the roads leading into the town and were winning the day—but the Earl of Warwick took us by surprise. He sent his archers through the back gardens of the houses. Our men panicked when they were attacked from the rear and York's men overwhelmed us before we could recover.'

'How was Edmund Beaufort killed?' I remember the handsome young man I had last seen in Windsor, the man who so nearly won Catherine's hand.

'I didn't see—but they told me it wasn't a fair fight. They say he was murdered by a gang of Warwick's men as he came out of the tavern.'

'And the king?'

Jasper has a distant look in his eyes as he recalls the events of that day. 'I heard the bell ringing in the market square—our signal to rally round the king. Warwick's archers were aiming at anyone near the Royal Standard and I saw good men die from a dozen arrows before they even had a chance to fight. Others threw down their swords in surrender and were cut down as they begged for mercy. Lord Clifford tried to reason with them, in the name of the king, but was dragged from his horse and hacked to death...'

'I heard the king was hit in the neck?'

'Thank God he was wearing his plate armour. There was a lot of blood, but it was only a flesh wound.'

'From the sound of it you were lucky not to be wounded.'

'I was lucky to be spared, Father. The Duke of York ordered me set free and I saw him on his knees before the king, begging his forgiveness.'

'So it wasn't quite the victory the Yorkist's claim?'

'It was, Father. They could have killed us all.' He curses to himself. 'They stripped the dead and despoiled their bodies, leaving them to have their eyes pecked out by the crows. They cut the throats of the wounded and ran riot, looting the town and raping any women they could find.'

I hadn't realised how close I had been to losing my son and see from Jasper's face that the horrors of the battle will live with him, just as my own memories of the siege of Rouen have kept me awake at nights. Now I understand why Jasper is so keen for us to visit the queen in Greenwich.

I would have thought any chance of him remaining loyal to York would have died that day at St Albans, yet I know Jasper spent many days with the duke after the battle, hoping to reconcile the opposing sides. His efforts have not been a complete waste of time, as the generous grants made by the king to my sons are the only ones not reversed by York's parliament as the duke rewards those loyal to him and punishes those who are not.

✱ ✱ ✱

The armed guards at the Palace of Placentia in Greenwich are vigilant and challenge us as we approach. It seems the queen is taking no risks and is expecting trouble from the Duke of York. It has taken us several days to make the journey from Bletsoe and I am weary from the long ride.

We are shown in to a sumptuous room in the royal apartments of the palace and told that the queen will see us shortly. High windows flood the room with light and provide views over the extensive gardens, where a high fountain in a classic Greek style is an impressive centrepiece. It feels strange to be in what was once the home of Duke Humphrey, who brought such hardship to me and my family. The room has been expensively redecorated since I was last here. Even the tiles on the floor have been replaced with new ones, alternating with the queen's yellow-gold marguerite emblem and the fleur-de-lis of France.

'Why is the king not here? Surely he should be with the queen and his son?'

Jasper shrugs. 'The Duke of York sent them all to Hertford Castle and now Henry insists on staying there.'

I can understand why. The king would remember happier times at the old castle in Hertford from when he was a boy, and I know it is in keeping with the king's austere taste. I can also see why the queen prefers the luxury of her palace at Greenwich. Easily defended, it has the advantage of quick access to the city by river. More than thirty miles north of London, Hertford Castle may suit the king but not Queen Margaret.

An usher arrives and leads us into the queen's private room where she waits with her ladies-in-waiting. We bow and she invites us to be seated. Although Margaret is only a year older than Jasper, the strain of the ten years since her coronation has left its mark. The beautiful young girl has grown into a strong, but bitter woman. I see she has put on a little weight since the birth of her son, but then so have I.

'I must congratulate you, Master Tudor, on your son's wedding.' Margaret's voice sounds strained.

'Thank you, Your Highness. How is Prince Edward?'

'He is well, considering our... situation.'

'That is what we've come to discuss.' Jasper glances at the queen's ladies-in-waiting, who are pretending disinterest. 'In private, if it pleases Your Highness?'

Queen Margaret dismisses her ladies-in-waiting. As they leave I note that Lady Alice is not among them, and realise I have not seen Juliette, although she is likely to be somewhere in the palace.

'I am grateful that you take the time to visit me.' Margaret smiles. 'It is good to be reminded I have family here in England.'

Jasper returns her smile. 'I have come to tell you we can no longer remain loyal to York, Your Highness. I wish to pledge my loyalty to my half-brother, the king and you, our queen.'

His words are no surprise to me, but I see they give comfort to Margaret. I recall the young girl I first met back in Rouen and the contempt of Richard, Duke of York. Jasper is right; it is time to show our colours. I know Catherine would have expected me to do what I can to protect her eldest son, his wife and their infant grandson Prince Edward.

'We Tudors are your family, Your Highness, and you can rely on our support.'

Margaret looks pleased. 'That means a lot to me. The king has so many enemies I no longer know who can be trusted.'

She turns to Jasper. 'The king told me you defended him bravely at St Albans. He needs good men such as you around him now.'

'Which is why we must bring him here from Hertford, Your Highness.' Jasper glances at me. 'We must raise an army to protect him from the Duke of York—and Richard, Duke of Warwick.'

Margaret tenses at the mention of Richard Neville. 'Warwick whispers in the ears of my few remaining supporters. I fear he will not rest until my husband is dead and York is made king.' She almost spits the words as she tries to control her anger.

Jasper seems taken back by the bitterness in her voice. 'His father, the Earl of Salisbury, has been made Lord Chancellor by York, so parliament is now under his control. I regret I will no longer be able to attend meetings of the council in Westminster.' He scowls. 'York puts me in an impossible position.'

'Your absence will be seen as a sign. They will try to take the lands Henry has granted you.'

'Let them try.' Jasper's voice has a new edge. 'I've been informed that one of York's supporters, a man named William Herbert, is mustering an army to support his cause in Wales.' He glances at me again. 'We Tudors will make sure he fails—and build our own Welsh army to rid England of those disloyal to the king.'

'I will pray to God every day that you succeed, Sir Jasper. Remind your men that my son, Edward, is the Prince of Wales and will one day reward those who protect his interests.'

'There is no time to lose, Your Highness. Every day this York parliament grows stronger by gifts of lands that rightfully belong to the Crown.'

Chapter Twenty-Three

I sit back in my favourite chair and smile as I reread Edmund's letter. The words are those of my eldest son, yet the hand is almost as perfect as Nathaniel's monkish script. The clue is in the frequent thanks to God. The letter has been written by Edmund's wife, Countess Margaret. I can picture Edmund dictating to her, while Margaret does her best to improve his sentiments.

I call Bethan and her mother. 'Come quickly, I have an announcement to make!'

Bethan looks intrigued and her mother stands drying her hands on a linen cloth. Little enough has happened in Beaumaris since my arrival and I am keen to share my good news. 'I am going to become a grandfather!' I wave the letter in the air as proof of my claim. 'My son Edmund is to become a father.'

Bethan laughs. 'I'd like to be the first to congratulate you, sir.' Her English is almost perfect now.

Her mother has practical concerns. 'You'll be travelling to see them when the baby is born, Master Tudor?' She still speaks only in Welsh, despite my efforts to teach her some useful words and phrases.

'I will. They are living in South Wales, in Lamphey Palace, one of the residences of the Bishop of St David's.'

Bethan looks wistful. 'Would you consider... letting me come with you, when you travel to see them sir?'

Her request surprises me. 'We will see, Bethan, we will see.'

Her mother gives Bethan a warning glance to stop her embarrassing me further. Bethan has told me how she longs to see more of the world, and she listened in fascination as I repeated Jasper's account of the battle of St Albans, gasping as I told her the York soldiers cut the throats of prisoners. Sometimes I am persuaded to tell her stories of my life in France when I was her age. Once I even described for her how Catherine's sword saved me from being taken prisoner by the Admiral of France.

After they have gone I remember Jasper's grim warning that Margaret is too young and frail to have a child. I know to my cost that childbirth is dangerous enough for a fully grown woman. Edmund's wife is still no more than thirteen years old and when I last saw her she looked like she would snap like a twig in a breeze.

I already have enough to worry about with my sons, as Jasper remains at the side of the king in Greenwich. His last letter was little more than a note, explaining that Edmund has gone to South Wales at the request of the Duke of York to establish royal authority. The whole idea seems odd, as although Jasper has his castle in Pembroke, Edmund has no particular interests in Wales.

My sons play a dangerous game, still seeming to support Duke Richard while secretly strengthening the position of the king. Jasper's note had been written so it would do them no harm if it fell into the hands of York sympathisers. I am reassured by news that the king has regained control of parliament, but I wonder how long Henry can preside over such an uneasy peace.

★ ★ ★

The yeomen arrive in the late evening and sit at my kitchen table devouring bowls of cawl as they do their best to answer my questions. I recognise them as Jasper's trusted men, who had travelled with us to Greenwich the day after Edmund's wedding at Bletsoe Castle. They brought a letter from Jasper and as I broke the dark wax seal I knew it must be something serious to justify them travelling all the way from London.

It still came as a shock when I read Jasper's news. Edmund had been arrested by William Herbert and supporters of the Duke of York and imprisoned in the dungeons of Carmarthen Castle. Jasper was able to use his influence to have him released, but it had been a close thing and marks the beginning of a dangerous time for us all.

'Tell me again, everything you know?' Their story is confusing, as it is part fact and, I suspect, part speculation.

One of the yeomen finishes his cawl and wipes his mouth on his sleeve. 'We heard Sir Edmund was doing well, sir.' He holds up his empty tankard as a sign to Bethan that more ale would be welcome. 'He took back the castle in Carmarthen for the king.'

The second yeoman drains his tankard. 'Word has it that Sir William Herbert surprised him with an army of experienced men. Sir Edmund had no choice but to surrender.'

'I know of Sir William Herbert. He is York's man. Is he still in Carmarthen Castle?'

'He is, sir—last time we heard.' The yeoman waits as Bethan refills his tankard. 'That's why Sir Jasper has gone to Pembroke Castle and asks us to escort you there, if you will sir.'

'Of course. It is a long ride, so get some sleep and we'll leave at first light.'

I find I am unable to take my own advice, as I am kept awake by troubled thoughts. York has showed his hand and

Fortune's Wheel has turned again. York is capable of overthrowing King Henry and I wonder what will become of my sons if there is a revolt. I look forward to seeing them both again and finally fall asleep with a new resolve. My life has lacked purpose on the peaceful island of Ynys Môn and now I have a new one.

I will fight to my last breath, risk everything I have, to make the country a safer place for my new grandchild, because if I don't we are lost. If that means taking on the powerful Duke of York and his self-aggrandising accomplices the Earls of Warwick and Salisbury, then so be it.

Bethan wakes me with a firm knock on my door and I realise I have overslept, although that is no bad thing. I am growing old and we have a long journey ahead. I remember agreeing she can ride with us. There are dangers, but we have two yeomen as escort and I am glad to have her company. Our journey will take us the length of Wales, so it is a rare opportunity for her to see more of the country. Bethan is already dressed in her riding clothes and her hair is tied back under a headscarf, reminding me a little of Juliette when I first met her.

'The yeomen are ready when you are, Master Tudor.' Her voice is cheerful and her eyes shine with anticipation.

'Thank you, Bethan. Has your mother packed something for us on the journey?'

'Mother has baked fresh loaves and wrapped a fine ham in muslin—and filled leather flasks with ale.'

'Good. Tell the men I'll soon be ready, if you will.'

After she leaves I dress in a warm doublet and riding breeches, with my cape to keep me dry if the weather changes. Peering from my small window I try to read the clouds. The late autumn sunshine is encouraging, but shrieking seagulls are heading inland and dark clouds gather on the far horizon. For once I refuse to see this as a bad omen for our journey as I am on the way to see my sons.

It takes us almost two weeks to reach Pembroke in South Wales. The weather remains fair, so we could have made better progress, but I decided to take the narrow, twisting pass through the mountains of Snowdonia. Although there is nothing there to mark the events of my youth, we stop at the foot of the highest mountain in Wales in memory of the men who fought so bravely for our country.

Further time is taken by the need for caution, as these are dangerous times. We rest only in small villages, avoiding larger towns such as Aberystwyth, where the castle is now held by York supporters. At last the massive stone towers of Pembroke Castle appear on the skyline and I say a silent prayer of thanks that we have arrived safely. High on a rocky outcrop overlooking the estuary of the winding River Cleddau, the castle is one of the few in the country which has never been breached by invaders.

As we ride closer I see the Royal Standard flying from the top of the keep, then realise it is Jasper's flag, with its blue border of golden martlets. I feel a surge of pride that this grand fortress, which has dominated the area since Roman times, is the home of my sons.

I look across at Bethan, who rides at my side. 'Not far now. What do you think of Wales now, Bethan?'

'Wales is bigger, grander—and more beautiful than I ever dreamed, Master Tudor.'

'You have done well, Bethan. It has been a long journey, but it is good for you to see your country.'

'I am grateful to you, sir, for allowing me the privilege.'

I smile in acknowledgement. No one would believe she only spoke Welsh when I first met her. It amuses me to see how she likes to use longer words than either of the yeomen we ride with. As we pick our way through the narrow roads leading up to the castle I decide we will stay a while in Pembroke, perhaps until the baby is born, as Lamphey Palace is only a few miles away.

The guards at the castle gatehouse tell us to wait while one goes to announce our arrival to Jasper. The guard soon returns and asks me to follow him to the chapel, while Bethan and the two yeomen are to be taken to the kitchens. As we enter the castle grounds we stop to stare in amazement at the activity within the open expanse of the inner ward, surrounded by high stone walls and overlooked by the enormous Norman keep.

Archers stand in rows and on a shouted command fire a devastating volley of arrows deep into the straw bodies of man-shaped targets lined up against the wall. Scores of men wearing sallet helmets advance in battle formation with long halberds, while elsewhere blacksmiths hammer new swords at makeshift forges.

Jasper is raising an army for the king within the privacy of the high castle walls, invisibly to the outside world. I remember my son promising Queen Margaret he would do so, yet to see so many Welshmen preparing for war is a stark reminder of the dangers the country faces.

I am led, alone, through heavy iron inner gates and see the great hall, with its new roof and freshly carved stone. My son has been busy with his improvements, although it is strange he has chosen to meet in the chapel.

A long, low-ceilinged room, the chapel has a small window at the far end and is lit by a row of yellow candles. It takes me a moment to adjust to the candlelight before I see Jasper stands with Countess Margaret at his side, her belly noticeably swollen with my grandchild. Their faces are grim. It is not what I expect and I feel a terrible foreboding as I realise something has gone badly wrong.

Jasper breaks the silence. 'Welcome, Father. It warms our hearts to see you again... but I regret I have to tell you the worst has happened.' He places a comforting hand on Margaret's shoulder. 'Edmund is dead.'

I feel unsteady on my feet and slump into one of the wooden chapel pews. My first thought is Jasper must be mistaken, but Edmund would be here to welcome me and he is not. There are only the three of us in the silent chapel. I look into Jasper's eyes for explanation, then into Margaret's and see the truth. My eldest son is dead and he will never see his child.

'How can he be?' My voice is a whisper in the silent chapel.

'He caught... an illness in Carmarthen Castle.' Jasper's voice is factual, drained of emotion. 'There was nothing anyone could do.' He glances at Margaret. 'I am sorry, Father, that you have arrived too late.'

'He is already buried?' It is all too much to take in.

'A week ago, on the first day of November in the choir of the Grey Friars Church, in Carmarthen. I have paid for a fine tomb, and for the friars to keep candles burning day and night and pray for his soul.' He glances at Margaret, as if for permission to say more and sees her nod. 'They told me it could be the plague, Father. We were not allowed to see him at the end, so even if you arrived earlier it would have made little difference.'

Jasper has grown into a warrior knight, with a hardness in his eyes that warns others not to underestimate him. I know how close my sons have always been and realise this lack of emotion is his way of dealing with his grief.

Margaret speaks, her voice soft in the quiet chapel. 'I am sorry for your loss.' Her hand moves self-consciously to her bulging belly. 'God willing, your son will live on through our child.'

It is almost too much for me, but I must reply. Margaret is thirteen years old, yet I am looking into the eyes of a strong, confident woman and recall telling Jasper that Margaret has Beaufort steel running through her veins.

'I am sorry for *your* loss, Lady Margaret. Edmund was a good son and...' I am too choked with sadness to continue.

They realise I need time and leave me in the chapel to mourn my son. I kneel at the simple altar, which is bare except for a large silver crucifix. The last rays of the setting sun cast a golden glow through the small west-facing window as I pray for Edmund's soul and curse William Herbert and his followers of York.

✷ ✷ ✷

I sit at the fireside in the great hall of Pembroke Castle, warming my feet in the heat from the blazing logs. We have done all we can and now are powerless to do anything other than wait. It has been a cheerless Christmas and New Year, marked by a solemn pilgrimage to pray together at Edmund's tomb at the church of Grey Friars in Carmarthen. I am proud to learn that a stirring elegy to the memory of my son has been written in Welsh by the eminent bard Lewis Glyn Cothi.

Now it is the end of January and snowflakes drift across the windswept inner ward as we wish for it to soon be over. Jasper has a man stationed outside Margaret's door, ready to run to him with news, good or bad. He has also secured the services of a skilled midwife, a local woman with a reputation for healing with herbs as well as delivering children, who has sat with Margaret since the first signs. That was well before noon and it is now dark outside, but still there is no word.

Jasper paces in frustration as he no longer tries to hide his concern for Margaret. The two of them have been inseparable since Edmund's death, praying in the chapel together, discussing news from London and walking within the castle grounds. Although Jasper is more caring than any husband, I have never seen signs of intimacy between them. I hope the day will come, but for now they have been united by concern for the unborn child.

'What is York up to now?' I try to occupy my son's mind until the agonising wait is over.

'I can't believe he has persuaded the king to appoint Warwick as Captain of Calais!' Jasper curses. 'I would never have allowed it if I had been there.' He frowns. 'The king's intentions are good. He tries his best to keep the peace and all they do is see it as weakness—and turn his goodwill to their own advantage.'

'I don't see why that's such a bad thing. At least Warwick is well out of the way for a while.'

'The garrison at Calais is England's only standing army. Now Warwick has control of it—and of the Channel—and of our last possession in France. It is the perfect base for him to prepare a revolt against the king—against us, Father!' Jasper's voice is raised to the rafters of the great hall.

'You can't be in two places at once, Jasper. The king has other advisors.'

Jasper stops pacing and turns to me. 'Before I came here I was the only one who remained loyal to the king.'

'Because of the queen?'

Jasper nods. 'The queen puts the interests of her son above everything else, even the best interests of the king.'

'That's understandable.' I stare into the fire and remember how passionate the queen had been about her family. That is the problem. Reading between the lines of my last letter from Nathaniel I know the queen has offended not only the powerful nobles but also the influential merchants who have the money to fund armies.

We are interrupted by hammering at the door and Jasper's man appears, breathless from his sprint across the inner ward. I fear I cannot take more bad news.

'Lady Margaret has given birth... to a healthy boy, my lord.'

Jasper hands him a silver coin. 'Did the midwife say if Lady Margaret is well?'

The man gratefully takes the coin. 'As well as can be expected.' He sees Jasper's frown. 'Those were her words, my lord.'

I understand the midwife's coded message and see Jasper does also. My son had been right, after all, at that wedding banquet in Bletsoe Castle which seems so long ago now. This is going to be a testing time for us all. I will always remember how Catherine looked after giving birth to our daughter, and how I saw the shadow of an early death in our newborn child's eyes.

'Let us go and see if the midwife has more to say?'

Jasper is already heading for the door and we hurry across the inner ward, oblivious of the cold, and up the winding stone staircase of the tower set aside for Lady Margaret's confinement. It is not spacious, but has the advantage of being well away from the men of the garrison.

Jasper knocks, and the door to Margaret's room opens almost immediately, as the midwife is expecting us. Margaret sits in a chair by the fireside holding her new son, who is wrapped in a white shawl. She is worryingly pale, but the gleam of triumph in her eyes tells us more than the midwife ever could.

'I have decided to name him Henry.' Her voice sounds weak yet content.

'A good choice.' I choke back emotion and beam with joy that I have lived to see a healthy grandson, a new generation to continue the name of Tudor.

Chapter Twenty-Four

Spring 1459

Soon after Henry's birth, Jasper asks to see me in his study, a high room in a tower with views overlooking the meandering River Cleddau. I join Jasper at the open window and together we watch as a tan-sailed barge attempts to moor at the castle wharf below. The river is tidal, with strong currents. The crew seems to be struggling as the barge approaches and shout to a man on the quayside who throws them a rope. One of the crew catches it and pulls the heavy barge into the lee of the castle.

Jasper turns to me. 'Sometimes I wish my life was as simple as theirs, Father. It would be good to let others worry about the king or whatever the Duke of York is up to.'

'You would never be content as a bargeman, Jasper.' I grin at the thought. 'I expected to find contentment in Beaumaris—but felt life was passing me by. It's in our blood, our restless quest for knowledge, learning and adventure.'

'Your martlet device.'

'*Our* martlet, Jasper—it is one thing you inherit from me.'

I sit in one of his comfortable chairs. The room is sparsely furnished, with a bare stone floor, a small hearth, two chairs and Jasper's desk. The desk is covered in neat piles of papers, letters to be answered and a few of Jasper's precious books. A goose-feather quill stands in a heavy bronze inkpot and an official document with a dark red seal is spread out on the desk. It looks as if Jasper was studying it and making changes when I arrived.

On one wall is a coloured parchment map of Wales. Imaginary sea monsters poke their heads from the blue-painted ocean, and the main castles feature as prominent, larger-than-life landmarks. The familiar castle at Beaumaris catches my eye and reminds me how far I have travelled from the peaceful solitude I had chosen. I have no regrets, as I am glad to spend as much time as I can with my new grandson.

I still see something of myself in Jasper, but we are quite different in character. Handsome and confident, he has been prepared well for his life as a noble. Even before the death of his brother, he was becoming the better leader of the two, with a talent for gaining the loyalty and respect of the men under his command.

'We need to talk about Margaret—and her son.' Jasper is serious. 'The midwife said both Margaret and her child were close to death. After such a difficult birth... it is unlikely she will be able to have another child.'

'That is unfortunate, Jasper—but thank God they both seem well enough now.' I feel a sense of loss as I recall the moment at Much Hadam Palace when I first held my newborn son Edmund in my arms. 'You are thinking little Henry needs a father?' I had been expecting this discussion. It will need a special dispensation, but Jasper and Margaret seem a good match.

'Lady Margaret's mother has already chosen a husband for her, and I have agreed to arrange it.'

'Margaret should observe twelve months of mourning before she starts planning another marriage.' It pains me to be reminded how soon life is moving on after Edmund's death, as if he never existed. I sit back in my chair. 'So who is this lucky fellow?'

'We thought to approach the Duke of Buckingham. He is proving a useful ally, helping me defend the Welsh Marches against York's sympathisers. Margaret will marry the duke's second son, Henry Stafford.'

'I see the sense of it. Buckingham is one of the few men left who can rival the power of York.' I look across at Jasper. 'Like Margaret, he is descended from the royal line, but as the second son, Henry Stafford has no fortune of his own.'

'He won't need it, Father. Lady Margaret's fortune will provide for them both.'

I think about this for a moment. 'Where will they live?'

'Margaret owns a manor house in Lincolnshire. She said she would consider moving there once she is remarried.'

I feel saddened, as Lincolnshire is a long way from Beaumaris, more than two hundred miles, and even further from Pembroke. There will be little opportunity for me to visit my only grandson.

Jasper seems to notice my concern. 'There is a risk we could lose the Richmond estates, so I've requested that the king makes me little Henry's legal guardian—and that he should receive his education here in Pembroke.'

I notice the glint in Jasper's eye. He has cleverly found a way to keep his late brother's son and me safely in Pembroke Castle, as well as protect Edmund's legacy. I was right to think he had plans for Margaret, but they have proved to be quite different from those I was expecting. Now I know Jasper will not rest until Margaret agrees to his plan.

✩ ✩ ✩

'It feels good to breathe fresh sea air again!'

Bethan pulls off her headscarf and lets the breeze flow through her hair as we reach the seashore. It is a bright spring morning and we have ridden ten miles east from Pembroke Castle along the ancient ridgeway to the coastal town of Tenby. I am officially here to check the progress with the town defences, although I am glad to see the waves rolling onto the long sandy beach.

A surprising turn of events has led to me spending much of my time with little Henry. Now an intelligent child of two years old, my grandson has his mother's Beaufort determination, as well as her frailty. After Margaret married Henry Stafford and moved to Lincolnshire Bethan has proved to be an ideal nursery maid for my grandson.

I had expected Bethan to want to return to her mother in Beaumaris by now, but she seems to be enjoying our new life in Pembroke. She is good company for me when Jasper is away on business, as he so often is these days, as she is always full of questions and keeps me active with our regular exploration of the local areas.

Our horses' hooves dig deeply into the sand as we canter along the deserted beach. Seagulls call overhead in the light sea breeze and in the distance we see the island of Caldey, home to a Benedictine Priory. We ride up a steep hill up into the town, which bustles with activity. It is market day and people have travelled from miles around. The numerous taverns are doing good business, and market stalls line the long narrow street leading down to the harbour.

We leave our horses at a stable and I visit my favourite tavern while Bethan goes to see the market stalls. I find a sunlit table by the window where I can watch people coming and going, and thank the landlord, who brings me a jug of frothy, bitter tasting ale.

Conversation drifts across from other men drinking nearby. Although some speak in the local Welsh dialect, most of the talk is in English. I overhear an argument break out when one of the men drunkenly calls Prince Edward the bastard son of a French whore. Others accuse him of being a Yorkist and eject him into the street. I drain my tankard and leave in search of Bethan, who I find at a dressmaker's stall.

She holds one of the dresses up for me to see. 'What do you think, Master Tudor?'

I smile at her youthful enthusiasm. She has been well paid but there is little to spend her money on in Pembroke. 'Too plain for you, Bethan,' I suggest. 'You should choose something with bright colours?'

The stallholder, a kindly looking woman, is listening and produces a dress in emerald green. 'You may try this one on, my lady, if you wish.'

Bethan laughs at the dressmaker's mistake, but I am not surprised. She has learned a great deal from Lady Margaret during the year they were together. Her voice sounds almost cultured now and she has more natural grace than some of the noble ladies I have known. She disappears behind the stall and soon emerges wearing the dress, which seems a good fit, accentuating her shapely curves.

I look at her appraisingly. 'That's perfect. You can pass for a lady anywhere now, Bethan.'

She buys the emerald green dress, as well as a woollen shawl to keep out the evening chill. 'I shall keep it for special occasions!'

We continue down the hill to the harbour and the smell of fresh fish fills the air. As we turn the corner we see the little harbour is alive with activity. The fleet has returned and men are unloading wicker baskets overflowing with fish. They use long ropes to haul their catch from the holds of the boats high up onto the stone quay, where the merchants of the town are already haggling for the best price.

One of the merchants recognises me and calls out. 'Good day, Master Tudor!'

I raise my hand in acknowledgement. 'Good day, sir. How is the progress with the walls?'

'They should be finished within the month or so, sir. You must come with me and see.'

We follow the merchant to the highest part of the town, where the old stone wall is being raised by the height of a man and made wider to create a walkway. Jasper started the improvements two years before and a team of stonemasons has been working on it ever since. The old moat has also been dug out to a width of thirty feet, and with the new gun ports, installed at Jasper's expense, Tenby is now one of the best defended harbours on this stretch of coast.

Looking down at the busy scene in the sheltered harbour below I realise this place is beginning to feel more like home than Beaumaris ever was. I have found unexpected happiness here with my grandson and Bethan. My only wish is that Jasper would be able to settle down without the shadow of York's rebellion looming over us like an unwelcome storm cloud.

Back in Pembroke Castle little Henry shrieks with delight as I carry him high on my shoulders in the spring sunshine. The grassed area of the castle's inner ward has become Henry's playground, as the soldiers are mostly away with Jasper, leaving only the men on guard duty at the gatehouse.

'Careful, Henry!' Bethan laughs and shouts to me. 'Hold on tight!'

'I have him—you fuss about him more than his mother.'

'When is Lady Margaret coming back to Pembroke?'

I carefully lower Henry to the ground. 'Jasper said she might be back in the summer.'

'That's a long time for a child. He will hardly recognise her.'

'I must admit I have mixed feelings about it. I didn't think she would agree to leave Henry behind.'

'I wouldn't have.' Bethan watches Henry toddle after the red leather ball, his favourite toy.

'As Lady Margaret is still under age, she is still officially Jasper's ward. I was surprised though, when the king awarded Jasper joint wardship of little Henry—but then I was surprised when you decided to stay on here at Pembroke.'

'You know the reason well enough, Master Tudor.' She looks at me questioningly. 'Have you said anything to Sir Jasper yet?'

'There hasn't been the right time.' The words sound like an excuse, although it is the truth.

Little Henry brings me his ball, which I take and throw a little distance for him. He toddles off in pursuit, his eyes shining with Beaufort and Tudor determination.

'I've hardly had the chance to speak to Jasper since he was appointed constable of Aberystwyth and Carmarthen. Even when he does come back he goes straight to Tenby.'

Bethan's expression shows she has heard it all before. When Jasper returns to Pembroke I must reveal my secret, something I have kept well, although if I delay any longer it will be too late. I know my son as well as anyone, yet I have no idea how he will react to my news.

I wait until we are alone one evening and all the servants are stood down.

'There is something I need to tell you, Jasper.'

'You're thinking of returning to Beaumaris?'

'No—well not yet at least.'

He smiles with understanding. 'You want to spend more time with little Henry?'

'And with you, Jasper.' I take a deep breath. 'Bethan...' I cannot look him in the eye. 'She is expecting a child.'

'Do you know who the father is?'

'I do.'

'You?'

'It was never my plan.'

'Bethan is even younger than I am.' Jasper sounds more amused than disapproving.

I'm unsure how to explain my actions to him. 'When I first met Bethan she'd never travelled further than the Wednesday market at Caernarvon. She has changed a great deal since then.'

'So it seems.' He raises an eyebrow.

'You didn't suspect?'

'Well, at least you were discreet. We have to keep this from Lady Margaret, of course, she would not approve of such a thing.'

'There is no need to tell anyone. I thought you deserved to know you are to have another half-brother—or sister.'

Jasper sits looking at me, his head tilted to one side, as if seeing me in a new light. 'I also have a secret—and this seems as good a time to share it with you as any.'

'You have finally decided to marry a rich widow?'

He gives me a wry smile. 'My secret is that you have a granddaughter, named Ellen—or at least that is what her mother would have me understand.'

Now it is my turn to look surprised. 'Where is she? How old is she?'

'It was a year ago, in North Wales. Her mother is a woman named Myfanwy.' Jasper smiles at a memory as he says her name. 'I would not say we are close.'

I understand, as Jasper has his own life to lead. 'I would like to meet her when we are next in the north.'

'Of course. I have made sure she is well provided for, Father—and we will do the same for Bethan.'

'I plan for her to have my house in Beaumaris. Her mother is acting as my housekeeper there...'

'I need Bethan here to care for young Henry. She is good with him—and I must return to London.' There is an edge to Jasper's voice now. 'I've been summoned by the queen.'

'Something's happened?'

Jasper remains silent for a moment. 'I fear we are on the brink of civil war.'

I have not concerned myself with developments in London. Nathaniel takes care with what he writes in his letters, in case they are intercepted, so it comes as something of a shock to hear my son's blunt assessment. Jasper publicly blamed York for Edmund's death when William Herbert was brought to trial, although he was speechless with rage when Herbert promised fealty to the king and was released without charge.

'What are you going to do?' Now I realise why Jasper been spending so much time away from Pembroke. As we had promised the queen, he has been strengthening the loyal garrisons, ready for war with the Duke of York.

'I've been given an apartment in the Palace of Westminster and am charged to protect it from attack, as well as help safeguard Prince Edward—and of course the queen herself.'

'What about the king?'

Jasper shakes his head. 'The king still doesn't believe York will lift a hand against him.'

'Even after what happened at St Albans?'

'Apparently so. My informers tell me York is mustering an army at Ludlow Castle. The man should be charged with treason, but the king won't hear of it.'

'Take care in London, Jasper. Nathaniel's last letter to me implied that the people are tiring of what they see as Queen Margaret's... interference.'

'Nathaniel is right. London is like a keg of powder, waiting for someone to light the fuse.'

'And you will be right in the middle of it?'

'I don't have any choice... I can't stay here and do nothing.'

'I want to help as well, Jasper.'

'Sorry, Father. There is nothing you can do, except remain here and keep little Henry safe while I am away.'

'Nathaniel has the confidence of the merchants in London and will be vigilant for the first signs of a rebellion. You should have him report to you?'

Jasper nods. 'I surely will. In the meantime you must see to the completion of the fortifications here, as we may have need of them soon. As well as York's army, Warwick has control of Calais and my agents tell me he's built an army of two hundred men-at-arms and at least six hundred archers. His father is doing the same at Middleham Castle in the north. They are planning to rebel against the king— and when they do we must be ready.'

☆ ☆ ☆

The midwife is certain the child will come soon, so I wait alone in the low-ceilinged chapel, on my knees in prayer. I say a prayer for Bethan and our unborn child and light a candle in memory of my eldest son, for it was in this chapel

I first heard of Edmund's death. Then I light a candle in memory of Catherine, the love of my life, and another for my daughter Margaret. The three candles burn brightly in a row as I mourn the loss of them all.

I hear the door open and turn to see the boy I paid a silver coin to bring me news of Bethan.

'The baby is born, Master Tudor.' His young voice echoes in the empty chapel.

'Is it a boy or a girl?'

'A boy, sir.' He glances back towards the tower where Bethan has been confined. 'The midwife says it would be in order for you to see him now, sir, if you wish?'

'Of course.' I follow the boy in the near darkness, thinking how strange it is to be in this situation again.

The midwife ushers me into Bethan's room. It is hot, as they have made a good fire to boil pans of water. Bethan is still in her bed, holding the little child tightly, as if to prevent him being taken from her. Her face is red and her hair tangled, but she is smiling and her eyes are bright when she sees me.

'I was thinking of calling him Dafydd, after my father— and Owen after you.'

I am relieved and will happily agree to any name she wishes. 'Is the child well?' My question is addressed to the midwife.

'It was a difficult birth, Master Tudor. The baby took a long time coming, but mother and baby seem well enough now.'

I thank her and sit at Bethan's bedside admiring my newest son. Now I have one more young life to worry about. The country is on the brink of civil war and I must do whatever I can to protect my growing family.

Chapter Twenty-Five

I wear my sword and burnished plate armour and sit astride my fine black warhorse. My sword has survived all my adventures and is the same one given to me by Catherine. My armour and horse are also gifts, along with grants of lands and a hundred pounds a year, from my grateful king. My son has raised an army from the loyal men of Wales, from Pembrokeshire, Carmarthenshire and Cardiganshire, as well as those from North Wales who have rallied to the cause.

The silhouette of Denbigh Castle crowns a steep rocky hill as the sun sets above the town, providing its Yorkist defenders with commanding views of the round-backed hills of Clwyd. The king has made Jasper Governor of Denbigh and ordered him to prevent the Duke of York's return from Ireland through Wales. I have command of the archers, good Welshmen whose lives now depend on my judgement.

Duke Richard of York licks his wounds in Ireland; the Earl of Warwick has fled back to Calais and anyone daring to support the Yorkist cause is declared guilty of treason. Everyone knows this, it seems, except for the men holding out in the castle on the hill. They have been under siege for more than a month, yet they are defiant and seem determined to hold their fortress for York, whatever the cost.

Jasper rides to my right, wearing a surcoat embroidered with the red, blue and gold of the royal arms to show his rank. At his side is his deputy at Denbigh, Roger Puleston, a resourceful and loyal supporter of Edmund's before becoming Jasper's right-hand man. Puleston's grandmother was Owain Glyndŵr's younger sister, Lowry, and he is related by marriage to the Tudors of Ynys Môn.

'It's time to end this. I have the king's authority to pardon any who surrender—and to execute any who don't.' Jasper has become hardened by relentless campaigning. It is clear from the way he says the words that he will do whatever is needed to protect the king and prevent another York rebellion.

I am tired and lean back in my saddle. I am sixty years old now and feel the ache in my bones. I shade my eyes from the bright evening sun and peer up at the castle in frustration. 'You mean to use heavy cannons?' I still remember the damage done by Nathaniel's cannon in Normandy. 'It will take time, but once the walls are breached, we have a chance.'

'The castle is no use to us in ruins.'

'Then what are we going to do?'

'A diversion at the gatehouse should keep them occupied while my men scale the wall at the rear—under covering fire from your archers.' Jasper sounds uncompromising.

'The wall is too high to scale, Jasper. Owain Glyndŵr attacked this castle in fourteen hundred with your grandfather at his side.' I glance across at my son. 'He failed.'

Jasper is silent for a moment. 'We must try, Father.'

Roger Puleston answers. 'The postern gate at the rear of the castle has a drawbridge and is overlooked by a tower, but it could be breached with enough men if we launch a diversion at the main gate.'

I am unconvinced. 'We could find ourselves trapped by a portcullis, with archers firing down on us.'

'I'm sure we will—but if the portcullis is raised we could jam it in position before they bring it down.' Puleston looks pleased with himself. 'I also have the firebombs prepared for *Y Ddraig*—that should make our diversion convincing.'

I had been watching them haul the towering wooden siege engine they call *Y Ddraig, the Dragon*, into place. Based on the French trebuchet, its giant catapult is designed to fling a missile high into the air and has a range of several hundred yards. Now Puleston plans to use it to throw his dangerous firebombs made from sulphur and pitch, mixed with iron nails and whatever else his men can lay their hands on.

'That decides it. We will attack the postern tower.' Jasper reins in his horse and puts his gauntleted hand on Roger Puleston's shoulder. 'You will lead the diversionary assault on the gatehouse. I want to use the cover of darkness—and have your men make as much noise as they can.' Jasper turns his horse and rides off to inform his commanders of our plan.

I ride back to the encampment which has become my home. Our base was only meant to be temporary, but now the grass has turned to hard packed earth under the constant trampling of heavy boots. Inside my cramped canvas tent I have only what I brought with me from Pembroke: a travelling bed, rolled up out of the way each morning, two woollen blankets, a linen undershirt and my leather saddlebags.

The place has a homely smell of soup and wood smoke and my squire, a young Welsh boy named Rhys, is having difficulty with our makeshift stove. A cooking pot is precariously supported over the fire by an arrangement of stout branches. Rhys stops what he is doing as I dismount and he takes my horse by the bridle, returning to help unbuckle my armour.

'Will you have a bowl of cawl, sir?'

'Thank you Rhys.' I tire of cawl, but it is all we have.

'Did you manage to find any meat to put in it?'

'Sorry, sir. I will try for a rabbit again tomorrow.'

I can't complain, for this is life under siege and we must live off whatever we can forage. Jasper is right. It is time to take decisive action, as I now wish we had never travelled to Denbigh. I should be back in the safety of Pembroke Castle, with my grandson Henry and my youngest son Dafydd Owen. Instead, we risk our lives besieging an impenetrable fortress and cannot return until it is taken. I dismiss the ghosts of the siege of Rouen from my mind and remember I once promised I would never again complain about my food.

I scan the battlements at the top of the castle wall in the dim light of a waxing moon, looking for any sign of movement. Rhys woke me early, as my archers had to find good vantage points before the main attack. They seem in good spirits, glad to be taking action after so many weeks of waiting and watching. Several of them sit behind heavy mantlets, black-painted, portable shields made from iron plates on a wicker frame to provide some protection from the castle's defenders.

Progress is slow because we must remain silent to prevent the castle sentries raising the alarm. Several of Jasper's men carry heavy logs, ready to block the postern portcullis gate. The idea sounded straightforward enough when Roger Puleston suggested it the previous day. Now the plan seems impossibly reckless and the castle walls have many arrow slits through which death could come at any moment.

Rhys hands me my iron sallet helmet. It is heavy and uncomfortable to wear, despite the cotton padding fitted inside, but now I am glad to put it on. I wait while he tightens the leather straps on my armour then I see the signal from the sergeant-at-arms. My men are ready now and all we can do is wait.

I say a silent prayer not for myself but for Jasper. I have little confidence in our chances of success, and if our attack fails it will be difficult for Jasper to escape to safety. Too late, I wish I had said more to my son, then the shuddering boom of a cannon sounds on the opposite side of the fortress. The diversionary attack has started and the hairs prickle on the back of my neck as I sense the real danger we now face.

The first of Roger Puleston's firebombs makes a flaming arc in the night sky with unnatural slowness, like a sulphurous, man-made comet, before descending out of sight behind the castle walls. I remember the damage done by a few burning arrows in Normandy and am glad not to be on the receiving end of *Y Ddraig*.

'Ready men!' I look at the tense faces of the archers to each side of me and shout to them as loud as I dare. 'Hold your fire until my command and choose your targets well!'

Jasper appears from the dark cover of the trees, followed by his hand-picked soldiers, who cross silently to the postern gate. As they pass I hear one of my men call. 'God be with the House of Lancaster!'

Urged on by Jasper, they disappear from view into the dark entrance of the postern gate. I wait for the shout of alarm, but none comes. It seems their plan is working, as more men make their way up the steep, rocky bank and enter the castle.

More brightly blazing firebombs curve through the sky and cannons flash and roar as Roger Puleston's men press the frontal attack but I worry now that Jasper has been trapped within the outer defences. I strain to hear raised voices and the clang of steel as a battle rages inside the castle.

An arrow stabs deep into the ground a few yards in front of me and a second embeds itself in the tree a few feet to my left with a dull thud. The defending archers have spotted us in the trees and are finding the range. It is impossible to tell in the darkness where they are firing from or how many men are shooting at us. One of the archers near me calls out as an arrow strikes him in the chest. He wears the thick padded coat the men call a 'jack' and is able to pull it out with his hand, but it is a close thing.

We must hold our position, although my men have yet to fire a single arrow, as without a target I have to tell them to hold their fire. Then I spot movement at the postern gate. At first I think Jasper's men have been beaten back, then realise they are Yorkist men of the castle garrison, escaping. Many are armed and some begin to aim crossbows at my men.

'Fire as you will!' The need for caution is gone now and I shout at the top of my voice.

A volley of arrows flash through the air, felling several of the fleeing men, then the others stop running down the steep embankment and throw down their weapons, raising their arms in surrender. The battle is over, for us at least. I see our arrow shafts sticking from the twisted bodies of the fallen and feel sad so many good men had to die.

Our victorious army makes its long journey home through the mountains of Snowdonia, leaving Roger Puleston and the men of North Wales at our new stronghold in Denbigh. Many of Jasper's men have served double the forty days they agreed under the commission of array. They are glad to return to their families, carrying booty looted in the king's name from the Yorkist Mortimers.

Jasper was wounded in the battle, but is well enough to ride at my side. He has said little about the fighting inside the castle, but I know it was hard won, as it took two days to bury the dead. Many men on both sides suffered wounds which may never heal. As we approach the castle at Harlech, our first stop, a young boy rides out to meet us.

'I have a message from the queen for Sir Jasper Tudor, Earl of Pembroke.'

Jasper turns to the boy. 'I am Jasper Tudor—and who might you be?'

'John Coombe of Annesbury, sir.'

'Why does the queen send a boy with her message?'

The boy looks unsure how much he should say. 'The king has been captured by York's army at Northampton, my lord, and the queen requires you to take her and his highness Prince Edward into safety.'

Jasper frowns. 'Where is the queen now?'

'In hiding, sir. She was robbed by her servant and the others ran off.' He glances over his shoulder in the direction of Harlech. 'There is only me left now, sir. She sent me to find you.'

'Take me to her.'

Jasper turns to me. 'After we have rested the horses I will escort the queen and Prince Edward with my men back to Denbigh Castle. She will be safer there than here in Harlech. You must return to Pembroke and help rebuild our army there. It seems we are truly at war now, Father.'

When I arrive at Pembroke Castle I am welcomed by Bethan, who leads young Henry, now four years old, by one hand and little Dafydd now aged two, with the other. My squire Rhys takes care of my horse and Bethan serves me a jug of ale and a trencher of fresh bread with a thick slice of ham in the great hall.

Little Henry wants to know what I have brought back for him, and I give him a buckler, a small round hand-shield taken from the Yorkist garrison. Henry is pleased with his gift and runs around the hall showing it to the servants like a trophy, which it is. Seeing it again reminds me of the great price that was paid for it.

'You have a visitor, Owen.' Bethan glances behind her. 'A friend has travelled here with news from London.'

Nathaniel steps into the room, dressed in a dark velvet doublet and wearing a gold chain around his neck. His hair is now silver-grey and he has put on a little weight, but his eyes are as sharp as ever.

'Good to see you again, Owen.'

'And you, Nathaniel. Have they thrown you out of London?'

'I left in something of a hurry, true enough. You've heard the news?'

'I've been travelling from North Wales for the past week. What's happened?'

'York's son, Edward, came to London with the Earls of Warwick and Salisbury at the head of an army of thousands. Any supporters of the king are considered fair game now and the looting has run out of control. This is the safest place I could think of.'

'You are welcome to stay here for as long as you wish.' I embrace my friend warmly. 'I'll be grateful of your help, as the men who fought with us in North Wales have all dispersed. We need to draw up a roll of all who can fight and make sure they are trained and equipped. I wish it was different, Nathaniel, but we must prepare an army to set the king free and put an end to this rebellion by the Duke of York and his supporters.'

✯ ✯ ✯

I shiver in the late January cold, despite my thick wool coat, as we ride through the normally peaceful market town of Llandovery. Local people line the long main street, a drovers' road, more used to flocks of mountain sheep than marching men, to cheer us on.

Small bare-footed children shriek with delight as Nathaniel throws them coins and a man with a drum joins the march, keeping time with a loud bass beat that echoes from the timber-framed houses. A young girl waves to Jasper and blows him a kiss. I feel a surge of pride in my son, and to be riding with the king's Welsh army.

Nathaniel stares up at the darkening sky. 'The rain will hold, God willing.'

'I'm glad of your faith, Nathaniel. If it rains these frozen roads will turn to mud.' I notice many of those cheering us on are women and children. 'Most of the men have joined our cause, which is heartening.'

'We don't have enough weapons—or padded jacks and sallet helmets for them all.' Nathaniel glances back at the straggling column of men marching behind us. 'Some are armed with butcher's knives and scythes, whatever they can find.'

Jasper rides ahead with Sir James Butler, Earl of Wiltshire and Ormond, his second in command. 'It's good Sir James has brought his mercenaries. If the Yorkists expect Welsh farmers armed with pitchforks, the sight of battle-hardened men from Ireland, France and Brittany will surely put the fear of God into their cowardly hearts.'

'I'll be glad when we join the queen's northern army. I heard she has a deal with the Scots to fight for us—and has mustered men of fighting age from every shire in England still loyal to the king.'

Nathaniel is no soldier, yet wears a sword and a steel breastplate, riding at my side despite Jasper's insistence that we are both too old and should remain in Pembroke. This is personal for me now, as one of those we ride against is the man I hold responsible for Edmund's death. Sir William Herbert surprised no one when he rejoined the Yorkist army.

Richard, Duke of York, the man who planned to usurp the king, is no more. Captured by the queen's supporters at Wakefield, his head is rotting on a spike over the Micklegate Bar in York beside the head of Warwick's father, Richard, Earl of Salisbury. Now Jasper's informers have told him York's young son, Edward, Earl of March, has sworn to avenge his father's death and rides with his army to meet us.

We have been marching hard for eleven cold days, only stopping when darkness falls and starting again each day at dawn. The rain never comes, although our breath freezes in the air as we march through Brecon and cross the River Wye at Glasbury into Herefordshire. The light is failing when Jasper's advance guard warns us the York army has been sighted near Mortimer's Cross, on the old Roman road near the crossing of the River Lugg.

Jasper turns in his saddle. 'We will camp here for the night. At first light I want you to take your archers and form a rearguard, Father.'

'You don't think we should try to avoid them? We should head north, under cover of darkness.' I allow myself to hope Jasper will consider my plan. A long march through the night would be preferable to a battle against the army of York's vengeful son.

'It's too late, Father. They must know where we are and it's impossible to move this many men without someone seeing us. I will try to negotiate terms if we have the chance—but we have to be ready to fight.' Jasper rides off into the gloom to warn his other commanders.

Nathaniel has been listening. 'If they wait for us they will have chosen the best ground.'

'We have God on our side, Nathaniel!'

I try to sound cheerful, but spend a restless night as the ground is frozen and because of a growing sense of dread. I have lost my wife, my daughter and my eldest son and feel the same stirring of fear, deep within my chest, as I sensed before we stormed the castle in Denbigh. My fear is for Jasper, who will risk his life to free the king.

In the morning we set off in silence. I ride with the rearguard, with Nathaniel to one side and my young squire Rhys to the other. Both are usually talkative, but now every man is lost in his own thoughts and vigilant for any sign of our enemy on the road ahead.

The attack begins with an ambush. As Jasper's vanguard turns a corner they are met by a storm of arrows. Several of his men are dead or wounded before they know what has happened. An arrow strikes deep into the neck of Jasper's horse and it rears into the air, throwing him from its back. He scrambles to his feet, drawing his sword, ready to fight. I see all this from the rearguard and shout for my archers as both sides engage in hand-to-hand fighting, making it impossible for my men to be sure of their targets.

The York men-at-arms take advantage of our confusion and hack at us with axes, maces and swords, slashing and killing without mercy. I see men throw down their weapons and run for their lives. Sir James Butler rides off, followed by many of his mercenaries. As I watch, our deserters are cut down and slaughtered like animals, their bodies thrown into the slow-flowing River Lugg. The Yorkists are in no mood for taking prisoners.

I can't see Jasper anywhere, but as I search for his distinctive surcoat with the red, blue and gold of the royal arms amongst the melee of fighting men I see a knight, a head taller than those around him. He wears full plate armour and is killing with such ferocity he cuts a swathe through our line. Then I realise this must be York's son Edward, avenging the death of his father.

Edward, Earl of March, could have stayed on his horse and watched the battle from a safe distance, as his army outnumbers ours by more than two to one. They are experienced, hand-picked fighting men, well-armed, with good armour, wearing the livery of York. I can see Nathaniel was right with his fateful warning. The enemy commanders had time to choose their ground well, as they drive Jasper's men towards the river at their back.

A troop of mounted knights appear from nowhere with a thunder of hooves and surround what is left of my rearguard, cutting off any chance of escape. I still cannot see Jasper anywhere, but I did see my young squire Rhys running for his life. Nathaniel is bleeding from a wound on his arm and looks dazed. Seeing me look in his direction he shakes his head. We throw down our swords and raise our hands in surrender.

Ten of us march, roped in a line, hands tied behind our backs. I am comforted by a rumour that Jasper has not been found amongst the dead and may have escaped with Sir Thomas Perrot of Haverfordwest. The man walking in front of me is John Throckmorton, a good man, loyal to the king and one of Jasper's commanders. Throckmorton is bleeding from a deep cut on his forehead and frequently stumbles, as he walks barefoot because someone has relieved him of his riding boots.

'With God's grace we may have the chance to reason with young Edward, the new Duke of York.' He glances back at me and spits blood on the path. 'I served Sir Richard Beauchamp, Earl of Warwick—that should count for something.'

There is hope in John Throckmorton's voice and I take my cue from him. 'I trust we can, John.' I decide not to tell him how I witnessed Edward slaughtering all in his path.

'Did you see what became of my friend Nathaniel?'

'Yes. He was led away soon after we were captured.' John Throckmorton glances back at the eight men roped together behind us. 'I pray we are not the only survivors.'

I am tired after our forced march of nearly twenty miles to the market town of Hereford, and my throat feels as dry as old parchment. We are made to wait without food or water in the dark cellar of a warehouse before being led out to the market square, where a crowd of curious onlookers has gathered, despite the wintry chill.

It seems we are to have some kind of show trial. I try to think what I will need to say in my defence and recall how I won a pardon from the king that day before the council in Westminster. There is always hope.

The executioner rips the collar from my doublet and throws it to the ground, then the crowd falls silent as I am made to kneel at the block. I close my eyes and prepare myself for the blow. There will be no last-minute pardon from the king. I pray my son Jasper will live to fight another battle and uphold the name of Tudor. Still waiting for the blade to fall I say a prayer next for my grandson Henry, that he will have a long and happy life, then I say a prayer of thanks that I will soon be joining my Catherine, the beautiful love of my life.

Er clybod darfor â dur
Newid hoedl Owain Tudur,
Gweilio Siasbr a Harri
Ei ŵyr a'I fab, yr wyf I

Although it is said that giving up steel
Changed the life of Owen Tudor,
To keep watching out for his son and grandson
Jasper and Henry, I will.

Ieuan Gethin, Welsh Bard, 1461

Author's Note

I was born near Pembroke Castle and recently visited the small room where it is said the thirteen-year-old Margaret Beaufort gave birth to Henry Tudor. I also stood on the pebble beach at Mill Bay near Milford Haven, imagining how Jasper Tudor would have felt as he approached with Henry and his mercenary army to ride to Bosworth - and change the history of Britain.

These experiences made me wonder about Owen Tudor, the Welsh servant who married Queen Catherine and began this fascinating dynasty. I felt a responsibility to research his story in as much detail as possible and try to sort out the myths from the facts. There are, of course, huge gaps in the historical records, which only historical fiction can help to fill. As well as there being no surviving record of Owen's marriage, no reliable image of him exists.

I thought it likely that Owen would have had at least one relationship before he married Catherine, as he was a handsome young man living in a household full of well educated women. Queen Catherine had several maids, Joanna Belknap, Joanna Courcy, Joanna Troutbeck and one called Agnes, whose surname is not known. There was also a French lady of the bedchamber named Guillemote. There is no evidence of a relationship between Owen and any of these ladies, but I decided it was possible and created the character of Juliette to represent the other women with whom he undoubtedly shared his life.

Similarly, the character of Nathaniel represents the many clerks and male servants that Owen would have befriended, lived and worked with. I also created the character of the Welsh priest, Thomas Lewis, after discovering Owen spent his time in Newgate Gaol with a servant and his chaplain.

I admit to a raised eyebrow when I realised Owen was almost sixty when he fathered a son, Dafydd Owen, with an unknown Welsh woman at Pembroke Castle. I therefore created the character of Bethan to make this possible. Apart from that, you will find that the real people and places referred to in this book are consistent with the historical facts as we currently know them.

I also had to address the often quoted stories about how Owen and Catherine met, such as Owen falling into her lap during a drunken dance. This story is based on sonnets written by Elizabethan poet Michael Drayton, more than a century later, which say, '*Who would not judge it fortune's greatest grace, Since he must fall, to fall in such a place*'. Perhaps it was not meant literally, but that Owen was lucky to be in close proximity to Catherine at such a lonely time for her. Drayton's sonnet may have been inspired by a work known as the *Chronicle of London* by William Gregory, a London skinner and mayor of the fifteenth century, who records Owen's last words as, '*that head shall lie on the stock that was wont to lie on Queen Katherine's lap.*'

Owen Tudor was buried in the chapel of the Greyfriars Church in Hereford, later pulled down after the Dissolution of the Monasteries. A plaque marks the spot of his execution in Hereford High Street, his only memorial. I would like to remember Owen, not as a victim of the Wars of the Roses, but as an adventurer, a risk-taker, a man who lived his life to the full and made his mark on the world through his descendants.

Thank you for reading as far as this. I would be grateful if you will kindly consider writing a short review on the site where you purchased my novel. It would mean a lot to me.

Tony Riches
Pembrokeshire 2015

Jasper

Book Two of the Tudor Trilogy

England 1461: The young King Edward of York has taken the country by force from King Henry VI of Lancaster. Sir Jasper Tudor, Earl of Pembroke, flees the massacre of his Welsh army at the Battle of Mortimer's Cross and plans a rebellion to return his half-brother King Henry to the throne.

When King Henry is imprisoned by Edward in the Tower of London and murdered, Jasper escapes to Brittany with his young nephew, Henry Tudor. Then after the sudden death of King Edward and the mysterious disappearance of his sons, a new king, Edward's brother Richard III takes the English Throne. With nothing but his wits and charm, Jasper sees his chance to make young Henry Tudor king with a daring and reckless invasion of England.

Set in the often brutal world of fifteenth century England, Wales, Scotland, France, Burgundy and Brittany, during the Wars of the Roses, this fast-paced story is one of courage and adventure, love and belief in the destiny of the Tudors.

Coming soon from Tony Riches:

Henry

Book Three of the Tudor Trilogy

Henry Tudor finds himself king of a divided country and decides to unite the Houses of Lancaster and York through marriage to the beautiful Elizabeth of York. This is his story.

Also by Tony Riches:

The Secret Diary of Eleanor Cobham

England 1441: Lady Eleanor Cobham, Duchess of Gloucester, hopes to become Queen of England before her interest in astrology and her husband's ambition leads their enemies to accuse her of a plot against the king. Eleanor is found guilty of sorcery and witchcraft. Rather than have her executed, King Henry VI orders Eleanor to be imprisoned for life.

✝

More than a century after her death, carpenters restoring one of the towers of Beaumaris Castle discover a sealed box hidden under the wooden boards. Thinking they have found treasure, they break the ancient box open, disappointed to find it only contains a book, with hand-sewn pages of yellowed parchment.

Written in a code no one could understand, the mysterious book changed hands many times for more than five centuries, between antiquarian book collectors, until it came to me. After years of frustrating failure to break the code, I discover it is based on a long-forgotten medieval dialect and am at last able to decipher the secret diary of Eleanor Cobham.

Also by Tony Riches:
Warwick
The Man behind the Wars of the Roses

Richard Neville, Earl of Warwick, the 'Kingmaker', is the wealthiest noble in England. He becomes a warrior knight, bravely protecting the north against invasion by the Scots. A key figure in what have become known as 'the Wars of the Roses,' he fought in most of the important battles. As Captain of Calais, he turns privateer, daring to take on the might of the Spanish fleet and becoming Admiral of England. The friend of kings, he is the sworn enemy of Queen Margaret of Anjou. Then, in an amazing change of heart, why does he risk everything to fight for her cause?

✟

Writers from William Shakespeare to best-selling modern authors have tried to show what sort of man Richard Neville must have been, with quite different results. Sometimes Warwick is portrayed as the skilled political manipulator behind the throne, shaping events for his own advantage. Others describe him as the 'last of the barons', ruling his fiefdom like an uncrowned king. Whatever the truth, his story is one of adventure, power and influence at the heart of one of the most dangerous times in the history of England.